'Outstanding prose is married to a suspenseful plot and a quiet humour' Amanda Craig, *The Times*

'Stands out for its original subject and plot…Each book takes McNish into new territory, and this one is both assured and thought-provoking.' Nikki Gamble, *The Bookseller*

'Tense, quirky and highly individual, this story has plenty going for it' Nicholas Tucker, *TES*

'A deft construction…McNish vividly portrays two worlds in the light of each other, creating a thin space between them that makes for a moving and thought provoking tale.' Huw Thomas, *Books for Keeps*

'A fascinating read' *Carousel*

'This neat combination of teen angst and behavioural ethics is … complex and charged.' *Sunday Telegraph*

'What a book. I simply couldn't put it down…a highly charged look at personal spirituality…the writing is effortless and elegant and as it slips between character perspectives, *Angel* never loses an air of authenticity. And at moments, it reaches the sublime. I loved it' Jill Murphy, *The Bookbag*

'This unusual fantasy is made plausible by a very strong depiction of the underpinning pattern of teenage anxieties and everyday angst' Lesley Agnew, *The Bookseller*

'Haunting and thought provoking' Lesley Agnew, *CY Mag*

'A fascinating read' Jo Griffiths, *Waterstones*

'If you love stories about friendship, this one's a must' *Bliss*

Also by Cliff McNish

The Doomspell Trilogy

The Doomspell
The Scent of Magic
The Wizard's Promise

The Silver Sequence

The Silver Child
Silver City
Silver World

Breathe: A Ghost Story

Angel

CLIFF McNISH

Orion
Children's Books

Acknowledgements

For permission to reprint lines from *Paradise*, grateful thanks are due to the author, Chaz Brenchley, and his agent, John Jarrold.

First published in Great Britain in 2007
by Orion Children's Books
This paperback edition first published in 2008
by Orion Children's Books
a division of the Orion Publishing Group Ltd
Orion House
5 Upper St Martin's Lane
London WC2H 9EA

An Hachette Livre UK Company

1 3 5 7 9 10 8 6 4 2

A catalogue record for this book is available from the British Library

ISBN 978 1 84255 629 0

Designed in ITC Giovani by Geoff Green Book Design

Printed in Great Britain by Clays Ltd, St Ives plc

www.orionbooks.co.uk

For Chaz Brenchley

PROLOGUE

Freya Harrison had always wanted to be an angel. Ever since she could remember she'd wanted wings instead of arms and a halo instead of toys. And perhaps dreams come true, because when she was barely eight years old an angel paid her a fleeting visit.

It was at least seven feet tall, with creamy-white skin, displaying itself in what she later recognized as the classic style: shining, fully-robed, its halo like a mane of golden sunshine.

And male. Definitely a man. Or was it?

Freya had to look twice to be sure. The body was certainly male, and so was the face-structure, but weren't those lips curiously soft and full, the contour of the eyes almost feminine? Six years later, having devoured everything she could find about angels, Freya knew the term to apply: *androgynous*. An appearance neither exclusively male nor female, but somehow both.

The visitation took place on a warm spring night. Freya had been fast asleep in her open-windowed bedroom when the curtains slowly swirled and there he was, like the perfection of a dream – a glorious angel in the dead of night. He was huge. He seemed too big for her room, or any room for that matter.

Despite which, awakening, she hadn't been alarmed, not afraid at all. On the contrary, it was as if some part of her had been waiting her whole life for him to deftly lift aside that thin bedroom curtain.

An angel. An actual angel.

To gaze in wonder upon such a thing.

She fell in love with his wings at once. Supple feathers. Tips as smooth as the afterglow of sunsets. Just seeing them had made Freya hunger for wide spaces. And when she reached out to touch them it was like dipping her fingers inside light itself.

But the way the bulky, complex wing-joints entered the shoulder-blades scared her. Creeping behind him to sneak a peek, she'd seen how twisted and gnarled it was back there. Didn't his shoulders hurt? Surely they must ache from having to hold up such big wings all the time?

'No,' the angel had replied. A subtle, airy voice. A dying eagle on a last flight over one more mountain might have sounded like this.

But it was what the angel did next that shocked her. For years afterwards Freya had trouble controlling her emotions whenever she recalled it. Because tears had sprung from his eyes. Tears that poured freely over his unblemished cheeks, across his sculpted lips and down his smooth throat.

'Are you sad?' It was all Freya could think to say at the time. 'What's the matter?' And wanting to comfort him, but not knowing how, she'd taken one of his wings, draping it around her. But it was too heavy to hold. That particular detail stuck in her mind – attempting to lift the wing, but unable to; hauling it up, but feeling it forever slipping away from her grasp.

Freya always berated herself for her childish fixation with those wings. Instead of the important questions she might have asked (Are you a messenger? Are you from God?) her eight-year-old self had simply put her cheek up against that sunset-drenched wing and doggedly hugged away.

In the end the angel had turned his broad back, preparing to leave.

'Don't go!' Freya had screamed, unable to bear the thought of losing him. 'What are you doing? Don't go without me.'

'I cannot remain,' the angel had answered. 'Someone is calling. I am needed elsewhere.'

'But *I* need you! Please! Stay with me!'

And perhaps if the angel had just flown away then, done nothing else, Freya might have been able to forget him. She might have been able to convince herself that his visit was merely the product of an overactive imagination or a peculiarly vivid dream. But how could she have dreamed up what happened next? For the angel had knelt – actually knelt – before her, lowered his proud, beautiful head to the level of her heart and peered inside there. It was such a physical experience that she'd almost felt the small bones of her ribs being moved aside. The gaze was direct, the way a knife is direct. Those eyes: eyes, she realized afterwards, that might have beheld God.

And then the angel had said this: 'There is greatness there, or could be. I see it. My brother is wrong about you. But I should not have come. You are too young. And even if you were older I was wrong to expect anything of you. Forgive me, Freya.'

A gentle kiss on the forehead, and he was gone.

She'd rushed to the window, of course, to see him fly, but he was already out of sight, those wings too fast for her.

Freya had waited for him to come back. She still remembered the exact spot under the window where she'd knelt down, her toes digging into the carpet. But as the hours lengthened, and there was no sign of him, a new worry had crept into her mind. It was dark out there. Maybe he was lost. Did angels have special eyes to see at night? Concerned that he might bump into things and hurt himself, she'd forced herself to stay awake so she could guide him if he got into trouble. All night she waited there, scrunched up inside her quilt, a cold little girl calling softly and forlornly into an empty sky.

Six years on, Freya was still waiting. There had been no second visit from the angel. For the first few weeks she'd opened her window wide every night, fully expecting him to return. Then she'd tried enticing him back, drawing colourful angel pictures and displaying a new one prominently on her pillow each night for him to see. When that didn't work either she borrowed a book from her local library. It contained a long list of angelic names. Perching it precariously on her knees, Freya spent an evening with her head stuck out of her bedroom window, doing her best to pronounce the long, tricky words.

If one of the names was his, he never answered.

In desperation, she finally took to placing squares of chocolate on her window sill, in case she could tempt him back that way. Did angels get hungry? But the night skies remained empty and every morning Freya woke up next to her window, alone.

A sort of madness set in then. An obsession. It was that last tantalizing remark. *There is greatness there, or could be.* It was hard to forget those words. Freya secretly sat in her room, entreating the angel to come back and tell her what he had meant by them.

Soon nothing would stop her leaning dangerously out of her window. When locks were installed, she smashed them. When sturdier locks were fitted she screamed at the top of her lungs until they were removed. For a while her dad could distract her by playing happy flying games – she'd run all over the house with him, arms wide, whooshing about – but soon even such diversions stopped working. Would the presence of a mother have made a difference? Her dad often wondered about that. But there was no way of telling. Freya never knew her mother. She died of cancer in the first year of Freya's life.

It was just after her ninth birthday that Freya finally refused to leave her spot by the window altogether. The crazy times started around then: the visits to the doctor, the specialist clinics, the endless child counsellors. But she only got worse. By the time all the cognitive and other therapies had been tried and had failed Freya had locked herself tight inside a private fantasy realm. It was a world where only the angels could reach her. And inside it, she wasn't just visited again by her angel. (Her guardian angel, she thought of him now. What else could he have been?) It went far beyond that. In her imagination, for over three years, Freya *was* an angel. Her mind constructed all the trappings: the wings, the velvety feathers, the male-female duality, the halo, everything.

Nothing could break her out of it.

Except that her dad had finally done so. His voice, both at home and in the various hospitals, kept tirelessly reaching out to her. Until one day, long after the doctors had given up hope, she'd heard him murmur her name and opened her eyes to find tubes extending into her arms and her dad blinking at her from the foot of a small metal-framed bed.

That was last summer. Another life, it seemed now. For here she was, fourteen years old, back at home again, hopefully for good this time. 'A brand spanking new girl,' as one of the merrier doctors put it. Generally clearer in her mind, anyway. Certainly it had been a long time since she'd flapped her arms around a hospital ward seriously intending to take off.

No more hospitals were needed, in fact, except the occasional outpatient visit. And if she still sometimes imagined herself becoming an angel – if that desire still burned like a hot little stake in her heart – so what? She was more in control of the urge now. Often she could go for hours at a stretch, days even, without thinking about angels at all.

She didn't leave her bedroom window ajar at night any more, either. The pane of glass remained permanently shut. She never opened it. Never. Not ever. Not even a fraction. Not even the tiniest crack for an angel to get its bright, strong fingers beneath.

Seven-fifteen, Monday morning. Definitely time to get up.

Freya yawned and threw the quilt off her bed. Hurrying to the bathroom before her sixteen-year-old brother Luke could beat her to it, she had a good soak under the shower, then concentrated on her hair. Her old waist-length dark brown locks, perfect for angel dressing up, were history. These days Freya kept it strictly cropped and dyed blonde. The most recent cut, a month or so ago, had been expensive – designer hairdresser's no less – but the new style, Dad said, was all part of putting the past behind her, and he'd insisted she got exactly what she wanted.

Back in her bedroom Freya experimented, trying something new, curling the hair ends under slightly. Then she got out her make-up case. By the time she finished, dreary morning November light was entering her window and Luke's alarm clock was jangling in the room next door. He let it ring and ring.

'Luke!' Dad yelled from downstairs.

Freya heard a great groan as Luke woke from his usual coma-like sleep, smashed his arm on the alarm and told it to shut up. Freya's own alarm clock was new. The one with the buzzing angel wings was safely lying on a rubbish tip somewhere.

'Hey!' Luke bashed the wall between their rooms. 'You seen the time? Get up.'

'I *am* up, you idiot!'

He grunted, then traipsed to the bathroom. A few minutes later Freya wandered downstairs, joining him at the breakfast table.

Before she could even reach for the muesli Luke leaned over and prodded at her still-drying hair.

'Leave it alone,' she told him.

'Very fetching.' Luke shook his head. 'All bouncy. Amy's going to love it.'

Amy Carr was one of Freya's new friends. Well, the beginnings of a friendship anyway. Recently she'd been attending school full-time again. Ashcroft High. A huge comprehensive where only a handful of teachers knew what she'd been like before, and none of the other students considered her a misfit or freak – or, at least, she didn't think they did. There was no more talk of angels, either. Freya was careful to make sure not one word on that topic passed her lips.

To begin with she'd just stayed in the background, studying how the other students behaved, especially the more popular girls. It was only when she was ready that she started cautiously bringing up subjects they were interested in – boys, music, TV, whatever. Things she'd missed out on and should have liked herself. Things, in fact, she *was* starting to like herself. It wasn't just an act any more. Boys were definitely interesting.

And in the last month, there'd been another new development – she'd been accepted into one of the more select social circles at school. She wasn't quite a fixture yet, but she was working on it. Amy Carr, just about the most admired Year 10 student, had made it obvious she liked her. And if Amy liked you, others found that they did, too.

Freya's dad entered the kitchen, a piece of toast dangling from his mouth. He narrowed his eyes at her. 'What have you done to your hair, then?'

'It's just a bit of a bob,' she said. 'Nothing special.'

'It looks really good.'

Luke yawned. 'Yeah, lovely.'

Dad poked him in the back of the head. 'You can talk. What do you call this scruff look, anyway?'

Luke wore his hair in a kind of long black tumble to shoulder level. There was no particular style that Freya could discern, though annoyingly it did suit him.

'It's called natural,' Luke answered.

Freya grunted. 'Oh, right. Natural. Like Tarzan. Should have seen the resemblance.' She reached across the table and picked at the wispy sideburns Luke was trying to grow. 'You might try combing it once in a while. Just to see what it looks like. Weird idea, I know.'

Luke scooped cereal into his mouth. 'I spend hours on this messed-up look, Freya.'

'The girls love it, huh?'

'You bet.'

They did, too.

Freya flicked a bran flake at him. He flicked it back.

'Don't take any notice of him,' Dad said to her. 'Your hair looks great.'

Freya was used to Dad's compliments. Every single moment of her recovery had been filled with them, deserved or not. This morning, as her gaze lingered over him, she thought he looked weary. Lately he often did. And after years of looking less than his age, hadn't he also started looking *old*? His sandy hair was thinning, and he wasn't as trim as he had been. Or had she been so preoccupied with her own recovery that she hadn't noticed the changes? The possibility shocked her a little.

'What's wrong?' Dad asked, seeing her pensive look.

'Nothing.' She touched his cheek. 'You look tired, that's all.'

A warning glance passed between Dad and Luke, obviously not meant for her.

'What's going on?' she asked.

For a second Dad shifted uncomfortably in his seat.

Then Luke came to his rescue. 'Freya, why don't you just leave what's left of your hair alone? Isn't that the point of having short hair – so you don't have to bother with it? Hey,' he added, laughing, 'remember all that talcum powder you used to sprinkle on your head, pretending it was angel glitter?'

Dad looked up slowly, guardedly. There was an unwritten rule of the house that angels were never mentioned. Recently, though, Freya had been deliberately nudging the boundaries, and Luke, aware of her growing confidence, had started joining in. Freya was glad. The angel stuff had kept her and Luke apart for years. It felt good being able to share a joke with him about them, chatting as if angels were nothing special at all. Freya felt secure enough to do that now. She wanted her dad to feel the same way, to see how well she was recovering.

'I saw an angel gift set last week,' Luke said. 'Did I tell you? A kind of portable toolkit. You're supposed to use it to get all connected with your own guardian angel. There were some crazy things inside, like fluffy invocation poetry and cheapo incense and candles. And also – get this – a titchy plastic cushion to sit on. I could just see some paunchy middle-aged bloke, scented candle in hand, trying to park his backside on it, invoking away.'

Dad laughed. 'That'll be me.'

'It was expensive, too,' Luke said. 'Real expensive.'

Freya propped her chin in her hands. 'Did you buy it?'

'Of course I did! I need all the spiritual help I can get!'

Freya grinned. Dad did as well, but only half-heartedly. He was clearly made uneasy by all the talk of angels. Freya didn't want him feeling that way. Taking his hand across the table, she told him seriously, 'You don't need to protect me any more. I'm all right now, you know.'

'I know,' he said, equally serious. He walked across to the calendar on the kitchen wall, tapped a date there. 'It's over six months since you started at Ashcroft High. Did you realize that?'

Freya knew exactly how long it had been. Until this year, occasional visits from a home tutor was all she'd been able to handle. Being stable enough to attend regular school had seemed an impossible dream. Looking at Dad, she thought back to the grimness of her last hospital stay. Most of it had been spent tied down with straps, heavily sedated, with a drip in her arm. The hospital staff had no choice about the drip. Freya had refused to eat. Angels don't need food, she'd explained. They live off the stars. Off light itself. Off twinkling sunshine.

Had that really been only a year ago?

'I'll never go back to the way I was,' she said, surprising herself with how emotionally it came out. 'I promise I'll never put you through that again. Are you listening?'

'Yes,' Dad said, gazing at her steadily.

'I mean it.'

'I know you do.' His look was confident, but also said don't commit yourself to such a promise yet.

Freya laughed to get the mood back to normal and finished off her muesli. Shortly after, Dad set off for work and Freya went back to her room. She spent some time gazing critically at her reflection in the dressing-table mirror. A hint of lip-gloss was in order. Most of the other girls were using it, so she'd started dabbing her lower lip before she left the house. Not too much. Just enough to lighten the naturally dark shade of her lips. After that she inserted some ear studs. It was a pair Amy Carr had picked out for her recently, and Freya was careful as she poked them in because her lobes were still sensitive. She liked the discomfort, though. Angels didn't wear jewellery. It was another sign of how much she'd put behind her.

A few minutes later Luke caught her standing in the hall-way, checking her profile, eyeing the studs. He didn't say anything, but Freya knew what he thought of Amy Carr.

'Hey, do what you like,' he said as she waved him away. 'Just make sure you don't turn yourself into her clone, that's all.'

'There's nothing wrong with Amy Carr,' Freya said. It came out more defensively than she wanted.

Luke shrugged. 'If you say so. I just can't help noticing the way the others in that little gang of hers follow her around like a bunch of lapdogs. Amy'll have you doing it soon as well if you don't watch out. Pirouetting. Licking the ground she walks on.'

'No way.'

'Yes, she will. It's all part of the entry criteria to join her nitwit gang. Do as she says, or you're out.' After a warning glare from Freya, he backed off. But he couldn't resist a final comment. 'Better make sure you don't smudge that make-up, Freya. Amy Carr won't like you if you don't look perfect.'

'Luke?' Freya said sweetly.

'Yeah?'

'Shut up.'

Freya left for Ashcroft High a few minutes later. She'd barely gone two steps down Cardigan Street when she spotted Albert, a local pensioner, making a bee-line towards her. She spent a few minutes chatting with him, then out of the corner of her eye spotted a couple of girls walking together further down the street – Vicky Stokes and Gemma Masters, two of Amy's crew.

Seeing who Freya was with, Gemma pulled a sour face.

Freya winced. Ouch. Not good to have been seen chin-wagging with an old man. Making her excuses to Albert, with two quick snaps of her heels she managed to get away. At the bottom of the street, crossing into Pottery Close, she fell into step with Vicky and Gemma.

Vicky was doll-pretty, with heavily-lacquered blond hair and unusually wide, almond-shaped green eyes. Gemma was brunette, and taller, with a big chest and a protuberant chin she tried her best to disguise. Freya felt both girls giving her a brisk, silent once-over, as if to confirm that she looked good enough to be seen walking with.

They sneaked each other an almost imperceptible nod.

'Ooh, look what you've done, Freya!' Gemma cooed,

touching her hair. 'It's a bob, isn't it? Looks really nice, doesn't it, Vicky?'

'It's lovely,' Vicky said, equally gushing, taking Freya's arm as though they were sisters.

Freya blushed slightly. The interest of both girls had only picked up when Amy started favouring her, but Freya couldn't help enjoying the compliments and attention all the same. Other girls they passed on the footpath were giving her mildly envious glances.

'Like what you're wearing,' Vicky said. 'New skirt, eh?'

'Mm.'

Freya had been made to realize that her standard school uniform required some gentle and not so gentle teasing into shape. A tighter skirt, for a start, and reduced length. A short tie as well, with an open collar, at least until you got into school. Today, in addition to her stud earrings, Freya had a modest opal pendant swinging from her neck. Her dad had given her the money to buy it only yesterday.

'Oh, that's gorgeous!' Gemma said. 'Vicky, take a look at what Freya's been hiding from us.'

Vicky paused her texting to take a look. 'Um, lovely.' She shook her head, glaring at her mobile. 'Darren's so stupid!' she growled. 'He was supposed to meet me after school yesterday, but he forgot. Can you believe that? He just left me standing outside the school gates where anyone could see me.'

'Chuck him,' Gemma said matter-of-factly. 'No. Wait. He's handy for money. Don't chuck him.'

Freya joined in the laughter.

'He'd better meet me tonight.' Vicky shook her head glumly and continued furiously texting.

'Who was that you were talking to outside your house, then?' Gemma asked Freya.

'Just a neighbour,' she said.

Gemma backed off, genuinely amazed.

'But he's an old man. What do you want to talk to him for?'

'He's OK.'

'No, he's not. He tried talking to me once. He's so short I could see his pink scalp.' Gemma grimaced. 'There was even some kind of white furzy stuff on it.'

'He's all right,' Freya said uneasily.

'No, he looks disgusting. No point defending him, Freya.' Gemma laughed. 'I saw him the other day, bending down to do up his shoelaces. You know the way old men always have those thin shoelaces that keep coming undone? What's the matter with them? Anyway, he had this really skinny leg, all veiny . . .'

'He *is* over eighty,' Freya said.

'I bet he smells.'

Freya half laughed. 'No, he doesn't smell.'

'Yeah, I bet he does. Old people always smell funny.'

'My grandma smells,' Vicky said, still texting. 'She smells of pee. She's incontinent.'

'Ugh! Shut up!' Gemma growled. 'Look, there's Amy!'

Gemma and Vicky gave a little wave in unison, and Freya copied them.

Amy was *the* attractive blonde of year ten. Naturally blonde of course, that had been made clear to Freya more than once. Tall and slender, her athletic legs ended in heels just this side of being banned at school. This morning she had a couple of the better-looking boys from Ashcroft High hovering either side of her. Glancing sweetly over her shoulder, she indicated that it was OK to be approached.

Freya and the other girls joined her, and the enlarged group swanned into the school playground, chatting loudly, joking and generally eyeing up the boys. They took up their usual position not far from the main entrance, where Amy could see everyone and everyone could see her. She hadn't paid Freya any personal attention yet, but that was normal.

'And who's this?' asked one particularly tall fit boy Freya didn't know, standing behind Amy.

'Ah, you like her, do you?' Amy said, laughing and turning to Freya. 'Naughty Year 11's after you, girl. Better watch yourself.'

Freya, flustered, smiled cautiously back.

'I'm Adam,' the boy said.

Freya nearly put out her hand to shake his, an old habit, then remembered just to give him a quick nod.

'Freya.'

'Nice to meet you, Freya.'

'Yeah.'

Gemma giggled, but a venomous glance from Amy stopped her cold. Winking at Freya, Amy said airily, 'See you later, boys,' and with a dismissive wave of her hand the males magically evaporated. The four girls peeled away together, everyone stepping neatly into line behind Amy.

'He's gorgeous, isn't he?' Gemma whispered in Freya's ear.

'Yes,' Freya replied, laughing.

'You know who he is, don't you?'

Freya gave her a vacant look.

'God, she doesn't know,' Gemma said. 'Bless her.'

'He's Adam Rix,' Vicky explained. 'Amy's ex. Used to be the most popular boy in the school before Amy dumped him.'

Amy shrugged. 'He still hangs around for some reason. You can have him if you want, Freya.'

'What?' Freya felt her face flush. Talking about boys was one thing, going out with them another.

Amy smiled mischievously. 'Yeah, you'll look good with Adam hanging off your arm.' She touched Freya's hair approvingly. 'You look older as well, since you cut your hair. Boys like that.'

Gemma and Vicky were miffed at being excluded from this exchange, but kept their silence and traipsed behind.

'What are you doing Thursday evening?' Amy asked, snapping open her mobile.

'I . . . haven't got any special plans.' Freya tried to sound cool. It was the first time Amy had invited her out after school.

'Good,' Amy said. 'I'll set it up now. Me, you, Vicky and Gemma. Does that sound all right?'

'Yeah.' Freya smiled.

Amy smiled back. 'Oh, and four boys, of course.'

Freya was aware of being closely studied. She'd never been out with boys and, although she might have tried to pretend she had with the others, Amy would see right through any act.

'Great,' she said.

'You got something to wear?'

'I . . . can find something.'

'Fine.' Amy turned to Vicky. 'You bring Darren, but make sure he's got plenty of money, or he can stay home.' Vicky nodded unhappily. 'Gemma, you pick Freya up.'

'What? But I live miles from her house!'

'It's not that far. We don't want her to have to come on her own, do we? First date and everything, she needs a chaperone.' Gemma capitulated, while managing to give Freya a filthy look. Freya didn't trust herself to say anything.

'Right,' Amy said. 'It's all set then. Eight o'clock. We'll meet outside Burger King.'

'I'll be ready,' Freya found herself promising.

'Gemma will pick you up at 7.30. Don't be late.' Amy laughed. 'I mean, you don't want to keep Adam waiting, do you?'

'Will he be there?'

"Course he will, if I ask him to be. Just make sure . . . what?'

A dark angel was staring down at Freya.

It was perched on a nearby factory roof, watching her.

Freya stumbled slightly. The angel was big – at least ten feet tall – and utterly black. Squinting, she tried to see it more clearly, but the sun's rays seemed to die when they touched it.

'What's up?' Amy wanted to know.

'Nothing . . . I'm . . .'

Images of angels had dominated Freya's hospital years, but nothing as terrifying as this. Aware of Vicky holding her up, she separated herself and glanced towards the roof again.

The angel was still there, staring at her. It hadn't moved. Its body was so impenetrably dark that the brickwork on the building beneath was nearly erased by the sheer depth of its shadow. Freya tried to make out the angel's features. There was a face of some kind there, but it was hideous – as if the angel had chosen the nose, eyes and lips of the most deformed people in the world to be its own.

It's not real, she told herself. It's not. Stand up straight. Don't let them see you like this.

She forced out a smile. 'I just felt dizzy . . .'

Vicky helped steady her. Gemma and Amy gave each other a suspicious look.

When Freya checked the roof again the dark angel was gone.

For ten minutes she concentrated hard on following the conversation between the other girls and acting as normally as she could. It's OK, she told herself. It's not the first time you've seen an angel. But it *was* the first time she'd seen an angel since leaving the hospital. It's fine, she tried to reassure herself. Forget it. The doctors said you were bound to still see them every now and again. It doesn't mean anything.

A sense of relief was just starting to gain hold when she felt a tap on her arm. With a mouth opening and closing like a fish, Gemma squealed, 'Oh – my – God! What on earth is *that*?'

For one horrifying second Freya was sure that Gemma had seen the dark angel.

Then she realized her mistake.

It was a girl.

An odd-looking girl, about their own age, had been left outside the main school gates. She wore what looked like an ancient boy's duffle coat. Below that Freya could just see white little-girl socks reaching down to her nondescript flats. Her face was small and pinched, her mousy hair unfashionably long and curly.

Her mother was with her, fussing away, scratching at a patch on her coat. Then the mother did something that made Freya gasp. She licked her finger and rubbed at the girl's cheek, as if she was a five-year-old who needed help cleaning herself up. The girl tried to stop her, but the mother held her hands and rubbed away at the cheek until she was satisfied.

The girl's face dropped in dismay, and Freya's heart went out to her. It was only a few years ago that she'd turned up to school herself, flouncing around in her own home-made angel wings held on with sticky tape. What was the woman thinking of, behaving like that in front of everyone? Didn't she know the rest of the kids would crucify her daughter if they saw this?

'Ah . . .' Vicky muttered, a trace of sympathy in her voice. But she soon changed her attitude once she heard what Amy had to say.

'New victim,' Amy announced. 'Oh, this is going to be good. This is going to be so, so good.'

Vicky tittered, giving Freya a suddenly scandalized glance. 'Look at her coat! Oh God, I wouldn't be seen dead . . .'

'She's coming in!' Gemma squeaked. 'Quick, move back before she contaminates us.'

The mother was gone. The girl, after briefly trying to measure the astonished looks she was getting, walked with slow dignity through the school gate.

Her eyes locked on Freya.

'What are you doing?' Gemma whispered, as Freya headed towards the girl. She grabbed Freya's arm, giving her a disgusted look.

Freya stopped. The duffle-coated girl stared hopefully at her, obviously desperate for someone to cling onto.

'The state some people let themselves get in,' Amy said loudly, making sure the girl heard.

Freya knew she'd made a grave social slip-up by approaching the new girl in front of Amy. She'd already behaved oddly when the image of the dark angel surprised her. She didn't dare make matters worse now. Feeling awful about it, she took one step back.

'Freya *was* going to talk to her,' Gemma hissed at Amy.

'Shut up,' Amy said. She patted Freya's cheek. 'She wasn't. You weren't actually going to say hi to her, were you?'

It was a test. Freya knew it.

She licked her lips. 'No . . . of course not.'

The duffle-coated girl, hearing this, made a funny little noise and shuffled off. She stood on her own, her eyes darting nervously around. Then she sidled up to a wall and hunched against it.

'Look, she's trying to hide!' Gemma said.

The girl shuddered. Pulling a bulky hood up over her head, she deliberately concealed her face. Seeing that, one boy laughed. For a while the duffle-coated girl just stood there, seemingly trying to become part of the wall. Then she abruptly clasped her hands together.

Shutting her eyes, she whispered something.

'Is she praying?' Vicky cried, copying Gemma's tone. 'I think she's praying! Oh God, she's praying. Actually praying.' She immediately got out her mobile, clicked a snapshot of the girl and started texting.

Amy never took her eyes off Freya.

Gemma was also glancing at her sceptically. 'You did want to say hello to her, didn't you? You *still* want to.'

'No' Freya answered. 'It's just that she looks so –'

'Cheap,' Amy said.

'Vulnerable.'

It was a mistake. Freya knew it the moment the word slipped out. Amy dug her nails into Freya's wrist, she was so irritated.

'She's just a scab, Freya Harrison,' she growled. 'We don't talk to scabs. Are you with us or not? God, I bring you in, give you advice, practically offer you a boyfriend on a plate, and you go mooning after some dirty gipsy scab girl.'

Freya mentally implored her to stop, but said nothing. She felt wretched about relying so much on Amy's opinion, but didn't dare challenge her.

The new girl had heard everything and cast her eyes down. Freya nearly walked over to her, but held back. If she went over now, the social status she'd worked so hard to develop would vanish instantly. She'd be back among the school misfits and freaks again. She couldn't return to that place, not after all the effort she'd made to get away from it. Despising herself, Freya looked at the ground, anywhere but at the new girl, and silently prayed for the bell to go.

Behind her, there were suppressed tears. Freya didn't turn around, though she knew who they were coming from. When the bell finally went, she felt Amy's nails relaxing. She'd hardly been aware that they'd been digging into her all this time.

Gemma was laughing, mostly at Freya now. As they walked towards the school entrance, Freya briefly got up the courage to look back.

The new girl, meekly pulling her hood up to hide her face, was running like a petrified little toddler out of the school gates.

That evening Stephanie Rice knelt in her room, burning with humiliation. To have run away like that! To have actually *run in tears* out of the school gates with everyone watching. How could she ever go back now? She couldn't.

Yet she had to. Her mother had made that quite clear. All the pleading earlier had made no difference.

'Choose another school!' she'd begged. 'Mother, please!'

'But we've tried all the others in our catchment area, you know that. There aren't any left. It has to be this one.'

'I'll go back to the last school. I'll try harder. The Headmaster liked me there. He said so. He –'

'I know he did. But given the reaction of the other students –'

'Mother, I can't go back to Ashcroft High! It's too late to make a good impression. Too many saw me running away.'

'Stephanie . . .'

'You shouldn't have been there. You made it worse. You made me look like a little girl, scratching at my face like that!'

'I'm sorry, darling. I didn't think, but . . . you wanted me to come inside with you. You *asked* me to.'

'I know, I know, I know!'

Stephanie knew it was ridiculous getting angry with her

parents. They didn't understand much about the real world. All her life they'd shielded her from it, kept her close to them, rarely allowing her out unsupervised. The few other kids they'd permitted her to be with were all hand-picked from families just like their own. Even the terms they preferred her to use – *Mother*, *Father*, instead of Mum and Dad – were oddly formal, though Stephanie had used them for so long now that she could hardly think of addressing them any other way.

Distrusting modern schooling, they'd educated her exclusively at home. All that had changed when Stephanie turned thirteen. Reassessing Stephanie's home environment, the authorities found it lacking, and forced her outraged parents to place her in local educational care. Stephanie could still recall how much she'd looked forward to that first day at a real school – a whiff of freedom at last. Until, that is, she blithely turned up at her first class wearing a hand-made blue cotton dress. And sparkly yellow hair grips. And plimsolls.

The kids laughed her straight out of the door at that comprehensive. By the next, Stephanie had wised up enough to ditch the plimsolls and hair grips, but she still couldn't shake off her home-grown naivety. Whenever she opened her mouth, the words always came out wrong, sounding quietly desperate.

A couple of students started pushing her around in her second school. Initially it was nothing much, just small vindictive nudges and shoves between lessons. But it soon escalated. Having no idea how to stop it, Stephanie changed her behaviour. The other students seemed to prefer a more confident personality, so she stopped playing the shy mouse and tried acting with a hint of defiance. When that didn't work either, Stephanie, totally confused now, just looked for ways to stay unnoticed. She kept quiet. She didn't speak unless she had to. She didn't ask for anything, didn't even try to make friends, though she would have loved a friend to talk to. Yet nothing changed. The other students still shunned her.

But at least I made it into the classrooms of those other schools, Stephanie thought. At least I *started* lessons. Today she'd barely made it through the gates.

She stayed in her bedroom all day, furious with herself about the way she'd panicked at Ashcroft High. ('Like a little girl, Stephanie, that's all you are! Too weird to make any friends. Fourteen years old, and you still can't do it.'). It was tempting to blame Mother for what had happened, but it wasn't Mother who'd fled in humiliation from the school, was it?

That evening, locking herself in her room, Stephanie ignored every attempt by her mother to get her to eat. She remained in bed until after midnight, her face covered with a sheet. Only much later still did she throw the sheet off and glance nervously up. And even then she didn't have the courage to look directly at the portrait hanging high on her wall.

The portrait was of an angel. Clad in a green tunic, with gold-rimmed eyes, the name *Nadiel* was emblazoned across his brass shield.

It was an old picture. Stephanie had bought it on impulse from a charity shop around her ninth birthday. Thinking back on it, she couldn't even remember why she bought it. In defiance of the strictness of her parents, perhaps? Or just for someone to talk to? In her less confident moments, Stephanie wondered if it was just that.

It was certainly an easy portrait for a lonely girl to grow fond of. In his left hand, the angel Nadiel held a dove of peace; in his other, a staff reaching up to seraphs in the heavenly firmament. His feet were shod in burnished bronze, and a smile played on his lips, and every day it was the same smile, beaming beneficently down.

As to when Stephanie started to convince herself that Nadiel represented more than a picture, she couldn't have said. All she knew was that as the years passed her casual interest in Nadiel's portrait turned into something more significant. It became a belief in the existence of angels. Whether that belief started in the cradle of her heart or her head she didn't know. But over time, gradually, she came to be increasingly sure that she was right. She almost felt it in her blood: angels were real; beyond the confines of the portrait, Nadiel and other guardians like him truly existed.

But if she had a guardian angel, why had she fled from school this morning? Before setting off for Ashcroft High, hadn't she put her absolute trust in Nadiel to protect her? Hadn't she placed herself in his hands, promising to stay calm no matter what the students did?

Yet at the first sign of opposition she'd caved in.

What did that say about the strength of her faith in her angel?

For many hours that night Stephanie knelt, staring at the floor in shame, asking for Nadiel's forgiveness. Then she decided that whispering apologies in her usual way wasn't enough. Not this time. She needed to be braver, to do something more direct. To apologize in person. Sneaking into libraries and bookshops over the years, she'd read literature on the subject of angels, and some of those explained how to bring your own personal guardian into a confined space.

A direct manifestation.

It wasn't something Stephanie had attempted before – she'd been far too nervous to try anything so dramatic. But now, lying in the darkness, she found herself thinking everything through carefully, recalling all the details of the ceremony she'd read.

She began by tiptoeing around her room, ensuring it was a fit area to receive an angel. This was vitally important: the surfaces all had to be sparkling and dust free, especially her window. Only after that was done did Stephanie clear a broad circular space on her bedroom floor.

Then, after making sure her parents were asleep so she would not be disturbed, she selected a candle. Stephanie didn't believe in all the mystical properties some New Age angel books ascribed to candles, but she'd got into the habit of lighting one when she was in trouble. This particular candle was cream-coloured, scented with rose and had never been lit before – a good omen. She closed the curtains, so that its naked flame would better illuminate her.

Like two quiet sisters, she and the candle faced one another in the near-darkness.

I'm ready, she thought.

Kneeling, she lit the candle, and held it between the fingers of both hands.

'I dedicate this candle to you, my guardian angel,' she whispered, closing her eyes to help her remember the words of the ceremony. 'I ask only that you work with your perfect abilities to help me.'

She placed the candle in the middle of the floor and lifted her arms up towards the centre of the room, palms outward.

'Each moment I know I am protected by my guardian angel,' she said. 'I believe in him and live in trust that he will attract only miracles into my life. I know he watches over me and creates an ideal path.'

Then Stephanie closed her eyes and imagined a funnel of bright blue light coming down from the sky to cover her home. She pictured in her mind four of the great archangels. One she placed at the north of the house, one at the south, one at the east and one at the west, near her own room. She imagined archangel Michael carrying his sword of flame, floating above the chimney of their house in all his glory, protecting it.

Then she slowly chanted:

'Michael, Who Stands with God, I ask you to guard and bless this house.

'Gabriel, Hero of God, who protects the entrance to Heaven, I ask you to guard and bless this house.

'Raphael, Healer and Teacher, I ask you to guard and bless this house.

'Uriel, Fire of God, I ask you to guard and bless this house.'

The final part of the ceremony was meant to be more personal.

To reinforce positive thoughts before she started, Stephanie picked a card at random from the pack of Angelic Affirmations she kept under her pillow and read it out loud.

'Security and safety.'

She picked another.

'Personal peace.'

Both seemed appropriate. She said the affirmations over and over under her breath. Then she fetched her diary. Throughout the years she had collected together a few lines to use on occasions like this. What followed came in slowly-delivered sentences between the flickering of the candle, with long breaths between.

'Fear cannot affect me here in this place.

'Fear means nothing.

'Fear has no dominion over the angels.

'I believe in Nadiel, my guardian angel. He loves me more completely than I can possibly know.

'As long as my guardian angel is with me, I can withstand anything.

'In love and light, love and light, love and light.'

Feeling dry-mouthed and nervous, Stephanie almost stopped. The books said that the final part of the ceremony had to be performed perfectly if she was to bring her guardian angel directly into the room.

Stephanie took her time, making sure she was focused.

First, she imagined herself surrounded by a cloud. Puffing

the cloud out, she pictured its supple bounciness surrounding her whole body. Then she turned the cloud a soft green colour, to represent Nadiel, and pictured the vapour of the cloud flooding down from the top of her head and shooting through her body. Only when that was done did she solemnly call her guardian angel into her presence.

'Nadiel, Nadiel,' she said in a wavering high voice, raising her face to the window. 'I'm here. Come to me.'

At first there was nothing. Then – stifling a gasp – she sensed an angel in the distance, floating on a waft of his own breath towards her. She could not see Nadiel clearly, but the books had warned her about this, and told her to feel for him instead in the perturbations of the air and the waters of her body.

She did so, and within moments sensed the luminescence of inhuman eyes entering her room. Stephanie trembled, but she did not feel afraid. Nadiel came alone, as if he existed only for her. She watched him soar into the room, raising his brass shield in greeting, and it was as if he was as excited to greet her as she was to greet him. He slowly lowered his arms to embrace her, and briefly she felt his love pouring into her, banishing all uncertainty – and forgiving her for doubting herself at school that day.

This was the moment in the ceremony when Stephanie was supposed to ask for advice. But now, in Nadiel's direct embrace, she felt too humbled, too overwhelmed, to request anything. 'Nadiel, I ask . . . I ask . . .' But she couldn't think; she was too grateful, too happy, too confused. Finally, however, she smiled, and lifted her chin proudly. 'Nadiel, I ask to be wrapped in your protection during this time,' she said. 'I need the students to accept me. I need to do the right things when I'm with them. Help me to. That's all I ask.'

For a long time after the ceremony was over, Stephanie stayed within the brightly charged atmosphere of the room, shivering with excitement. She'd called for her guardian angel, and he had come – of course he had! Angels didn't ration out their affections like people, she thought. They came when you needed them.

Clenching her fists, she was filled with sudden renewed determination to face the students of Ashcroft High. But even with the presence of Nadiel such a recent memory, Stephanie's courage didn't last for long. Courage is a mercurial property. Although she could picture herself marching confidently past the students next morning, head erect, Nadiel like a lion of strength beside her, Stephanie didn't truly believe she could do it. Not really.

Realizing that, and angry with herself, she took the portrait of Nadiel off her wall, pressed it against her chest and asked to be loved. She didn't even know where that stray request came from – some hollow of her heart, perhaps – but she couldn't deny it mattered to her.

What kind of love, though? It wasn't more of Nadiel's love she was after. Nor that of her parents. With foreboding, almost dread, she realized it was the affection of the students at Ashcroft High she craved.

Stephanie lay in the dark, thinking about them. She wanted

them to like her, but she was still terrified about confronting them at school tomorrow. And the longer she lay there against her pillow, the more obvious it seemed to Stephanie that love itself was too much to expect. Love was far too much too ask from a bunch of students she'd never even met. So instead she wished for something smaller. She wished for a friend. But a friend seemed too much to expect as well, so Stephanie limited herself to asking for acceptance. Finally, as the night hours dwindled, eating up the last of her confidence, she wished only not to be laughed at. Then she wished for less, since that was not going to happen. She wished, after they'd finished laughing at her, that the students would leave her alone.

Shortly after Stephanie fell asleep, a real angel entered her room. It was not Nadiel, angel of gold-rimmed eyes and burnished feet, who did not exist except in Stephanie's imagination. It was a far greater and more beautiful angel than that. And as it stood over her bed, looking down, its feathers tinged with the afterglow of sunsets, the light against the pale walls increased and magnified. But even if she had woken, Stephanie would not have seen it, for it was not light from this world.

The angel bent towards her and still Stephanie did not wake. Only in her dreams did she feel the soft drift of feathers wrapping themselves around her small head, giving her, for a while at least, peace.

Freya waited for the return of the dark angel. Such a horror-creature could only be a throwback from her imagination, and it terrified her that she could conjure up something so frightening, but she was determined not to dwell on it. She didn't mention it to anyone, least of all Amy, Vicky or Gemma. All three were ruthlessly practical in outlook. In fact, that was partly why she gravitated so strongly towards them. There was none of the stuff of angels around anyone who hung out with Amy Carr.

At school, Freya kept a cautious look-out for the vulnerable, duffle-coated girl. She felt guilty about the way she'd ignored her, but was also relieved not to see her scared little face pop through the gates again. If Amy caught her chatting to anyone like that her punishment would be swift and vicious. She'd already become distinctly cooler towards Freya since the incident in the playground. There'd been no more mention of Thursday's night out, or meeting up with the good-looking Adam.

For the rest of that week, Amy repositioned the gang right inside the school gates. Freya knew it was so she could be among the first to confront the strange girl if she ever came back. But Freya suspected that Amy had more subtle games in mind as well – not least of which was probably to use the new girl to test her loyalty. Luke had warned Freya about something, when she first started hanging around with Amy. 'Don't get on Carr's wrong side,' he'd told her. 'From what I've heard, none of Amy's old friends are allowed to walk quietly away once she gets fed up with them. She destroys them if she can. Are you ready for that?'

Freya wasn't ready for it, and as each new day passed she felt more relieved that she'd avoided a showdown. Through a judicious amount of praise she managed to rebuild some of Amy's confidence in her, too.

Her reward came on the following Tuesday.

'Sorry you couldn't make the last night out,' Amy said, as if Freya had uninvited herself. 'Anyway, we're going out again tomorrow if you're still interested. Adam certainly is.' She gave Freya a knowing look and they both laughed. 'He asked about you last week, you know.'

'Did he?' Freya tried to look neutral.

Gemma, standing beside Vicky, gave Freya a jealous look.

'Mm,' Amy said. 'Very put out you weren't there, he was. When I told him you'd probably be out with us tomorrow night he couldn't wipe the grin off his face, could he Gemma?'

Gemma chewed her lip, pretending not to hear.

'Don't worry about our Gemma,' Amy said. 'She's just a bit sulky 'cause she's been dumped by her boyfriend.'

'Ah, there, there,' Vicky said. 'He wasn't any good anyway.' She smiled, reaching into her handbag. 'Gems, you've got a massive spot coming out on your neck. I can give you something for that.'

'Shut up!' Gemma groaned. 'He didn't dump me! I wasn't even seeing him, really. Anyway, *I dumped him*!'

'Right.' Amy winked at Freya.

For the rest of that morning, Freya concentrated on her lessons. Through sheer hard work she'd been able to rise up to the top set in English, but she was still struggling to catch up in most other subjects. Amy, of course, was in the top percentile of every group. Freya doubted that any teacher would dare put her anywhere else.

As for Gemma and Vicky, they were in the highest English set this year, but were only middling in other subjects. Vicky was actually in the bottom class for nearly half of her lessons, a fact Amy sometimes alluded to, never to Vicky's advantage. 'At least she gets to see Darren a lot,' Amy muttered privately to Freya once.

Shortly before they broke up for lunch that day, Amy sauntered across a school corridor to face Freya. 'You'll be very interested in the conversation I just had,' she announced.

'Oh?'

'Yep. I just told Adam to dress up especially nicely for you when we meet up. Told him you like him, but that you have high standards. The highest.'

Freya was horrified. 'You shouldn't have said anything like that.'

'Why not? Don't worry, he loved it. I told him I wanted him

panting for breath and full of expectation. You know what boys get like when you talk to them like that. He could hardly stand still.'

Freya inwardly cringed, her face flushing.

'Don't thank me then,' Amy grunted.

'Don't be silly,' Freya said, trying to stay cool. 'You know I appreciate it.'

'And so does he,' Amy replied. 'He was drooling at the prospect. From what I can see you're well in there, girl.'

Freya wasn't sure she wanted that yet.

'What's he like?' she asked nervously.

'Like any other boy, I suppose. He's a good kisser, if that's what you mean.'

'I didn't mean that.' Freya laughed, though her heart was racing.

'You haven't kissed anyone before, have you?'

Freya found her eyes roving the corridor. No one else was listening.

'Don't worry, I won't tell anyone,' Amy said. 'We're friends, aren't we? I wouldn't do something like that.' She took Freya's arm and smiled, whipping out her mobile. 'You should get some practise in, though. I'll ring up Gemma's ex, shall I? He's free these days. You can practise on him. He's got nice lips. I bet he wouldn't mind.'

'Don't!'

They both grinned.

'Anyway,' Amy said, putting the mobile away and squeezing Freya's wrist, 'we'll have a good time. I just hope it's not too cold. Gemma never puts enough clothes on, if you know what I mean. See you around eight then, yeah?'

'Yeah.'

'Don't forget Gemma's picking you up. Be nice to her. She won't have a boy, so she'll be miserable. Unless she can find a new one today. I wouldn't put that past her, either. She's a fast worker when she wants to be.'

Freya nodded.

Amy stepped back and studied Freya approvingly. 'Mm. I think we're going to look nice together, walking down that high street with two gorgeous boys hanging off our every word. It won't just be Vicky and Gemma looking at us.'

Freya felt a thrill run through her. That was Amy's gift: she could be cruel, but she could also shine a light on you that seemed to offer everything.

'Are you bringing someone along as well?' Freya asked her cautiously.

'Of course.'

'Who?'

'No one you know. I don't bother picking from the boys at school these days. Gets messy.'

Freya laughed, and Amy, adjusting the bag on her shoulder, wandered royally off down the corridor, bestowing nods on one or two younger girls. They smiled back, grateful for the moment of attention.

It was lunchtime at Ashcroft High, and Year 7 student Sam Davenport, eleven years old, was passing a derelict warehouse on his way back home for lunch. He'd just crossed into a side-street when he had the misfortune to bump into Jeremy Tate. Tate was a sixteen-year-old thug who'd been steadily building up an aggressive reputation at Ashcroft High for a couple of years. It didn't take much to irritate him. Sam had a lock of blond hair that fell limply across his brow. The lock made him look like a fresh-cheeked junior schooler. That, plus the fact that Tate had a mate with him he wanted to impress, was enough of a reason to set him off.

He tripped Sam up as he walked past. 'Just where do you think you're going, you clumsy little git? You've made my shoe dirty. I'm not very happy about that.'

The other boy grinned like a shark.

'Lick it off,' Tate said. 'Then I'll pardon you.'

Sam gazed at Tate, trying to work out if he was serious.

'Go on,' Tate said. 'Or I'll kick your teeth out.'

Sam swallowed. Situations like this were new to him. He'd heard about Tate – who hadn't? But what should he do? He couldn't lick the shoe. Anything he said would only make it worse, though. So he said nothing.

'No?' Tate slowly took off his jacket and rolled up his sleeves. 'So it's a kicking, then. Unless you reconsider the shoe option. See, I'm trying to be fair about this.'

Sam put his head down and tried to just walk on.

Tate barred his way. 'Hey, goldilocks, I'm talking to you. You're showing disrespect. I don't mind, but my friend here is really touchy and sensitive when it comes to that.'

Sam screwed up his courage. 'Are you going to let me

through?' he managed to whisper.

'Are we going to let him through?' Tate mimicked his tone. 'Should we let him through?' Laughter. 'Of course we'll let you through. We'll let your leg through before we break it, then your arm . . .' Sam weakly pushed at Tate, to get by him. 'Oh, you gonna fight back, eh?' Tate slapped Sam's head twice. 'Brilliant. Come on!'

Then, behind them, a new figure emerged.

It was Luke. On his own way home for lunch, he'd come across the scene by chance.

'Oh, how brave,' he said. 'How fearless of you, Tate. I'm so impressed. Building your reputation on Year 7s these days, eh? Two of you against one as well. Hold those heads up high.'

Tate glanced at him malevolently.

'Stay out of this, Harrison.'

'Or you'll do what?'

For a moment Tate was obviously deciding – fight or not?

Luke could see it, and knew he'd miscalculated. He didn't want to fight. The sudden, unexpected threat of violence also made him remember only too well what it felt like to be cringing in this Year 7's position. At about the same age, Luke had been quietly and methodically beaten up by a fifteen-year-old boy every week for several months – an ordeal that only ended when the boy's family left the area. Most of the blows Luke endured at the time had been to his body – out of sight, easily hidden – and so much crazy stuff had been going on with Freya around then that even Dad hadn't realized the worst of it.

Glancing now at the blond boy quaking beside him, Luke

could see the sheer relief on his face – relief that he was here to protect him. Luke understood that only too well. All those years ago he'd dreamed of a situation like this arising – some bigger, stronger kid appearing out of the blue, stepping in to rescue him.

He knew he couldn't just let Tate do what he wanted. But this situation wasn't quite the same, was it? He'd been up against a single older boy. Tate came with another member of his gang. If they attacked together he wouldn't stand much chance.

Luckily the other boy was edging away, ready to back off, and Tate, seeing that, swore and decided to retreat. He sauntered off, then gave vent to a free rein of curses once he was at a safe distance.

Luke smiled back, but he had trouble keeping the smile intact. Tate would remember this. Being humiliated. Especially in front of a Year 7. The whole situation gave him an uneasy feeling about the future.

When Tate was out of sight, Luke knelt down beside Sam.

'You all right?' he asked.

'Yeah.' Sam hung his head. 'They didn't hurt me. But I didn't stand on his shoe,' he blurted. 'I didn't do anything. I didn't!'

Luke nodded, gazing up at the rows of houses either side of the street. It was unusually quiet for this time of day. No one was anywhere near them now that Tate had gone. The street looked deserted. Looking around, Luke felt a chill and wondered what was wrong, what was making him feel so uncomfortable. Maybe it was just a delayed reaction from the confrontation with Tate, all those violent memories coming back. Or maybe it was the street itself, the emptiness, the absence of people, that made Luke think of his Dad, and of other silences, his own. He considered events that might be ahead.

I can't let it drift on like this, he decided. Freya's got to know. Dad's wrong to delay this. I'll tell her now. While I've got the nerve.

He knew exactly where he'd find Freya. Amy always dragged her gang to the same places at lunchtime. 'You hungry?' he asked the boy standing patiently beside him.

Sam nodded.

'Come on, then.' Luke clamped a hand on his shoulder. 'Just a little detour. Then I'll get you home.'

Amy lived too far away to go home for lunch, but she never fancied the press of the Year 7 and 8s cramping her style in the canteen so the gang tended to spend lunchtimes hanging around the local shops. Freya met up with her and Vicky in their usual spot near the sports hall before setting off.

Gemma, however, was missing.

'She's cruising,' Amy said with a grin, offering no further explanation.

They eventually found her standing outside a video rental shop, eating an open bag of chips. Between mouthfuls, Gemma was eyeing up some nearby boys hopefully.

'Stop it, Gems,' Vicky said, from a few feet away. 'Your tongue's hanging out.'

Gemma laughed. 'Do you think they like me, though?'

'Yeah, 'course they do. But you don't even know them.'

'I know one of them a bit. I think so, anyway. That one with the big nose, he's called, yeah him, don't point you idiot, he's called –' Gemma screwed up her face, trying to remember, then laughed. 'Big nose. Yeah, that's his actual name – John Bignose.'

'God, you're shameless,' Vicky tittered.

'Watch this,' Gemma said, glancing at Freya.

· 44 ·

She sauntered up to a group of five boys. They were sixteen or seventeen year olds. Anyone younger would have been beneath her attention. Smiling, she nonchalantly ignored four of the boys and offered the best-looking one a salty chip.

'Thanks,' he said, seeing that wasn't all she was offering.

Amy shook her head in admiration and smiled at Freya. 'She's a fast worker, all right. I told you so.'

The good-looking boy took several chips, then said 'Cheers' and turned back to his mates, pointedly ignoring Gemma. The other boys laughed. Gemma, drawing in a deep breath, retreated with as much dignity as she could muster.

'The cheek!' Vicky exclaimed.

Amy just grinned, and Freya covertly joined in with her, but she knew she'd have died if the same thing had happened to her.

Gemma, though, hitching up her skirt a little, wasn't done. Another boy, a bit spotty but on his own this time, stood nearby. He accepted a chip with great surprise and eventually, many chips later, took the hint.

'She'd rather go out with any old ugly thing than have no one for tomorrow night,' Amy sighed. 'It's sad, really. Not like you, Freya. Pretty thing like you could probably have had that first boy. Not that you need him. I've got you a hand-picked boy for our night out, haven't I?'

Freya blushed. Then she noticed a commotion starting up outside a nearby shop.

'Whath up?' Gemma asked, mouth full of chips, swivelling her eyes with great interest.

A bunch of kids were lined up outside the newsagents, backing away from someone.

'Ugh, mouldy tramp,' Gemma said.

It was a woman. Freya estimated that she was probably in her mid-thirties, an average age to be begging round here, but she didn't look like a tramp.

'She's filthy,' Amy said.

Freya looked more closely and saw that the woman was, in fact, clean.

'What's the matter with her?' Vicky wondered.

With one hand the woman clutched a navy-blue plastic bag filled with possessions. Her other hand was busy reaching out to all the kids within range, trying to hand them something. As each one backed away from her, often with exaggerated shrieks of fear, she turned hopefully to the next. She smiled as she did so. It was an unusual smile because her teeth – every single one – were either totally black or missing.

'Oh – disgusting!' Gemma groaned.

Freya had to admit it did look disgusting.

'Nnnn?' the woman said. 'Nnnn?' She kept saying that over and over, while trying to push some kind of note into each person's hand. No one took it. Some students, once they got over the initial shock of seeing her, were laughing. A few backed away in revulsion. One boy started kicking her bag.

Freya expected the woman to turn on the boy. Instead she just gave him that big gappy black smile and held out her note, as if her life was in his hands.

Freya nearly went forward to find out what she needed, but

was aware of Amy's gaze on her. 'She might be hurt,' she suggested. 'She might need medicine.'

'From a newsagents?' Amy snorted. 'Don't be stupid.'

The woman kept mouthing the same unintelligible words, and holding her little note out in the wind.

Freya wanted desperately to see what the note said, but didn't move. The woman, however, was widening her net to include everyone within reach and her eye alighted unerringly on Freya.

She stiffened as the woman lurched her way.

'Go on, then,' Amy said, giving Freya permission. 'Let's see what's in that manky note of hers.'

Up close, Freya expected stale breath from the woman. She was shocked to find that her breath smelled of – sweets. The woman was even younger than Freya had first thought. She had light blue, slightly distracted eyes, and unkempt dark hair. Except for her teeth, she was pretty, but her mind obviously wasn't quite in the right place.

Freya smiled at her.

'Her teeth are all decayed,' Amy said. 'Maybe she's looking for a dentist.' Some kids laughed. Amy thrust out her hand to take the note.

The woman gave it instead to Freya.

'What does it say?' Vicky asked, intensely curious, but trying to keep her distance from the woman.

The note, in neat capitals, read: LICORICE ALLSORTS, PLEASE. THANK YOU.

'What's that mean?' Vicky chewed the inside of her mouth.

'I don't know,' Freya admitted.

The woman reached into one of her coat sleeves and pulled out a fiver.

'Whooah!' Amy said. 'She's rich, Freya. Take it quick, and run. Go on, I dare you.'

Freya offered the woman a puzzled frown.

The woman had clearly seen the look many times before, and sighed like a lost child.

'She wants you to get her some sweets, you idiots.'

The voice belonged to Luke, calling from the other side of the road.

Freya was surprised to see him. Unable to stand Amy Carr, he normally stayed well away from her at all times.

Walking straight up to Freya, he checked the note still dangling limply from the woman's fingers. Gemma continued to ply the spotty boy with chips, but kept half an eye on Luke. She'd always fancied him.

'Lovely to see you, Gemma,' Luke said, cutting across her as she leaned towards him. 'Too many chips in your mouth for that smile, though.'

Gemma immediately clamped her mouth shut.

'The woman's been hanging around town for a few days,' Luke whispered in Freya's ear. 'Her name's Davina. God knows where she's from, but if you try hard enough you can just about understand her. She's got this thing for sweets. Trouble is, the shop owner says she puts everyone else off coming in, so he won't sell her any. Nice of him, eh? Someone wrote this note for her. Apparently she only likes one particular kind of sweet.

She wants you to go into the shop and buy them for her.'

He looked at Freya expectantly.

So did everyone else, including Amy.

Freya knew Luke was seeing if she'd act independently of Amy, and was suddenly furious with him for testing her in public. She swallowed, wanting to help the woman, but paralyzed by the frosty look on Amy's face.

'Oh, I see,' Luke muttered, glancing at Amy. 'Yeah, I see all right.' He turned to Davina. She was beaming broadly at him, oblivious of everyone else around her. 'Licorice allsorts?' Luke examined the note. 'Must taste good, eh?' Davina guffawed, sounding like a horse. 'All right,' Luke replied, taken aback by her reaction. 'Here goes.' He took the fiver and went into the shop.

Freya, along with everyone else, became intrigued by whether or not Luke would manage to get served. If the owner suspected the sweets were for Davina he'd probably refuse to sell them. Everyone watched though the window as Luke went through different stages: first simply asking for them, then arguing, and finally digging into his pocket and handing over a lot of money.

'Can you believe it?' he muttered to no one in particular as he left the shop. 'He charged me double!'

With everyone's eyes still on him, he gave Davina her fiver back. Davina was mortified and mouthed her protests so much that Luke eventually only offered her the change. Looking suddenly shy, she gave him a small kiss on the cheek. It made Luke cringe, but Davina didn't seem to notice. Rolling her eyes, she thrust her long, rather elegant fingers into the bag of sweets and popped one into her mouth. She instantly started making loud, sucking sounds, completely unaware that everyone was watching her. Or not caring, Freya thought. In a world of her own.

Davina also offered Luke a sweet. He politely declined, and Freya saw him walk off to join a nervous-looking blond boy across the street – but not before favouring Freya with a scathing glance. Then he sighed and came back across the street.

'I need to talk to you,' he said.

'Not now.' Freya was aware of Amy's gaze.

'She's busy,' Amy snapped. 'Talk to her later.'

'It's important,' Luke said.

Freya knew Amy didn't like the fact that Luke had taken so much of the limelight in the last few minutes. If she ignored her and spoke to Luke now it would be seen as a sign of disloyalty.

'It can't be that important,' she whispered. 'You could have told me this morning, or –'

'It *is* important.'

'Luke – not now.'

Luke's voice was edged with irritation. 'Freya, are you telling me you're so scared of what this dumb lot thinks that you won't talk to your own brother?' He let his eyes stray unashamedly to Amy.

Amy understood exactly what he was implying. She gave him a glacial glare, followed by a thin-lipped smile. The smile was aimed at Freya. It was obviously an ultimatum – be loyal now, or you're out.

Freya felt her face flush. She had no choice any more about what to do.

'I'll talk to you at home,' she said coldly.

'But –'

'Later, I said!'

Luke glanced once more at Amy, shook his head, then headed back towards Sam. Freya turned around and walked away from the scene with the others as fast as she could, her heart racing.

'Seven-thirty tomorrow,' Amy said, patting her hand, clearly pleased with her behaviour. 'Gemma will pick you up, remember. Make sure you look nice.'

Staring straight ahead, Freya nodded tightly.

Then she sensed – what was it?

Something immensely powerful, travelling across the sky.

The dark angel flared its enormous wings, landing on a steeple behind Freya. Each wing rose and fell without grace, a wet slap of matted filth. The angel's head was grossly misshapen. It had once seen a deformed woman with a head that shape, deliberately chosen it for itself, then gone window-shopping among the worst of humanity for its other features.

The angel's blank eyes fell on a side-street. A robbery was taking place there. A man stood on his own, arguing, resisting the robbery. The thief, a teenage boy, had a knife concealed in his jacket. He hadn't taken it out, but he was thinking about it.

The dark angel could have intervened. Instead it flew across town, a reconnaissance, seeking out Stephanie Rice. It found her hiding near a library, still too scared to face the students at Ashcroft High. She'd been lying to her parents about attending school for weeks. The dark angel could have eased her passage back to school. There were ways for an angel this powerful to do almost anything. But it chose not to. Instead, it flew back across town and sought out Freya again.

Freya Harrison: the girl who sensed angels in the world.

The dark angel watched her as she walked back into the school grounds, trailing behind Amy. The angel smiled to itself. It enjoyed the way Freya twisted and turned her shoulders, sensing it up there in the sky, but unable to locate it.

You don't want to find me, the dark angel thought. If I ever pay you a visit, Freya Harrison, you will wish with all your heart I had not.

It turned its head. Its blank eyes pinpointed Luke and Sam Davenport.

It saw Jeremy Tate and three others gathering to intercept them.

There was violence in Tate's mind.

The angel could have intervened, but it did not.

✳

Luke made a quick assessment. Tate and three others from his year were lounging against a wall, obviously looking for trouble. There was no sign of the kid who'd backed off earlier. Tate had replaced him with someone Luke didn't recognize.

A showdown.

Fear shot through Luke as soon as he recognized the set-up. He had no control over his reaction – he could almost feel the chemistry of his blood changing. He was eleven years old again, fists crunching into him. Giving his head a brief shake, he tried to clear it. You're nowhere near that young any more, he told himself. Get a grip.

He'd never expected Tate to move so fast. But I should have done, he realized. Tate obviously wanted immediate retribution for earlier. And the fact that he'd brought along new members of the gang showed he meant business.

What to do? Just wait for Tate to provoke the inevitable fight?

Keep moving, Luke thought, his nerves jumping a notch. They might let you past.

Walking towards Tate, he sensed Sam tightening up beside him. 'Don't worry,' he said. 'They won't touch you while I'm here.'

'Are you sure?'

No, Luke thought, I'm not.

He slowed down, measuring up the boys. He'd never been involved in a situation like this. He had no idea how well he could take care of himself in a serious fight. Against four, he knew his only chance was to run. But how fast could Sam run? In any case, it was too late to run. Their feet had already carried him too close to Tate for that.

Brazen it out, Luke thought, all his old terrors about being beaten up resurfacing. Brushing against his, Sam's hand was hot and sweating profusely. Luke remembered exactly what it felt like to sweat that much.

Stupid to get involved, he thought. Stupid. Stupid. Was

there a way out of this? If he turned round now, they'd be on him in seconds. Bluffing his way out was his only chance.

'Oh, more of you this time,' he said, trying to keep his voice steady. 'Sure you don't need any extra help with this Year 7, Tate?'

Tate smiled. 'It's not him I'm after any more.'

At those words, a band of sweat rolled in a long cold line down Luke's spine. He was trembling as well. He hoped it wasn't visible. His only chance was to provoke Tate into a one-on-one fight, but he realized he was scared even to do that. 'Tell you what,' he said, trying to keep his voice under control, 'let's do this one on one. Just me and you.' He doubted the challenge would be accepted – Tate couldn't afford to lose the fight in front of so many witnesses – but at least it brought everything out in the open. Tate's not going to be able to hide behind his henchmen anyway, he thought. Not without them knowing that's exactly what he's doing.

Sam huddled behind Luke, as far from Tate as he could get.

Tate rested nonchalantly against a brick wall. He looked almost happy.

Who am I kidding? Luke thought. He must have played this game a hundred times.

'I can fight if I have to,' Tate said. 'But that's why I've got this lot.' He thumbed towards the gang, gave Luke an appraising grin. 'I tell you what, Harrison, let's see what you've got. You're coming on the big man, but I don't think you've got any real guts. Let's see. First choice: you can take all three of my lads on. A straight fight. We'll see what a man you are then – and so will you. You might do better than you think. I'll even let Sammy-boy here go free and never bother him again. You hear that. *Never bother him again*. If you agree to fight, that is.'

Tate let Luke absorb that. 'Or,' he went on, 'and listen care-fully, now – you can hand Sammy over. We've got a bit of unfin-ished business, him and me. Bit of shoe-licking to do, etc. If you give him to us you can go free, Lukey. Walk away. Just like that.' Tate smirked. 'What do you say? It's entirely up to you.'

Luke felt his knees buckling. 'You fight me alone, you cow-ard,' he murmured.

'Oh, *I'm* the coward, am I?' Tate laughed out loud. 'It's all right, Harrison. I know you're not up to a fight. It's obvious you're really looking for a way out. So I'm giving you one. We're not going to do too much damage to the boy anyway, are we lads?' The others grinned. 'Naturally, we'll do more to Sammy than we would have that first time, before you stuck your mouth where it wasn't wanted, Lukey. He's put us to a bit more trouble, thanks to you. So we have to do some stuff to him. You understand. But it's OK. We'll take very good care of him. Off you go now.' Tate gestured dismissively in Luke's direction, not even looking at him any more.

One of Tate's gang reached out a long arm for Sam.

Sam bucked and screamed for Luke, clutching at his shirt.

'Tate . . .' But Luke did nothing. He couldn't. He was too scared. He couldn't face these four. Would they hurt Sam? No. He knew that wasn't true, but he kept repeating it to himself. He had to or he would have collapsed in front of them. He tried to galvanize himself into action – a push, a shove, something aimed at Tate – but he still couldn't do it. The proximity of the other boys froze him. Even knowing he'd have to face them later at some point he was too frightened to act.

Still screaming, Sam was plucked from Luke's side and bundled up to Tate. Another kid manhandled him around the corner and clipped his face to shut him up. Sam pleaded for Luke's help. The other three gang members watched Luke with contempt for a moment as he stood there, then followed Tate around the corner.

'Don't hurt him,' Luke found himself feebly mumbling. 'Don't hurt him.'

Somewhere out of sight Tate howled with laughter.

After school that afternoon, Freya was in her room, thinking about the dark angel – had she really felt him watching her? – when Luke came crashing into the house.

The front door banged, and she heard swearing.

As she rushed to the landing her dad was also there, coming out of his bedroom. He rubbed sleep out of one eye, pulling a dressing gown hastily around his shoulders.

'Dad?' Freya was surprised, not knowing he'd been in the house.

'What's going on?' he yelled downstairs, shrugging off her questioning look.

'Nothing,' came a vehemently suppressed voice. 'Not one thing. Absolutely bloody nothing.'

As Freya hurried towards the voice, between the wooden banisters of the staircase she caught a glimpse of Luke turning away from her, obviously holding back tears. She'd never seen him cry before, and she stopped where she was for a moment, in shock.

'Luke, are you . . . are you hurt?'

'Hurt?' He seemed to find the question darkly amusing. 'No, no one seems to have hurt me, Freya. But let's make sure, shall we? Let's be *certain*.' Balling his fist, he smashed his knuckles against the living room wall. The force of his blow left a graze of blood behind.

'Luke!' Freya yelled.

Dad gave Luke some space, studying him carefully. 'What on earth happened?'

'Nothing,' Luke grunted, pulling his school jacket open. 'I'm OK, aren't I? Don't I look OK? No damage done to this body.' He slammed his forehead against the living room wall so hard that Freya felt the impact through the floor.

Dad stepped forward and said firmly, 'Let's talk about this upstairs.'

Luke shook his head no, breathing heavily.

'Tell us what's wrong,' Freya murmured. 'Luke, please. Why won't you – '

'Shut up!' he growled. 'Shut up, will you! Just damn well shut up!' He twisted his face away.

'Hey!' Dad said. 'Don't speak to Freya like that.'

Luke turned on him. 'Why not? Why do we always have to talk in whispers around her? Isn't she old enough to be told things? Eh? Isn't she well enough yet?'

Dad gave him a warning glance.

Luke ignored it. He stabbed a finger at Freya. 'I told you to listen to me earlier! But you wouldn't, would you?'

Seeing Dad's expression, Freya knew that something vitally important was being concealed from her. That frightened her even more than Luke's self-destructive behaviour.

'I'm listening now,' she whispered.

'Luke! That's enough!' Dad snapped. 'Not one more word.'

'All you cared about was what Amy Carr made of it all,' Luke raged at Freya. 'Why the hell wouldn't you listen to me?'

'I'm sorry,' she said, before Dad could stop Luke. 'What is it? Come on. Tell me.'

'I can't say it now, can I?' Luke gritted his teeth. 'Jesus, Freya, are your eyes never open?'

Freya glanced between the two of them, finally settled on her dad.

'What does he mean?' she demanded. 'What's Luke hiding? What are *you* hiding?'

Dad didn't look at her. Instead, when Luke seemed about to open his mouth again, he thundered, 'I said that's enough!'

Freya had never heard Dad raise his voice so strongly. Even Luke was visibly taken aback. Shaking his head, laughing grimly at some interior thought, he rubbed the wet smears off his knuckles onto his shirt, seemingly finding the sight of his own blood funny.

The next moment Dad was bundling him upstairs, past Freya.

'Both of you stop it, and tell me what's going on,' she insisted.

But neither did. And now that Dad had hold of him, Luke clearly just wanted to get away, out of everyone's sight. He protested when pursued to his room, but Dad disregarded that, followed Luke inside and firmly shut the door.

Freya stood in the corridor, feeling excluded. She heard a quiet exchange between Dad and Luke, and had a few moments to wonder what they might mean before Dad came out again, alone this time. 'I'm going to get changed,' he said, gathering his dressing gown around him.

Freya waited for him downstairs on the sofa. Something was going on, something she'd missed entirely. What was it? And what was wrong with Luke? Had –

The dark angel was nearby.

Freya suddenly sensed its presence – like an extra weight leaning up against the house.

Turning around, knowing it was somewhere behind her, she felt the hairs on her scalp slowly rise. Then she pinpointed exactly where it was: pressed like a tide against the living room window to her left. She stayed still this time, not daring to look that way, preparing to run if she had to.

When Dad came down, fully-dressed now, he saw the disturbed, frozen look on her face.

'Freya, what's the matter?'

Freya could almost feel the dark angel pushing its distorted head up against the glass pane. She sensed the fury there, the hatred. The window would not stop it. Nothing on earth could prevent this angel from smashing its way through and harming her if it wanted to.

Dad peered in the direction she was angled away from.

'You're seeing an angel, aren't you?'

Freya shook her head, trying to conceal it from him.

'Oh, Freya.' Dad's face collapsed. 'You suppose I can't tell by now when you think you're in the presence of angels?'

She made herself check the window.

The dark angel, if it had ever been there, was gone.

She sat upright on the sofa, terrified. She felt like a little girl again, her whole world unravelling.

A malevolent angel. A blackened, deformed angel, stalking her.

It couldn't be real.

But part of her almost wanted it to be. Because then at least she wouldn't be going crazy. Freya suddenly saw the white doors of the old hospital wards shutting behind her again. She saw the smooth smiles of the nurses, the doctors reassuring her as they stretched the straps tightly around her arms. Was this new angel just an elaborate offshoot of her old fantasy? Whatever it was, she couldn't bear the prospect of returning to the hospitals. If the doctors there knew about this horror-vision, they'd never let her out.

'It's happening again,' she whispered, her whole body trembling.

Dad was quiet for a minute. Then he said, 'Is it like before? Are you seeing them all the time, or only now and again?'

'Don't ring the hospital.'

'But –'

'Dad, don't phone them. Not yet. Please.'

His face dropped. 'All right. Not yet. I won't ring them . . . unless you think I should. Or unless' – he raised his eyes again – 'unless I have to.'

Freya stared at him. Even with the dark angel haunting her thoughts, she could see how tired Dad looked. What was wrong with him? The middle of the afternoon, and here he was, at home, sleeping, obviously exhausted.

'Dad,' she said, 'I know you're holding something back from me. What is it?'

'Nothing,' he replied. 'Really, it's nothing you need to worry about.'

'So why won't you tell me?'

'I will. When I'm ready.'

'When you think *I'm* ready, you mean. You're too afraid to tell me, because you think I can't cope with anything. I can, you know. Is it to do with you? Or Luke? Or –' She stopped.

The dark angel was outside again – at the rear of the house this time. Freya glanced left, trying to determine its exact location. She ran to the back door.

Nothing there. Just the flap of the wind.

Standing with her hands over her face, she stood near Dad, shaking.

I can't control it, she thought. I can't. But I have to.

Dad came up behind her, but even before his hand found hers she knew she had to get out of the house. She didn't want to stay there feeling terrified about dark angels. She wanted to be with friends. If this new angel was about to dominate her thoughts the way previous angels had, she wanted at least one night out with the girls and Adam first. An evening on the town. A few carefree hours. She could keep her mind intact for that long, couldn't she?

'Talk to me,' Dad said.

To convince him to let her go out, Freya lied. She didn't mention the darkness of the angel. She said it was an ordinary angel she'd seen only once. And she promised him the friends she'd be with tomorrow evening would never leave her on her own. They'd be with her the whole time, and bring her straight back home if anything went wrong.

Her dad let her finish, then gazed shrewdly at her. Freya was certain he was going to keep her in the house for at least the next couple of days. Instead, he went upstairs to check on Luke.

'Is he all right?' Freya asked when he came back down.

'No. But he will be. Just leave him alone tonight. Whatever the problem is he doesn't want to share it with anyone.'

'Not even you?'

'No. Anyway, come on, we're going out.'

'Out?'

'Yes. And it's late. We need to get a move on.'

'Where are we going?'

'Just get your coat.'

He took her shopping. Evening clothes shopping in the town centre with Dad. It was a while since he'd last done that, knowing she preferred to shop with friends these days, and Freya should have felt embarrassed, but somehow she didn't. 'Take your time,' he said, insisting on letting her choose any clothes she wanted for tomorrow's night out. 'Just get whatever you like.'

At first, worried about the cost, Freya searched through the cheaper outfits, picking out a sensibly-priced pair of smart jeans and an inexpensive light grey top. But then her eye fell on a beautiful magenta John Rocha suede jacket in a designer shop. Dad, seeing where she was looking, said, 'It's yours.' The price was high, but he didn't hesitate as he handed over his credit card. 'You can't afford that,' she whispered, but he just stuffed some cash in her hand. 'You'll need that tomorrow as well. If you're seeing a boy, that is.' Freya stepped back in surprise, not having mentioned anything about Adam. It made Dad roar with laughter. 'Don't be so surprised,' he said. 'I was vaguely young once, you know. What else do you need?'

When they finally got back home, Luke was still upstairs. Dad went in to see him and their subdued voices occasionally reached Freya over the next hour, but she couldn't hear what they were saying.

Then she heard Luke opening his door. Creeping downstairs to the living room, he turned on the TV for some late-night football highlights and then remained down there for much longer. Dad left him alone this time and so did Freya. She desperately wanted to know what had happened to him, but suspected that Dad was right and she should leave her questions until Luke cooled off. As she was thinking this, she realized that she'd gone all evening without once seeing the gruesome face of the dark angel. Would it leave her alone tomorrow as well? What were the chances of that?

Just one night, she thought. That's all I want. Go away for that long.

To banish any thoughts about the dark angel, she brought the image of Adam to the forefront of her mind. What did she really know about him? Nothing, except a few minor details she'd wheedled out of Gemma. 'Amy wasn't his first girlfriend, anyway,' Gemma had informed her. 'I reckon he knows quite a bit about girls, if you know what I mean.' The comment had brought a grin out of Freya at the time, but she wished now that Gemma hadn't told her anything. Or that Adam knew nothing about girls. That he would be just as apprehensive as her.

Too nervous to eat anything, she had an early bath. Then she sat down at the dressing table in her room and laid out all her new clothes. Trying various lip-glosses out against the grey top, she settled on a dark pink shade, not too shiny. She squirmed into the black trousers and eased the John Rocha magenta jacket around her shoulders. It was about the fifteenth time she'd tried the jacket on already, and each time it looked fantastic. Laughing nervously, Freya hung it up in her wardrobe, then tucked Dad's cash into the tiny suede handbag he'd slipped in as an extra during their shopping trip.

Before she went to bed, she gazed uncertainly in the bedroom mirror at her reflection. Would Adam prefer her hair curled or flat? Not much left to curl or play about with now, of course. At least with her hair short he'd see plenty of her neck. Don't be stupid, she thought. You haven't even said a word to him, why would he be looking closely at that? But Amy's words about how keen he was were lodged firmly in her mind, and Freya couldn't help thinking about him. What was he doing right now? Thinking of her? Did boys spend as long worrying about what they were going to wear and say as this? No, she decided. Not Adam, anyway. He was old enough to have dated loads of girls. If Gemma was right, he probably wouldn't be nervous at all.

As soon as she woke next morning, Freya was certain the dark angel was outside her room. She sensed it flowing against the door, its breath on the wood, waiting for her to discover it.

No, it's not there, she told herself. Nothing is there. It can't be.

But she wasn't sure. She was so frightened it might be that for ages she couldn't even bring herself to open the door. It was only after Dad and Luke left that she felt the angel's presence drifting away from the house again.

Freya arrived late at school, tired and not groomed to anything like the usual standard Amy expected, but no one commented on it. She soon found out why. There was a buzz of anticipation around the gates. Gemma, grabbing her arm, gushed that someone had spotted the weird, duffle-coated girl hanging around near the sixth-former's annex.

Amy insisted on everyone getting over there fast, but there was no sign of the new girl, and Freya was relieved. She didn't want to be tested again by Amy. Not today.

The morning passed uneventfully. There were no more sightings of the dark angel, and by lunchtime Freya was feeling steady enough to tell herself that she might never see it again, or that she could cope if she did. Over lunch break, she made her excuses to Amy and searched around for Luke, but he wasn't in any of his usual places, so she couldn't question him about yesterday's events. After school, she waited for him again at home, but he didn't return until late, and then he rushed straight up to his room, barging moodily past her.

By seven-twenty that evening Freya was dressed and ready to go out on the town. Well, almost. Smoothing down the back of the John Rocha jacket, she double-checked that she had Dad's money zipped inside the silk-lined pocket of her handbag. 'You won't need money,' Amy had explained earlier that day. 'Adam will do all the paying.' But Freya was determined to go halves.

Ten minutes late, Gemma rang the doorbell.

Freya, already hovering outside her room, took a deep breath and hurried down. Luke, though, with mischief in his eyes, launched himself ahead of her and reached the door first.

Gemma was pleased to see him. She'd prepared an especially dazzling smile just in case he was there to see it. It took her a lot longer to notice Freya waiting behind him. 'Hiya,' she said at last, glancing over his shoulder. 'Oh, great jacket!'

Luke moved sullenly aside and let the girls kiss cheeks.

Gemma's outfit, Freya noticed, left little to the imagination. Despite the cold weather she wore a denim mini-skirt and white knee-high boots with heels so high she could barely stagger in them. Her only concession to the weather was a gold puffa jacket with a hood the size of an igloo.

'Ah, cute,' Freya said, spotting the small teddy-bear bag rocking on her shoulder.

'Yeah, lovely,' Luke sneered. He saw a boy with borderline acne and badly-combed hair waiting uncertainly behind Gemma. 'You going out with her tonight?' he mouthed silently over Gemma's shoulder. The boy nodded. 'Keep an eye on your money,' Luke said, not caring if Gemma heard. The boy blinked several times. Luke turned back to Gemma and said, 'Wonderful to see you. Dressed for the weather, I see. Sure you won't be too hot?' He didn't let her in.

Freya wanted to get away as fast as possible from the log-jam at the door and Luke's flaky mood. Then she noticed Dad standing between the living room and kitchen. He was watching her from a distance, staying in the background. The quietly confident smile he gave her was the perfect antidote to Luke's sarcasm.

Smiling at Dad, she grabbed Gemma's arm and hurried her away up the street before Luke could say anything else.

They shot off down Cardigan Street, the spotty boy dragging behind. Gemma didn't bother to introduce him and, after a while, cut adrift from the two girls, he started whistling to himself.

'What's that weird noise you're making?' Gemma quizzed him, her heels stamping sharply on the pavement.

The boy didn't answer.

Freya took another deep breath and kept them moving.

The wind picked up once they reached the wider town streets. Even in her jacket and jeans Freya felt cold, and she could tell the others were as well, but Gemma stoically put up with it, leaving her jacket undone. She's on the make again, Freya realized. Even on her first night out with this new boy she's keeping her options open for something better. Part of Freya couldn't help admiring her nerve.

Reaching into her teddy-bear bag, Gemma sent a text to Amy to say they were heading into town. She still didn't bother introducing the boy to Freya. By the time they got near the high street, Freya nudged her into an acknowledgement.

'So who's this?' she whispered. 'Your new beau?'

'Oh, him?' Gemma gave the boy a startled look, as if she'd just remembered he was with them and was having second thoughts about keeping him around. 'His name's Malc.' She said it quickly, obviously afraid he'd open his mouth and say something stupid if he was allowed to introduce himself.

'Nice to meet you,' Freya said.

'Cheers,' Malc replied, looking glum.

They soon reached the town centre. Amy and her latest boyfriend, Chaz, a chisel-featured Portuguese waiter about eighteen years old, met them outside Burger King. Freya caught Amy's attention and arched her eyes approvingly. Amy nodded with equal approval at Freya's jacket.

Amy wore a red stringy number, brushed black jeans, black ankle boots and a long dark coat. But the thing Freya noticed most of all was her bag – a genuine Gucci that must have cost a small fortune. 'Mm,' Freya said, making sure Amy knew she'd noticed, but also gazing round nervously. Adam wasn't anywhere in view.

'Don't you worry, he'll be here soon,' Amy said. Her tongue jutted squarely in her cheek. 'He'd better be anyway, or there'll be trouble.'

With the wind whipping at their heels, they strolled along the town centre high street. It was as covered in wrappers, half-eaten takeaways, dog excrement and general rubbish as it always was at this time of night. Vicky, wearing a khaki jacket buttoned up to her neck, ferreted Darren away and stood near the post office with him, busily rummaging inside his pockets. It was the first time Freya had seen Darren outside of school, and watching the way Vicky was giving him a tongue-lashing made her feel sorry for him. He was the same age as Vicky, but shorter – a point Amy never tired of mentioning – with a badly-shaven head Vicky preferred him to keep hooded.

'Is that all the money you brought, after what I told you?' they all heard her muttering. 'God you're so useless, Darren.'

'Well, what about you bringing some for a change?' he hissed back.

For that she nearly clipped him round the ear. He gave her a truculent stare, but said nothing else.

After Vicky took whatever money she could get from Darren, they headed for a stroll down to the end of the main parade of shops. Gemma made a point of being nice to Malc until he coughed up for burgers, chips and Coke for everyone, and then, like a happy mirage, Adam arrived from a side-street, all wrapped up inside a handsome black leather jacket and Pierre Cardin jeans. He immediately took up a spot not far from Freya's right thigh and asked if he could sip her Coke. She said he could.

Freya was so anxious not to say or do anything stupid that she only hazily remembered the details of what followed. She needn't have worried. As the evening wore on it became obvious that Darren was the main source of entertainment, and that Amy only allowed him along – and even encouraged Vicky to keep going out with him – because he gave everyone something to laugh at.

After they'd had enough shuffling up and down the high street, Adam suggested going inside another little café. He offered to buy Freya a raspberry muffin with her mochaccino (which she accepted). Once, when she thought Freya wasn't looking, Gemma thrust herself in a certain way at Adam, her jacket buttoned perfectly to show off her assets. Adam, Freya saw, pretended not to notice, which for some reason sent a thrill right through her.

Despite nothing much of significance happening or being said, she realized that she was enjoying herself more every minute. She was incredibly nervous about saying the wrong thing, but Adam seemed to be just as nervous. He even spilled his Coke all over his shirt, and at one point, answering a simple question from Malc, got all tongue-tied with his answer until Amy flicked a peanut at him to make a laugh out of it. And half way through the evening Freya also realized something else: she hadn't seen the dark angel.

Stay away, she thought. Don't you dare. Not tonight.

The hours skipped along in a warm haze. Chaz and Adam

were cool and articulate, while Darren and Malc were the opposite, keeping the amusement levels high. At one point Malc insisted on showing them the home-made tattoo of a donkey he'd had engraved on his arm. 'See, like a donkey 'cause everyone else's got an animal like a panther or a lion or whatever, so it's different,' he said, and while they all (including Gemma) laughed at that Darren pulled his pants part-down and showed them all the drunk-for-a-dare pony tattoo on his right thigh.

'What about you, then?' Freya dared Adam. He joked that his tattoo was in a place he couldn't show her, and Amy was just about to suggest where when Freya said no, it's OK, she'd find out for herself. She couldn't believe how daring she'd been in saying that, and as the others grinned approvingly she realized that although these weren't maybe the most perfectly matched group of people in the world she was loving being with them.

Nothing could spoil the evening for her, even when Darren and Malc began fighting over which character was hardest on TV's *World Wrestling Entertainment*. Following their scuffle, Malc somehow ended up falling over and cutting his hand. Blaming Darren, he chased him down the backstreets of the town, and the others, caught in the moment, followed, running across a road bordered with corrugated steel barriers and down under the railway arches until they had to stop, gasping, with their hands on their knees.

That was when they found they had run in to a bad part of town. Some guys in bomber jackets and pale grey cotton hoods were swapping packets of something in a dingy alley, and gave them a murderous look. So they kept walking, past derelict shops and toddler's nurseries blasted with graffiti. There were all sorts of dodgy people around, obviously ready to make trouble if you dared look at them. Except that Darren was looking, of course, and someone across the street was answering him back. Darren didn't like that, and started mouthing off, acting the tough street-boy, but it wasn't washing, it was just making things worse. And suddenly they were all running again, being chased over some low railings this time, back towards the town centre.

Freya, frightened but exhilarated (no one would really get hurt, would they?) found herself being pushed from behind by Adam and vaulting with him over some low bollards into a cul-de-sac. They collapsed noisily down behind some black sacks of rubbish smelling of the local greasy spoon café and hid until the pursuers gave up the chase.

It was late by then, and really cold, a gusty wind swirling around the dead-end street, but Freya hardly noticed because somehow she was lying back against some broken breeze blocks, and Adam was kneeling above her.

He smiled in a friendly way, his teeth flashing, his breath sharp, and Freya, unable to believe what she was doing, found her arms reaching up towards him, pulling him down and giving him a kiss. He kissed her back, then pulled away a little embarrassed, breathless, and she liked him all the more for that; and after they'd kissed again, more slowly this time, he listened to the street, took her hand and in one powerful motion hauled her to her feet.

They ran together back to the town centre. They couldn't find the others at first, but somewhere in the distance, making them laugh, they heard Vicky's unmistakable high twang screaming at Darren to just shut up about a kebab and take her home.

8

Three days later, halfway through Freya's double English period, there was a sharp rap on the classroom door. Mrs Baldwin, the Headmistress, popped her head inside. 'Are you ready?' she asked the English teacher, Miss Volhard.

Obviously expecting the interruption, Miss Volhard stood up and smiled. 'Of course. Bring her in.'

A few seconds later there was furious whispering, some kind of coaxing going on back in the corridor. Then Mrs Baldwin reappeared, looking slightly frazzled, holding firmly onto the shoulders of a duffle-coated girl. She held her with both hands, as if afraid the girl might take flight if she didn't.

'Everyone, this is Stephanie Rice,' Mrs Baldwin announced. 'She's new to our school, and I'm certain you will all want to give her a warm Ashcroft High welcome as she joins us this morning.'

One boy clapped, but it soon petered out when someone kicked him under the desk.

Stephanie stood rooted at the back of the class.

'It's all right,' Mrs Baldwin whispered. 'You'll be taken care of here.' With the tiniest of shoves, she propelled Stephanie forward and left the room.

Stephanie nearly followed her out. Cast adrift, she glanced longingly at the closed door. Then, wobbling, she took a deep breath and turned to face the class.

Freya looked at her, then quickly looked away again. Caught by surprise, she was torn between wanting to offer the girl a desk nearby and ignoring her.

'Why not come up here near the front?' Miss Volhard suggested. 'Have this seat near me.' When Stephanie didn't budge one or two members of the class giggled. 'It's all right,' Miss Volhard said, keeping up her best imitation of a smile. 'There are plenty of spare desks at the back – that's right, take the one near you. Just sit there until we can find a more suitable place.' She glanced around the class, looking for support. 'Freya Harrison, will you sit next to Stephanie please?'

All eyes turned, daring her to refuse.

'Yes, miss,' Freya said, dragging herself away from her middle-row seat next to Vicky. She brought her bags and books and sat beside Stephanie, aware of the class studying her every move.

Stephanie blinked at her.

Freya gave her a noncommittal nod.

'There now,' Miss Volhard said. 'Stephanie, you can take your coat off if you want.'

Stephanie just hunched the duffle coat more closely around her shoulders. Further giggles, and this time the middle row of students started whispering.

'That's enough!' Miss Volhard growled. Her voice wavering, she said to Stephanie, 'Fine, fine. Keep your coat on then, if you prefer.'

Stephanie looked for courage from somewhere, and Freya gave her it – a fleeting, tiny smile, but enough to get Stephanie to start peeling off the heavy coat.

Underneath it, she was wearing a school uniform – but it was the *wrong* school uniform. Even the colour was wrong, brown instead of green. Unsuppressed laughter broke out all over the classroom. A few students gave Stephanie outraged glances.

Freya was among those feeling pity. She knew there was no chance now that Stephanie would be treated normally.

Stephanie pulled nervously at her blazer, looking straight ahead. Her fingers twiddled with a brooch on the right pocket of her shirt. The brooch was made from hand-crafted glazed clay. It showed the figure of an angel, wings fully spread. Across the angel's body a series of symbols was engraved. Freya recognized the format. It was something she'd discovered herself while trawling the internet in the past – a personal name those interested in angels create to represent their angelic signature.

Don't let Amy see it, was Freya's first thought. Stop touching it. Don't give yourself away.

'Less of the childish tittering would be nice,' Miss Volhard said to the class.

Freya whispered to Stephanie over the noise, 'It's all right. Don't worry. It won't always be like this.'

Under the desk, Stephanie reached out to seize Freya's hand. Her clutch was cold and vice-like.

Freya stared directly ahead, hoping no one could see.

'Hey everyone, be quiet,' said a silky voice from the front of the class. Amy. 'Don't all be so horrible,' she chided. 'It's not easy starting your first day at a new school.'

That stopped everyone. Even Miss Volhard glanced at Amy in surprise.

'Actually,' Amy said sweetly to Stephanie, 'I'm really interested to hear about your background. You're not from round here, are you?'

Miss Volhard stared uncertainly at Amy, but allowed her to continue. Stephanie opened her mouth, then shut it again.

'It's all right,' Amy said. 'We won't bite. Tell us.' Her eyes sparkled with amusement. Freya noticed Gemma and Vicky exchanging puzzled glances. They were always one step behind whatever Amy was planning. A few others in class smiled, knowing from experience that Amy had something bizarre in mind.

Leave her alone, Freya thought. Please leave her alone.

Stephanie's large eyes blinked at Freya, then her freezing hand released slightly and she stood.

'You don't need to do that,' Amy said. 'But if you feel more comfortable standing before me be my guest.'

General laughter.

'That's enough,' Miss Volhard said, realizing that Amy obviously hadn't started this for altruistic reasons.

'I've been educated at home,' Stephanie managed to whisper, still standing.

'I'm sorry?' Amy cocked an ear. 'I didn't quite hear that.'

'I said we . . . my parents educated me at home. For English we studied Shakespeare. We did . . . all the major tragedies together, and some of the comedies.'

'That's why she's with us in this set,' Miss Volhard told them. 'Her English level is extremely high. In fact, some of you could learn . . .'

No one was listening.

'Comedies, eh?' Amy's tone was still amiable. 'Mm. I like comedies, too. Do you mind if I ask you a little question? I'm sorry, but it's been bothering me. What's that nice brooch you're wearing? It's very pretty. Does it mean something?'

Freya gave Stephanie a warning glance, but she missed it.

'It's my angelic sigil,' she said.

All movement and noise in the class stopped.

Miss Volhard tried to gesture at Stephanie to sit down, but she carried on, encouraged by Amy's nod and the silence of the room.

'I came up with the design myself,' she said. 'It represents who I am, sort of my angelic name, just in a different form.'

A few guffaws broke out, but no one said anything.

'Go on.' Amy was still smiling.

'That's quite enough out of you,' Miss Volhard growled.

'No, no,' Stephanie cut in. 'I want to explain – if people are interested.'

'Oh, we are,' Amy said. 'Definitely.'

Everyone waited. Freya glared at the teacher to put a stop to this, but Miss Volhard seemed unsure how to steer the discussion back to normality. The class held their breath, spellbound by the weirdness of the conversation.

'I used an old mystical method to come-up with the design, called Gematrian,' Stephanie said, heartened by Amy's ongoing smile. 'Each character represents a number which can be transliterated into letters to make up a name.'

'Can I have a sigil of my own?' Amy said, keeping a straight face.

'Of course you can,' Stephanie answered. 'Er, excuse me, but what is your name?'

'Amy.'

'Thank you, Amy. It's not hard to do, especially a short name like yours, with only three letters. I'll help you if you like, but really there's no right or wrong way to design your personal sigil as long as the final result feels that it represents you. You can use anything, really, your favourite colours, symbols or even animal shapes, whatever feels right.'

There were a few seconds of absolute silence in the class-room.

Then pandemonium broke out.

Freya saw that Stephanie couldn't understand why everyone was laughing at her. Vicky and Gemma were shaking their heads in admiration at Amy. Amy gave them a high five.

'It's OK,' Freya whispered to Stephanie. 'Just sit down. You can't talk about angels like that in class. I'll explain how it works afterwards. Don't listen to them.'

'No,' Stephanie murmured, confused. 'I want them to understand.' She thought of Nadiel, and made herself stand.

Seeing that, most of the class fell silent again.

'I'm not ashamed of my belief in angels,' Stephanie said in

a high, breathless voice, desperately gathering her thoughts. 'Angels are present throughout all religious writings. Not just the Bible, but in Islamic texts, Buddhism and all the great faiths. Some of the descriptions of them in the Hebrew Apocrypha and the Pseudepigrapha are so beautiful that they make your heart soar.'

Everyone was quiet in the class now. Even Amy had stopped laughing. This was too weird to be funny.

Stop it, Freya thought hopelessly. You've already gone too far.

Stephanie pressed ahead, deciding to trust in Nadiel and let her strong feelings guide her.

'Some people believe . . . that if you could list out the names of all the angels you would know the face of God,' she said. 'According to many of the great Medieval European scholars there are seven hierarchies of angels. The seraphim are the highest, followed by the cherubim – '

Freya gripped Stephanie's leg under the desk, trying to stop her.

'Stephanie, that's enough,' Miss Volhard said firmly.

'No, please let me finish.' Stephanie forged on, hoping that Nadiel would help her find the words to carry the class with her. 'Beneath . . . the Seraphim . . . no, I said them already, did-n't I? . . . Beneath the Cherubim, excuse me, are the Ophanim, the Dominions, Virtues and Powers –'

Stephanie could see many of the students laughing at her now. Not knowing what else to do, she ploughed on forlornly.

Gemma nudged Amy. 'Hey, Stephanie, are there any angels in this room?'

Stephanie thought about that. 'In this class? I . . . believe so. I've read that that in every ray of light angels are present.'

One boy found that hilarious and couldn't stop laughing. 'My dad works in sewage,' he said. 'No light down there.'

'He . . . will still have a guardian angel.' Stephanie glanced down, belatedly aware of the pressure of Freya's hand on her ankle. 'What should I do?' she whispered, seeing the students openly mocking her.

'Ignore them,' Freya said over the classroom hubbub.

'My dad's a plumber,' another boy remarked, folding his arms. 'Find an angel for that.'

Stephanie chewed her lower lip, thinking hard.

Miss Volhard was trying to get some kind of order, but it was impossible.

'There is a protective angel associated with every trade or hobby,' Stephanie said, clearing her throat. 'I think a plumber would fall under engineering. The angel is Kemuel.'

The whole class cracked up.

'Just sit down,' Freya said, trying to pull Stephanie back to her seat.

'It's true!' Stephanie shouted, suddenly feeling frightened. 'There is a book of angelic hobbies and pastimes. You can even dial it up on the Angel Lady phone line. I've got the number somewhere . . .'. She rummaged in her bag, trying to shut out the laughter. It was too late to pretend she'd been joking. They wouldn't believe that. What else could she do but press on and trust Nadiel?

'Does your dad work?' she asked the nearest student, trying to recover.

'Yeah,' the boy replied cautiously.

'What work does he do?'

'He's – I'm not telling you. Shut up.'

'Please tell me what he does for a living.'

'Leave me alone, you nutter.'

'I'm just trying to illustrate the principle that – '

'Shush,' Freya murmured. 'It's all right. You can't convince them. You can't.'

'I've got a nice hobby,' Amy announced. 'Internet chat surfing. I can never find the right boy, though. Who's the angel for that then?'

More laughter.

'My dad's a truck driver,' someone else yelled. 'Who's his angel?'

Stephanie said nothing, but was clearly trying to come up with an answer.

'My mum makes doll's houses,' Vicky piped up, grinning away.

'I know that one,' Stephanie said, relieved. 'Doll makers are in the charge of a number of angels. Azrael, Chamual, Gabriel, Jophiel and Uriel. According to the book I read . . .'

But she couldn't go on. The laughter was drowning her out.

Realizing that they were all laughing at her now, Stephanie put her hands over her eyes. The next moment she murmured an affirmation over and over again. 'Security and Safety. Security and safety. Nadiel help me. Nadiel help me.'

'I'll help you,' Freya whispered.

Stephanie stopped and gazed at her.

'I'll explain later,' Freya murmured so no one else could hear. 'Meet me at six o'clock outside the school. They don't understand.'

'Do you?'

'Yes.'

From somewhere amid the confusion, Miss Volhard took Stephanie's arm. 'I think you'd better come with me for now. At least until they calm down. Come on.'

When Stephanie just stood there blankly, Miss Volhard half lifted her away from her seat, guiding her out of the class.

Freya sat still amid the general uproar. Breathing deeply, she focused on the whiteboard. Some of the class were still rocking in their seats. Amy stared thoughtfully at Freya, clearly wondering what she'd said to Stephanie. Shaking her head, Freya tried to smile and shrug it off as nothing.

Miss Volhard marched Stephanie straight to the Headmistress's office, telling her to stay outside while she went in to explain what had happened. Stephanie fled the moment she was left alone. Running out of the school gates, she headed in no particular direction, just trying to get as far from Ashcroft High as possible.

Eventually she found herself on the edge of town, lost amid streets she'd never heard of. What was she going to do? The teachers were bound to ring home. She was rarely allowed out unaccompanied after dark under any circumstances by her parents. Once they knew what had happened Mother was certain to keep her indoors.

Ignoring the painful stitch in her side, she thought about Freya. Freya Harrison – a girl like herself, someone who understood about angels. Stephanie could hardly believe how excited she felt. And how could their meeting be a coincidence? Why else would Nadiel have allowed her to suffer such humiliation unless it was to meet this particular girl?

Thanking him silently, Stephanie checked her watch. There were still several hours to go before Freya had agreed to meet her. Stephanie agonized over what to do, then decided not to risk going home. I'll just stay somewhere out of sight in town, she thought. Years of obeying her parents meant that Stephanie felt guilty about that, but another part of her felt elated. Why should she go home? Why did she have to seek their permission to talk to Freya? Couldn't she have one friend they hadn't picked out for her?

With no money for food, she found a damp bench in a dreary park, overlooking a cemetery and an infants' playground. Buttoning up her duffle-coat, she settled down to watch the children playing.

It was about an hour later when the feather fell into her lap.

It drifted gently in a wavering line from somewhere in the sky. A lone feather, small and grey.

There didn't appear to be a bird up there. Was the feather from Nadiel, leaving a sign to let her know he was with her? Stephanie blinked at the sky. Picking the feather up by its short white stem, she twirled the soft edges against her fingertips and allowed herself a small smile.

That lunchtime Freya made a lame excuse to Amy and the others and trudged back home, thinking about Stephanie. On the way she also kept a look out for Luke. He'd been surly and was avoiding her questions lately, locking himself in his room at night, only emerging every now and again to spend time with Dad. He seemed to be doing that a lot lately, hardly going out at all. Freya was so lost in her thoughts about him and Stephanie that it was only as she shut the front door behind her that she realized the house wasn't empty.

Her first thought was that the dark angel was inside. Someone or something was definitely moving in the kitchen, shuffling around.

'Luke?' she murmured.

But it wasn't Luke. It was her dad. He was sitting in the kitchen with the blinds down, wearing only his underwear and a T-shirt. As Freya entered, he snatched his dressing gown from a nearby chair and put it on, clearly not expecting her.

'Hi, gorgeous,' he said, putting some energy into his bearing, straightening up. 'This is a surprise. I thought you always stayed at school for lunch these days.'

'Usually.' She put her bag down. 'What are you doing back home this early?'

'Half day at work.'

'Mm.' She concentrated on making herself a toasted cheese sandwich, her mind full of Stephanie.

Once Dad got over the initial surprise of seeing her, Freya noticed he stayed quiet. He was obviously waiting for her to talk to him about whatever was on her mind. But she didn't want to go over the business with Stephanie. She wasn't even sure what she thought of it herself, let alone how to describe it to Dad. 'I'll just take this to my room,' she said, starting towards the stairs.

'Just a minute.' Dad looked as if he was about to reveal something, then his expression changed. 'Listen,' he said, 'I'm not going to ask you this every time I see you, so there's no need to avoid me or anything, but what about . . .'

The word *angel* was left hanging in the air.

'Dad, please –'

'I just need to know you're OK,' he said more firmly.

'I am.'

'Are you?'

Freya hesitated. What was she supposed to say? No, Dad, the angel is black and terrifying – ring the hospital.

She wished that she hadn't admitted seeing an angel at all now. She didn't want him worrying about it. She didn't want to have to talk about it, either. Standing there, she attempted to formulate an answer he'd accept.

'It's all right,' he said. 'You don't need to make something up, just to get me off your back. I know it's not like the old days, when I'd hold you and sometimes the angels would just go away.' He smiled, embarrassed. 'I'm not much use when it comes to shutting them out any more, am I?'

'It's . . . not that,' Freya answered carefully. 'But you're right, I'm not a little girl now. Holding my hand doesn't make them go away any more. I wish it did. I have to get through this on my own.'

'Why on your own?'

'I can't keep relying on you.'

'Why not? You think I'll break?'

Freya hesitated, then walked over and kissed him. 'It's not that. It's just that . . . I can't come running to you as soon as I get a problem. I've got to start dealing with the angels on my own. If I can't find a way to fight this without you, I might . . . might never leave the angels behind.' It was a strong statement, and Freya hadn't meant it to come out so emphatically, but

· 88 ·

when it did she realized that she meant it.

'You don't know that,' Dad said, disturbed by her answer. 'It's still early days, and this is your first relapse. You're being way too hard on yourself.'

'Am I?' She held his hand. 'All right. Maybe I am.' She wanted to find something to say that would reassure him, but couldn't find the words. Smiling uncertainly, she kissed him again and made her way out of the kitchen and upstairs.

As soon as she left Dad fell back into his former weary posture in the chair. Well, he thought, what did you expect? That she'd just fall into your arms and it would be all better again?

He dragged a hand through his hair, feeling how thin the strands were becoming, and also feeling the dull ache in his side, knowing it would only get worse.

10

'Hey, Lukey-boy!'

Luke was sitting on a wall about a mile from Ashcroft High, just about to dig into a lunchtime bacon roll, when he heard Tate's voice boom out. He didn't look up. He'd spent the last few days taking different paths in and out of school, trying to avoid the scorn of Tate and his cronies. Trying to avoid Sam as well. How could he face him after what he'd done?

'Ah, don't be scared,' Tate said, sauntering over. 'I'm not going to hurt you. I heard you were hanging around here, out of the way. You've been quite hard to find recently. I just wanted to show you my cheery new servant.'

Luke glanced up to see Sam standing next to Tate. He was holding two school bags, one obviously Tate's. There were a couple of bruises on the side of his head. Seeing them, Luke winced.

'Nasty, aren't they?' Tate said, tutting. 'Accident on the way home. Mummy bought that story, anyway.'

Sam gazed into the distance, not looking at Luke.

'The bag's just a little extra penance,' Tate noted. 'I hate carrying my own, don't you?'

Luke checked around him. There was no one else on the

street. None of Tate's usual crowd. After their last meeting, Tate clearly felt confident enough about seeking Luke out for a bit of fun without their help. He was right. Even without the others to back Tate up, Luke felt scared. He tried to get a grip on that. In a straight fight could he handle Tate? Maybe. He knew he'd never get a better chance than this. But he still couldn't take it. He stared miserably down at the ground.

A group of year 8 boys from Ashcroft High were getting closer on the other side of the road. One of them pointed, recognizing Sam.

I'm roughly the same size as Tate, Luke thought, forcing himself to raise his eyes. If I can take him on and defeat him in front of witnesses his reputation will be finished. Could it be as simply done as that?

But he couldn't turn the thought into action. One of the year 8 boys was laughing at him now. Luke didn't look to see who it was. Rumours about the way he'd abandoned Sam had obviously spread among the boys.

'Shut up,' said a furious voice. 'You just shut up!'

It was Sam. He'd put down both bags and was shouting angrily at the kid across the street, defending Luke.

Luke found himself standing. Tate's humiliation was bad enough, but the shame of having Sam defend him was too much to accept. He had to get away.

Tate saw the flight-instinct in his bearing, and held up his hands in a mock fighting stance. 'Ooh, not running off, are you? Come on, one on one. Isn't that what you wanted?' He did a little dance, holding onto Sam's arms, jiggling him like a puppet. 'Come on then, Lukey, don't run off . . .'

Sam wrenched an arm free and swotted Tate's neck with the back of his hand.

'You little –' Tate thumped him in the belly.

Luke felt himself move. He took two steps forward and struck Tate forcefully in the face – a straight uppercut, a single, loaded punch that sent blood spraying sideways from Tate's nose and Tate himself sprawling on the ground.

Tate lay there, clutching his nose in disbelief.

The Year 8 boy on the other side of the street stopped laughing. Luke stared at his fist. He couldn't believe the venom he'd put into that punch. Sam's eyes were wide, astonished, wondering what Luke would do next. Luke had no idea. But plenty of kids were watching and would report whatever it was.

Tate put a hand up to his bloodied nose, dazedly started to rise.

Luke bent towards him. He wasn't intending to strike Tate again, but Tate thought he was and made a feeble squealing noise. A few kids, hearing it, laughed.

Sam stood back, blinking at Luke in awe.

'I'm not scared of you, Harrison,' Tate growled from the ground.

Luke looked closely at him, saw that the opposite was true. He motioned Sam over. 'You OK?'

Sam nodded. He couldn't take his gaze off Tate's messed-up nose. Tate prodded it, and from the way he flinched Luke knew it was probably broken.

Wiping his leaking nose on his jacket sleeve, Tate gathered himself. Sizing up who was watching, he muttered privately to Luke, 'OK, listen. This is the way it works. I get up. I hit you, not that hard, but you fall over, and you *don't* get up. Everyone sees that. I then walk away with Sam here. I'll leave you alone afterwards. That's it, over between us. But if you don't do exactly what I say I'll have my boys take their time over you. It won't just be the fun and games I've had with Sam, either. You understand?'

Luke nodded. He thought about it. The adrenalin rush that had made him leap at Tate was subsiding, but it wasn't gone yet. Putting his face close to Tate's, he whispered, 'No. You leave Sam here.'

'What?'

'You heard me. I'll let you go, but you're not taking Sam.'

'He has to come with me.'

'No. Go without him. And before you do, tell these kids watching you're never going to touch him again.'

'You know I can't do that.' Tate spat out some blood. 'This is your last chance to get out of this. I'll bust you up.'

Luke raised his fist again and Tate recoiled, holding up his arms to protect himself.

'Don't like the thought of that again, eh?' Luke said. 'You don't mind dishing it out, though, do you?'

Tate tried to get up, but Luke held his arm, pinning him down.

'Hit him again,' someone said – the same Year 8 who'd laughed at Luke earlier.

Luke was tempted. He wasn't scared of the version of Tate lying spread-eagled at his feet. But then what? If he pummelled Tate into submission, some time down the road Tate would find a way to take it out on Sam as well as on him. He had to get the focus away from Sam completely. But how?

'Shut up and listen,' he told Tate. 'I could finish you off right now. And then your pathetic little reputation as a hard man will be gone for ever, won't it? Here's what we do instead. Leave Sam alone from now on, and I won't touch you. Do you understand? We'll just go on as if none of this ever started.' He clipped Tate round the ear. 'Well?'

Tate's eyes narrowed with interest. 'OK, deal, yeah.' No argument. Instant agreement.

Luke was surprised, suspicious as well. He wanted to keep Tate pinned until he knew he could trust his word, but he couldn't exactly leave him lying there with blood all over the pavement once he'd agreed to his terms. Besides, the rest of Tate's gang couldn't be too far away. This had to be finished rapidly.

He allowed Tate up. Tate tried aggressively shrugging him off, but Luke held his collar and shoved his cheek against the pavement.

'All right,' Tate murmured. 'Yeah, yeah, I agree. I'll leave him alone.'

A handful of boys who'd stayed to watch snickered at Tate lying there. What next? Luke thought. Do I just let him go? Is that it?

With no further reason to hold onto him, he released his grip on Tate's arm. Tate backed off and took out a tissue, dabbing ineffectually at his nose. Luke sensed he'd made a mistake somewhere along the line, but couldn't decide where. He glanced at his fist, which had somehow led him to this place, then back at Tate. 'You'd better mean it,' he said.

Tate finished dusting himself off, held the tissue gingerly against one nostril and slowly – with as much decorum as he could manage, not much – walked off up the street. He was watched by Luke, Sam and at least a dozen other boys.

When he was far enough away to know he could run without getting caught, Tate stopped. He turned. He faced Luke and shouted at the top of his voice, 'I'm going to take you out, Harrison. For this I'm really going to do it properly.' He studied the other boys standing around, to make sure they'd heard the threat and understood it. Then, spitting blood out in his direction, Tate leveled his gaze at Sam. 'Hey!' he yelled. 'You like the sight of this, Sammy? You listening? Enjoy it while you can. You're a dead boy.'

After school that day, Freya was still deciding what she would say to Stephanie Rice when Amy called.

'Hi,' Freya said.

'Hi to you, too.' Amy couldn't keep the chuckle out of her voice. 'What have you done to my ex, then?'

For a moment, Freya wasn't sure what she meant.

'You mean Adam?'

'Too right I mean Adam. Get this. Not only has he arranged a night out for us all again this Tuesday – and let me tell you, that boy never arranged anything while I was going out with him – but he's practically begging me for your mobile number. You want me to give it to him?'

'Er . . .' Freya's heart was doing odd things. 'I suppose.'

'You suppose? I'll tell him you're dead enthusiastic then, shall I?'

'No. I mean I am, of course. Yes. Give him the number. Definitely. Yes.'

'OK, OK, take a breath or two, I get the message.' More chuckles, then a sly tone crept into Amy's voice. 'So what about that Stephanie Rice, then? You two were chatting away in class earlier. Like twin sisters, you were.'

'No, no,' Freya muttered, taken aback by the shift in conversation. 'Only because I had to sit next to her.'

'That's what I thought. Tricky position you were put in there.'

'Mm.' Freya fell quiet, knowing this was Amy's way of warning her to stay well away from Stephanie.

'Ooh, you've gone all quiet on me,' Amy said. 'You must be lovesick, Freya. What did you do to Adam the other night to get him so hot and sweaty, anyhow?'

'Nothing,' Freya said.

'So why's he drooling over you, then?'

'I don't know.' Freya knew she was playing a dangerous game, withholding information from Amy. But she was determined that her kiss with Adam would remain a secret between them.

'Look, we're girls together, aren't we? Friends?' Amy didn't bother disguising her annoyance now.

'Of course. It's just . . . that there's nothing to talk about.'

'Nothing *you* want to talk about, you mean. God, Freya, I gave him to you, and the first chance you get you shut me out.'

'I'm not doing that,' Freya said, trying to recover. 'Look, we ran away from that dangerous part of town together, just like you did.'

'And?'

'That's all.'

'All you're prepared to tell me, obviously,' Amy said irritably. 'Well, anyway, got to go. Other boys to kiss and all that.' She broke the connection before Freya could say anything else.

Freya stood looking at her phone. Amy was furious, but she would think about how to deal with that once her heart stopped capering around. Adam wanted to see her again. He wanted her number. Amy had used the word *drooling*. Typical Amy exaggeration, but Freya would have given anything to have been a bird sitting in on their conversation.

I'm not ready for this, she suddenly thought.

But another part of her wanted it more than anything.

Why hadn't she asked Amy for *his* number? She could have texted him, just said 'hi', something like that, friendly but neutral, seen what happened. Regretting that, but deciding not to ring Amy until she'd cooled off, Freya passed an hour or so in a haze thinking about Adam. Closing her eyes, moistening her lips, she discovered that she could still remember exactly what that second kiss had felt like.

When she next checked her watch it was quarter to six.

Time to meet Stephanie Rice.

Freya wavered, nearly decided not to go. It wasn't just that she preferred to think about Adam. It was because meeting Stephanie was dangerous. Not only would Amy make her life impossible if she found out, but Freya was genuinely scared of sparks flying when she and Stephanie came together. The mention of angels, which so amused the rest of the class earlier, had sent her own mind spinning, reminding her of everything she'd once loved and left behind. She couldn't afford to go back to those places.

I can't become Stephanie's friend, she thought. But I will help her, whatever Amy says. I'll show her the basics. A few tips on how to act and what to say at school. I can do that much.

She arrived slightly late at the location they'd agreed to meet. Stephanie was hanging back beside the bushes to the left of the school gates, still in her brown school uniform.

'Didn't you go home?' Freya said, amazed.

Stephanie shook her head. She looked cold, her long mousy hair plastered to her face where she'd been caught out in a shower earlier.

'Have you eaten?' Freya asked, torn between pity and the awkwardness of the situation. Another little shake of the head. 'I've got some money,' Freya told her. 'I'll get you something. Wait here.' She glanced up and down the street to make sure there weren't any kids around who might spot her, then headed to a local shop. Returning, she handed Stephanie a bar of whole nut chocolate and some salt and vinegar crisps.

'I can't go back there tomorrow,' Stephanie suddenly yelled, blinking at the school gates. 'I won't. I don't care what Mother says!'

'Shush,' Freya said. 'Keep it down.' In one of the adjoining school sports fields a group of boys were playing rugby. Freya didn't recognize any of them, but she couldn't be sure they weren't in her year. If this rendezvous got reported to Amy the only friend she'd have left would be Stephanie herself, trailing behind with her angel symbols. The callousness of that thought brought Freya up short. It was just the sort of remark Amy would have made.

Stephanie said hotly, 'Don't shush me. I'm not a little girl!'

'I know. Just keep your voice down.'

'Why? Ashamed of me, are you?'

'I'm here, aren't I?' Freya answered, annoyed now. 'Come on, we need to go somewhere more private.' She kept a decent distance ahead of Stephanie until she could find a secluded side-street, then ducked into it. Stephanie followed her, and stood suddenly looking meek, head down.

Seeing that, Freya softened her tone. 'All right,' she began, 'I'm going to tell you . . .' She stopped. Tell Stephanie what? All her angel experiences? That was too much. But as Freya started ordering her thoughts, choosing memories, selecting what to say, a strange thing happened: as soon as the word *angel* left her lips for the first time, the entire story poured out of her. Freya didn't mean it to. She only intended to highlight bits of her past to help Stephanie with a few aspects of classroom behaviour. But she found that she couldn't stop herself. Even when she tried to limit the flood of words, they splurged forth, her whole life lost among the angels flowing out in one long and increasingly tearful confession that went on and on. It was a story she'd been holding back for years, waiting for a sympathetic ear, and Stephanie proved exactly that, quietly listening in wonder. The only thing Freya kept to herself were the recent sightings of the dark angel. She wasn't ready to talk to anyone about those yet.

When she'd finished, Stephanie took over the conversation, telling Freya about the rules of her parents: their love, but also the isolation, the way strangers were frowned upon, all the restrictions. Freya let her go on, fascinated by her background, and when Stephanie finished Freya wished there was more. Who was this strangely animated girl who'd come into her life? In the end, temporarily with nothing left to say, they both found themselves gazing at each other, feeling oddly at ease, their cold breath mingling.

'I was thinking of not coming here today,' Freya said. 'I'm so glad I did.' She sighed, feeling light-headed after unburdening herself. Then she was serious again. 'I'm all right now about the angels, Stephanie. The staff in the hospital made me realize I'd never been visited by one. I just wanted to be, that's all.' She pulled a sheepish face.

Stephanie gave Freya a huge wide smile, stepped across and hugged her. A long deep hug, arms all the way around her back.

Freya was surprised, but didn't object.

Then Stephanie disengaged herself and stood back to look at Freya again. She laughed, a little titter, jumping up and down on the spot.

'What is it?' Freya said, confused, but laughing back.

'Don't you see?' Stephanie exclaimed, clapping her hands. 'You're the reason why Nadiel made me go to your school, even though I begged him to keep me away. It was so I could meet *you*.'

Freya gave her a bewildered look.

Stephanie clutched Freya's arms, lifted them up, then released her again. 'Freya, angels *do* exist! They do! Of course they exist! You were right about them.'

'No, Stephanie, you don't understand.'

But Stephanie wasn't listening. Her face shone with

excitement. 'I knew it!' she murmured. 'Something drew me to you right from the start. Don't you see, Freya? It's not an accident we met. We were meant to. You keep denying angels in your life, but your guardian angel holds the vision of your highest outcome even so, wanting you to achieve it. That's why he brought you to me.'

'What?' Freya stepped back. 'Stephanie, this has nothing to do with angels. You're wrong. Please listen – '

Stephanie whipped a small grey feather out of her bag. She placed it in Freya's left shirt pocket. 'This is for you,' she said. 'From an angel.' She smiled again. 'You should have seen your face shine when you described the way your guardian came through your window,' she exulted. 'Of course a real angel visited you! But Freya, for me *you* are a kind of angel as well. Look, you're here, like an angel would be, just when I need you to be . . .'

'No, Stephanie, that's not true. Please . . .'

'It *is* true. And you're enjoying talking about angels, aren't you? You're enjoying it a lot.'

'No, no . . .' But Freya suddenly realized with a yawning horror that she was. It was years since she'd felt as happy as she had while describing all her angel memories. Feeling dizzy, she said, 'Stephanie . . . please . . . I have to go now. I must . . .'

Stephanie caught her hand as she tried to pull away. 'You can't fool me, Freya Harrison. Your real fear is that you won't see the angel who visited you again, isn't it? That's what you're really terrified of. Not of seeing angels, but of *never* seeing them again.' She watched Freya's reaction, then said earnestly, 'I'll help you. You need to get in contact with your guardian angel again, that's all.'

'No!' Freya shouted it this time, suddenly frantic to get away.

'Still denying it?' Stephanie glanced sideways up at Freya. 'Don't you know that when a person needs help the anxious thoughts they send out create a bridge of light which the angels use to help that person? That's why I'm here. Nadiel sent me.'

'But I'm here to help *you*!' Freya said, her mind whirling. 'That's the only reason I came.'

Stephanie gave her a knowing smile. 'No. I think I was meant to help you, Freya. Guide you back towards the truth.'

Freya's mind reeled. What was happening? She had to get away. Stephanie stood there with that smile still breaking out on her face, thrusting angels at her as if they were a blessing. Freya closed her eyes, fearful that if she listened any more she would lose her mind.

'Come to my house,' Stephanie urged. 'We don't need those others at school. Wait, what's wrong?'

Freya was running, trying to put some distance between them.

'It's OK!' Stephanie said, trailing behind. 'Where are you going? I know you're scared. But it's OK. It's all right. You're not on your own any more. The angels –'

'Go away!' Freya begged. 'Do you hear me? I don't believe in your stupid angels!'

Stephanie stepped back as if she'd just been slapped. 'No, it's OK,' she said, trying to hitch her smile back up. 'You're just in shock, realizing the truth about the angels again. Don't run from me. You know I'm right. In your heart, you do. I'll be your friend. I'll help –'

'No, I won't be your friend,' Freya said. 'You want me to believe in angels again. I can't do that. I'm sorry. I can't.'

'But you *want* to. I can see that. It's all right, Freya.'

'No, it's not all right! It's not!' Freya shouted it this time. Wherever she turned Stephanie was in her face. 'I don't want to have anything to do with angels, do you hear! I nearly went *insane* thinking about them before! Don't talk to me about them. And at school . . . if Miss Volhard asks, say you want to sit somewhere else. I mean it. If you try to sit next to me . . .' Freya felt her mind returning to all those years wasted in hospital. 'I can't be with you, Stephanie. I'm sorry . . .' She started running again.

Stephanie stumbled and fell into the border of a garden.

'It's OK, Freya,' she murmured, struggling to get up. 'I just want us to be friends. I won't talk to you at school or try to sit next to you. I won't embarrass you. We can just see each other outside –'

'No,' Freya said, stopping, in tears herself. 'No, we can't.'

Stephanie slumped back on the grass, her left cheek pressed up against the soil.

'What's the matter?' Freya asked. 'What are you doing?' She tried to haul Stephanie up but Stephanie just lay still, staring at her.

'I'm not trying to hurt you,' Freya said. 'It's just . . . I can't do this. I can't talk about angels. Please try to understand. I've been really ill. I can't be like that again. Just get up, will you?'

She dragged Stephanie from the mud and grass with both arms.

Stephanie's face was half covered by sodden leaves, but she didn't seem to notice or care. 'Look at you!' she cried, a pale smile appearing from somewhere. 'You can't help yourself, Freya. Even now, you're helping me, just like an angel would.'

Freya, breathing heavily from the exertion of lifting Stephanie, felt her falling again and caught her under the arms. It was dark and cold, the moon hidden.

'You see?' Stephanie whispered. 'That's why you reached down for me again. That's why you're reaching right down here into the mud and grass. You're holding me up. You can't help yourself.' A breeze suddenly blew Stephanie's hair, making it stand on end. 'An angel's spirit is moving through you, Freya. Otherwise, why would you be here at all?'

'Oh, Stephanie, it's not that,' Freya said. 'You poor thing. You're lost, aren't you?'

'Not any more,' Stephanie murmured. 'It's you who is. Can't you hear an angel?'

Freya stumbled away from Stephanie, not looking back. She spent the rest of the evening in her room, trying to shut her mind to everything that had happened. All that sloppy business with Stephanie writhing around on the grass! How could she befriend someone like that? She couldn't. But she *wanted* to. Desperately trying to deny that to herself, Freya realized that all she really wanted to do was sit down with Stephanie in the darkness and talk all night about angels.

What had happened tonight? Freya couldn't believe the feelings running amok inside her. How could Stephanie affect her so much, stir up so many old emotions so easily? Was this all her recovery amounted to – something a single conversation with one deluded girl could tear apart?

When Luke called her down to eat Freya made an excuse, staying in her room, but even then she couldn't settle. Her gaze kept shifting nervously to the window as if Stephanie herself might be out there, standing on the footpath, her small white teeth catching the moonlight.

It was after midnight by the time Freya, still wearing her clothes, finally managed to doze off on top of her bed. She slept fitfully, waking every hour or so, falling in and out of dreams.

It was only when she woke for the fourth or fifth time that she sensed something was wrong.

At first she thought it was just the discomfort of lying for so long in her clothes, and all those dreams making her feel hot and thirsty. Then she realized it had nothing to do with those things.

An unaccountable need to defend herself was racing through her blood.

Jumping up off the bed, Freya stared wildly round.

Who was there? Stephanie? No, it couldn't be Stephanie.

Freya's eyes flicked around the bedroom. Nothing seemed out of place. There were no signs of any disturbance. Her jumper was on the dressing table, exactly where she'd left it earlier. Unfinished Maths homework lay next to her chair.

Then she realized that something was *outside* her room.

The corridor light always projected a thin yellow slit of brightness under her door. Today, that strip was broken by a dense black shadow. Either a large object had been placed against the door – or someone was standing there.

'Dad?' she said automatically, clearing the hair out of her eyes.

No answer. Gazing more closely, Freya saw that a stationary object couldn't be making the shadow because it was moving. The ends of the dark segment wavered, as if they were part of a living thing.

Suddenly she sensed it clearly: something inhuman was standing at the threshold of her room – something stunningly alive, capable of anything.

Freya was aware of her hands shaking, of her hair swaying back and forth on a breeze that had not been in the room earlier. Where was the breeze coming from? At the same time she felt compelled to open the door.

In the middle of the corridor, waiting for her, was the dark angel.

Up close, it was even more terrifying than she recalled from her first encounter. The insides of the angel's eyes were all shadow: ovals of elemental darkness. Their hollows suggested blindness, but the angel was not blind. Little motions, twitchings, of its misshapen head, showed that it was following Freya as she staggered back towards the far wall of her room.

She frantically shifted her gaze over the angel's face. It was male, but each feature was hideous, a gross contortion of flesh.

The angel took a stride towards her. It drew its wings into the room. It lowered its deformed head under the lintel. Then it shut the door, and somehow Freya knew that no sound she made after this would be heard by Luke or Dad or anyone else in the world.

'Scream if you are going to,' the angel rasped. 'No one will hear. I have arranged for us to be alone, dear one.' It lifted a wing, wafting a fetid stink towards her.

The rational part of Freya's mind tried to pretend the angel wasn't there. She'd learnt some useful techniques during her time in the hospitals, ways of deflecting her thoughts from angels. She employed one now.

The dark angel waited for it to fail.

'What is it you feel when you look upon me?' he asked.

Hatred, Freya thought. Hatred of me. Hatred of everyone. The emotion bursting out of the angel was so tangible that it invaded the room. Discharging like a glutinous liquid, it trickled over the surface of the carpet, clogged the air, flowed like a poison up the walls. In whatever direction the angel moved, its hatred spread.

If this angel had a soul, it did not want anything to look inside it.

'You think I have no soul?'

Freya, realizing her mind had been read, backed up against the wall.

'I don't believe you're here,' she murmured.

'Trying to wish me away? I don't blame you. I am your nightmare. I am everyone's worst nightmare.'

'You aren't real.' Freya closed her eyes.

Suddenly – terrifyingly – the angel laughed. It was joyless, a madman's cry. 'Would your imagination really conjure up a vision like this? Better believe what you see.'

Freya stared more closely at the angel's face. It looked neither old nor young, but ravaged by something she couldn't understand. And yet there was a trace of something else under the features as well – hidden until she looked closely, almost beautiful.

'Ah, your species loves to think of us as beautiful, doesn't it?' the dark angel said. 'Spirits of purity, grace and light. Most can't bear the thought that we might be mortal, with failings and weaknesses. That would make us a little too much like you.

And you don't want your guardian angels to be anything like that, do you?'

Freya glanced at the angel's wings. They were filthy, scraping like bone across the floor. Surely they weren't capable of flight?

'You're wrong,' the dark angel said. 'Humans base everything on appearances.' He twisted his profile to her, executed a grotesque pirouette. 'You like the angelic look I have assumed for you today? The androgynous features, with matching toga? It's been all the rage since a few dull western painters made it up in the middle of the nineteenth century. Now we have to come to you approximating it, or you all shrivel up in fear.'

Anger seeped through Freya. It wasn't her anger, but the angel's. It was entering her, infecting her, like it had the room. There was so much fury, and nowhere for it to go except inside her. Part of her sensed that the dark angel wanted that – to overwhelm her, so she could do nothing except scream.

Sliding along the wall, she collapsed onto her bed.

The angel settled its bulk beside her and patted her cheek. It was exactly the gesture Amy Carr used when Freya did something she liked.

'Is this what angels really look like?' Freya managed to murmur. 'Like you?'

'You're not ready for an answer to that,' came the reply. 'I may have become the shame of angels, but I'm not a terrorizer of children yet. Not quite.'

'I'm not a child.'

'Not the child you were, that's true. Remember that eight-year-old girl, Freya? The way you waited up night after night for an angel to come back when everyone tried to stop you? You had such passion then. But I prefer the limited thing you are now.'

Freya saw that the dark angel took genuine pleasure in telling her this. The comment brought her shockingly back to reality. Surely no angel from her imagination would ever have said it to her? At the same time, something made her pity what was in front of her.

'You can't see inside my mind yet,' the angel said. 'Or can you?'

He lunged across the blankets and forced back the lids of her eyes. Seizing her head in his gnarled hands, he examined her from several directions.

'What do you want?' Freya screamed.

'To prove my brother wrong.'

'I don't understand.'

'Of course not. You're only a child.'

He cupped her face harshly. His nails hurt. Freya couldn't free herself from his grip.

'Get off me!' she yelled.

'Pain,' he said. Freya tried to pull away again, could not. 'Yes, you are sensitive to your own pain, aren't you? Poor little Freya: abandoned by her nice creamy-white angel. He visited once but he never came back.'

The dark angel released her with a contemptuous sigh.

Freya leaned back against the headrest, appalled by him.

Bending towards her, the angel plucked the small grey

feather Stephanie had given her from the pocket of Freya's shirt. He held it up against his own wings.

'Do any of you honestly believe such feathers as ours willingly leave our bodies?' he asked scornfully. 'Or that they could ever bear to be parted from each other?'

Freya stared at him, not understanding, just wanting him to leave.

'Remember all those questions you were too awestruck to ask my brother?' the angel said. 'Here's your chance. You may never have the opportunity again. Or shall I go?' He laughed, knowing she desperately wanted him to.

Freya's blood pounded. She couldn't hold off the angel's anger.

'How can I see you?' she demanded, forcing herself to focus.

No reply from the angel.

'Is it because I'm a child? I've heard young people often see angels more easily than adults.'

'A myth invented by adults who want desperately to believe in the innocence of childhood. Next question.'

'Am I . . . am I unique, special in some way?'

The angel smiled. Black teeth within black gums. 'Ah, the answer you've been seeking all these years. The only question that really matters, eh?' He imitated the voice of the first angel Freya had seen. *There is greatness there, or could be.* Is that what you want to discover, Freya? What my brother meant by that? Is that what your little heart needs to know?'

'Yes,' Freya whispered.

'Answer it yourself.'

'I can't.'

'Then ask another question.'

'Are angels here to help us? To ease our way through life? To guard us from harm?'

'Do I look like a being that would guard you from harm?'

'Yes,' Freya found herself saying, not sure why.

'Ask another question,' the angel replied, with sudden fury. A blister appeared on his left cheek, then collapsed.

'Are you from God? Are angels the messengers of God?'

'No, unless we do that bidding unwittingly. Perhaps the godhead exists. Some of us believe, others not. In that way, at least, we are not so different from your own species.'

The angel grinned, showing more of his teeth. Freya didn't let that distract her, though she knew he was trying to. She sensed something extraordinary behind his mask of bitterness.

'Why are you so dark?' she whispered. When no answer came she studied his sagging wings, reaching for the truth. 'You've done something terrible, haven't you? Something awful. That's why you look like this.'

The dark angel didn't reply, but for the first time his feathers stopped moving entirely.

'What have you done?'

The angel said nothing. His shadow was utterly still. 'I realize what Hestron, my brother, sees in you now,' he whispered uneasily. 'But he is still wrong about you. You'll never be capable of what he thinks.'

'What does he think I can do?'

No answer.

'Is Hestron the name of my guardian angel?'

The dark angel laughed. 'What makes you think you have a guardian angel? Why do so many of you believe we would devote our whole lives to your small existences?'

'But you do, don't you?' Freya murmured.

Her insight shocked him. The dark angel stepped back, as if momentarily afraid of her, or what she could do to him.

Hestron, Freya thought. The creamy white angel who first visited me is called Hestron.

'What does his name mean?' she asked.

'Hestron means treasured by all. And my brother is. But he should not be wasting his time with you.'

'What does your name mean?' Freya demanded. 'Hated by all?'

'My name is Mestraal,' the dark angel said. 'That, at least, is the closest I can make it in your inflexible language.' He unfurled a wing, and for a second, beyond the darkness that absorbed light, Freya saw a glorious spark that made her gasp. She saw the raw power he had been hiding from her, almost as if he was ashamed for her to see it. Mestraal emanated extraordinary strength, a magnificent energy.

Freya was suddenly frightened again. She cast her eyes down; she couldn't help herself.

'Don't do that,' he rasped.

She couldn't lift her face. 'What does your name mean?' she whispered.

'It means the fairest,' he said. 'Most loved.'

And with that he wrapped himself in utter darkness and was gone.

13

Stephanie spent the whole of the evening after her meeting with Freya being exhaustively cross-examined by her parents. They wanted an explanation for why she had stayed out so late, and wouldn't let her out of their sight until they were satisfied.

Making her peace with them as best she could, Stephanie was finally allowed upstairs to get changed out of her damp school uniform. She had a hot shower, slipped into her dressing gown and lay sprawled across her bed. Curling up inside the blankets, normally it was the argument with her parents that would have dominated her thoughts, but today that was the furthest thing from her mind.

What an evening! What an extraordinary evening! She'd met no one like Freya. Even her name was musical. A soft gap between the 'y' and the 'a'. Frey-a. All softness. Stephanie kept whispering it to herself. And how could their finding each other be an accident? She hadn't even asked Nadiel for a friend, but he knew her inner heart, of course he did, and he'd given her the chance of one anyway. All she had to do now was find a way to gain Freya's respect. But how could she do that? She'd seen the cold rejection in Freya's eyes earlier. How do you gain someone's trust when you remind them of everything they've put behind them?

I behaved stupidly in front of her as well, Stephanie thought, recalling the way she'd rolled around in the grass, mud and leaves clinging to her face. And hadn't she actually begged Freya to become her friend? How shameful and desperate-sounding was that? Amy and the others are her real friends, Stephanie thought. Freya doesn't even know me. I'm nobody. I'm somebody you run away from.

Chewing her lip, she reached under her pillow and picked an affirmation card at random from the pack she kept there. 'Triumphant energy', it read. Stephanie whispered the words over and over to the portrait on her wall.

Then she fell silent and nervous again. Was it already too late to get Freya to like her? Had she acted too weirdly? The possibility haunted her. No, she told herself. I can make it better. I'll behave more normally from now on. I can do that. And I'll trust in Nadiel.

Struck by a happier thought, Stephanie switched on her bedside light. A gift, she thought. I'll make her something. Why not? Freya wouldn't expect that. Something special, just for her.

Hunting around the room, Stephanie quickly selected paper and pens from her stencil set, thinking about the details. What colour should Freya's sigil be? Red for passion? Mm. Not quite right. Purple, perhaps – dark blood: forgotten fire, but coming back to life . . .

Stephanie got out her scissors and two or three of the specialist angel reference books she kept under her bed. Then she put them aside, deciding instead to let her imagination show her the way. Everything will be all right at school, she told herself. It doesn't matter if I make mistakes. Nadiel won't let me make too many.

I'm going to save you, Freya Harrison, she thought; I'm going to save you and you're going to save me.

She finished making the gift and popped it into her school bag. Then, on second thoughts, she wrapped the gift in paper, so no one else would see it when she handed it to Freya.

The moon and a few stars winked through the clouds outside her window. Stephanie gave up on any idea of sleep and sat up in bed, thinking about how much she needed to change to get Freya to like her. Perhaps the best option was to get the other students to like her *first*. That way Freya would find it easier to be her friend.

So I'll do that, Stephanie thought. I'll become friends with them all. Why not? Nadiel will be with me. I'll show Freya what a person with an angel at their side can be like.

Unable to settle, she hopped out of bed and padded along the dark corridor into the kitchen. Heating up some malt-flavoured milk, she sat on a chair, sipping her drink slowly in the dark. Something told her that tomorrow was going to be the hardest day of her life. Was that just her fear talking, or was it Nadiel, whispering words of wisdom, preparing her for the ordeal ahead?

It was cold outside. A breeze blew in through a gap under the front door, chilling her bare toes. The cup of milk slowly cooled in her hand. Clutching for the last of its warmth,

Stephanie willed only courage into her mind.

I'm scared, she thought, but I mustn't be.

To maintain her confidence, she closed her eyes and conjured up a powerful image of her and Freya together. She saw them as close friends, laughing – even mocking – the other students, they were so clearly immune to everything but their affection for each other.

I won't give you a reason to be ashamed of me, Freya Harrison, Stephanie thought. I won't sit next to you, not until you're ready. And I won't say a word to you or anyone else unless you want me to. Your secrets are mine. Do you think I'm a weak person? I'm not.

She watched the moon for over an hour, wishing she could stay forever within its simple transparency of light. Then she got out her pens again and drew a picture of Freya – an empty outline figure this time. Stephanie sat there for a while, deciding what to put in the space where the heart should be. Herself? Nadiel? In the end she just drew a small dotted empty heart-shape, waiting to be filled, and kissed it.

The remainder of the night was sleepless for Freya. She lay in bed, terrified. First Stephanie – weird, angel-obsessed Stephanie, the mirror image of what Freya herself used to be like – followed by the dark angel's visit.

Had she imagined him? Surely Mestraal had to be real. He seemed too appalling for her to have made up. Yet even Mestraal fitted the old pattern of her angels in a twisted way. Hadn't he mentioned her specialness? Hadn't he hinted that there was something unique about her? How likely was that?

There is greatness there, or could be. Is that what you want to discover, Freya? What my brother meant by that? Is that what your little heart needs to know?

And yes, she'd whispered. Yes. Yes. Nothing else had mattered.

The last thing Freya wanted was to be alone this morning, but she didn't dare go downstairs and join Luke and Dad at breakfast. She was too scared of how Dad would react. She knew she wouldn't be able to control her emotions if she saw him, and if anything slipped out about Mestraal he'd be straight on the phone to the hospital – what choice would he have? But staying in the house – with the possibility that

Mestraal might be waiting for her in one of the rooms – filled her with equal dread. At least at school there'd be company.

Dad and Luke both left the house earlier than she expected. Hearing them go, Freya jumped out of bed and was out of the front door within a few rushed minutes.

Cardigan Street was busy with commuters heading for work as she set off. Glad of the anonymous company, Freya's eyes darted right and left, searching for Mestraal.

This is what I used to do, she realized, coming to a halt. Walk along, checking for angels.

But in those days I *hoped* to see them. I wanted to.

She started to shake. It *is* happening again, she thought. I *am* sick. Mestraal isn't real. I just think he is.

Glancing up, she saw Gemma some distance down the street, and ran towards her, suddenly desperate for any kind of human company.

'Hey!' Gemma complained, as Freya collided with her. 'You trying to kill me? What's the matter?'

Freya didn't trust herself to say anything.

Vicky joined them nearer the school and exchanged a look with Gemma. 'Boy trouble,' she mouthed silently, then parted the hair on Freya's crown, genuinely concerned. 'Come on, you can tell us what's wrong. Is it something to do with Adam? Oh, poor thing, he hasn't dumped you already, has he?'

Freya shook her head. The last thing she wanted to think about now was Adam.

Vicky said, 'Come on, Gems, you know what to do. Girls together.' She parked herself on one side of Freya and firmly

· 120 ·

grasped an arm. Gemma took Freya's other arm, and the three of them set off in a line down Robert's Road. Vicky tightened her grip as they walked along, and despite everything that had happened last night, or perhaps because of it, Freya found herself relishing the solidarity and comfort of physical contact with both girls. I love you both, she thought, knowing it wasn't true, but meaning it all the same.

The warm, supportive atmosphere lasted until they reached school. As they neared the front gates Amy swam into view, talking animatedly with Adam.

That jerked Freya out of her angel reveries.

Adam offered Freya a tiny, guilt-laden smile as he scurried off, and Amy fell alongside the girls.

'Well, someone really *did* enjoy themselves the other night, didn't they?' she chuckled, squeezing Freya's arm.

'What?'

'A good snogger, isn't he?' Amy laughed at Freya's shocked expression. 'No good trying to keep secrets from me, Freya Harrison. Can't have that, can I? You forced me to find out more. Any boy can be made to talk, if you know how to persuade them.' She grinned. 'Adam's not a bad start-up boyfriend but don't expect loyalty, if you know what I mean.'

Freya stood there, open-mouthed.

'Oh, don't look so gobsmacked,' Amy said, pushing Freya's chin back up. 'A boy can't keep anything from me if I really want to know.'

Freya was devastated. How could Adam have mentioned the kiss, betrayed her so unthinkingly?

'Boys,' Vicky sighed, with feeling. 'What can you do with them?'

Amy took Freya's arm gently, as if it was one of the others who'd been hurtful. 'Ah there, never mind, plenty more where Adam came from. Oh, I forgot to give him your mobile number, by the way. If you still want to go out with him you've got my permission, of course.' She smiled. 'Easy enough to find you another boy, though. In fact, if Gemma's going to spend all day hanging around the fish and chip shop again, maybe you can nab hers.'

Gemma arched her eyebrows angrily, but held her tongue in check. 'I've got Malc,' she said sulkily as they walked through the school gates.

'No you haven't,' Amy said. 'He chucked you. I *heard.*'

'That little . . . he's such a twat,' Gemma growled, stamping her foot.

'You let him kiss you.'

'No, I didn't!'

'Chaz saw you both, behind Pizza Express.'

'It wasn't a real kiss! Anyway, I dumped *him* ten minutes later so it doesn't count. I dumped him first, right!'

Amy laughed and held up her hands. 'All right, all right, no need to get so defensive. We believe you.'

Thinking about Adam, Freya felt nauseous. She couldn't get his casual little wave out of her head. The next moment the image of Mestraal shot into her mind as well, and she closed her eyes.

Amy took the gang to their usual vantage point inside the

school gates. Freya could guess who Amy was waiting for.

'What about that Rice girl yesterday?' Gemma said, wanting the spotlight off her. 'Reckon she'll be back, Freya?'

Freya said nothing.

Vicky's voice rose an octave. 'God, you don't think she will, do you?'

'I'd rather die,' Gemma said.

'Oh, I hope she does come back,' Amy murmured. 'And I'm not the only one. Freya liked her, didn't you? Chatting away yesterday in class. Got a soft spot for Stephanie Rice, I reckon.'

The other two immediately swivelled to glare at Freya.

Freya thought of home, and wished she'd stayed there. Just get through today, she told herself. She held grimly onto that, saying, 'Look, Stephanie's just an odd, confused girl, that's all. Don't be horrible to her if she comes back.'

'Oh, we wouldn't do that,' Amy said.

Stephanie slid unobtrusively through the school gates shortly before nine a.m. At first Freya feared she might run straight across the gap between them to be with her. Instead, pointedly ignoring Freya, she strode instead to the opposite side of the playground near the computer block. Five or six girls were congregated there in a loose group. Stephanie edged closer to them, a couple of tentative shuffles.

'Ah look, she's trying to fit in,' Amy said. 'It's so sad. You should go over there, Freya, tell her we'll be her friends.'

Freya ignored Amy. She could see Stephanie apologetically

introducing herself to various strangers. They all shunned her. News about what happened yesterday had already spread rapidly through the school, and even without her brown uniform many of them recognized who she was.

Stephanie kept trying. After each group rebuffed her, she took a couple of deep breaths and approached the next. Then, once all the kids near her had moved away, she turned to girls in pairs or alone. One Year 8 girl melodramatically started running when Stephanie bumbled over. Another told her to shove off. The voice carried clear across the playground and several boys laughed. Stephanie smiled uncertainly back at them.

Stop it, Freya thought. It's too late to get them to like you.

That's when she saw Mestraal.

He was standing on the sports hall roof, his black wings folded along his flanks.

Freya shrank back, almost fell over.

'What's wrong?' Vicky asked, as Freya clutched at her.

'Nothing, nothing.' A retch rose in Freya's throat. She stood there, trying not to be sick. When she glanced back up at the roof again Mestraal was gone. Vicky stayed close to her, helping get her to a wall where she could sit down.

Gemma and Amy gazed suspiciously at each other.

'I wouldn't want to be Stephanie Rice, would you?' Vicky said conspiratorially in Freya's ear. 'No one liking you. Imagine that. She'll be in our English group again today, I suppose.'

'*You'll* certainly be seeing plenty of her, that's for sure,' Amy replied, not liking the way Vicky had suddenly paired off with Freya.

'What do you mean?' Vicky asked.

'I mean she's bound to be in all the remedial classes.'

The insult to Vicky was so obvious that even Gemma, used to a slow trickle of them coming her way, was shocked. 'I'm just saying,' Amy went on smoothly, 'that it'll be the perfect opportunity to get your own back on Darren after the other night. You can inflict Stephanie on him.'

Vicky gave her a narrow-eyed look and let it go.

Gemma stared into the distance.

Freya wasn't listening. Had Mestraal really been there? She peered up again. There there was no sign of him.

'You look like you've seen a ghost,' Vicky said. 'You all right?'

'No. I think I need to lie down.'

'You're already sitting down,' Amy said. 'The bell will be going in a minute.'

'I need to lie down now.'

Giving her a sceptical look, Amy shrugged and they moved to a small bench, where Freya could stretch out. Vicky stayed next to her, asking questions which Freya fended off.

Across the playground, Stephanie was still trying to make friends. Everyone was avoiding her now. The whole area marked out for the basketball pitch was a rectangle of emptiness. Stephanie stood in the centre of it, uncertain which way to turn next. Her gaze briefly flicked to Freya, then away again.

'Ah, she's looking for you now, Freya,' Amy said. 'She wants to come over, you can tell. But she's shy. Why don't we encourage her? Make her more comfortable?'

'No,' Freya groaned. 'For God's sake, for once will you just leave her alone!'

Colour drained from Amy's face. Vicky, in the middle of texting, almost dropped her phone in shock. Gemma held her breath. Neither of them had ever heard anyone raise their voice to Amy that way. What would she do?

'What did you say?' Amy demanded.

Freya felt her face redden. 'Just . . . just leave her alone, that's all.'

'*Leave her alone*,' Amy mimicked. '*Leave her alone*.' She glared at Freya. 'Go on, invite her over,' she hissed in her ear. 'You want to, don't you? You're her new little friend, aren't you? Admit it.'

Freya looked up. Mestraal was fanning the air like a ghoul over the sports hall roof. The nausea rose again in her throat, and she choked slightly, holding it back.

'What's that?' Amy cocked her ear. 'Did you say you *do* want to become Stephanie's new angel friend? Is that what you said?'

'Don't be stupid,' Freya muttered, keeping her head down.

'Stupid? I'm not stupid, Freya Harrison. Are you calling me stupid now? Is that what you're doing?'

Freya shook her head, still not looking up.

Amy kept her pinned under a withering glare, then released her. 'Well, that's all right then,' she said loudly. 'Glad to hear it! Vicky, Gemma, come with me, will you?'

Both girls jumped to attention and followed Amy away.

Freya's head spun. She didn't care what happened to her in that moment. She felt like fainting – actually wanted to. I'm going to be sick, she realized. Images of Mestraal's flailing wings assailed her. Then a notion entered her mind – that if she could just get through today without seeing Mestraal again she wouldn't be drifting back to what she used to be like. She knew the idea was ridiculous, but she clung to it.

Although the bell hadn't gone, she stood up and unsteadily made her way to the main school doors. Vicky, some distance across the playground, stepped forward to help her, but Gemma yanked her back.

Amy's face was full of spite as Freya passed. 'That's right,' she said. 'Better hurry. Stephanie's running this way, trying to catch you up. You don't want that to happen, do you?'

Freya didn't look back to see if it was true. She bolted through the door, heading straight for the nearest toilet.

Freya spent the first two periods lying down in the school's sick room. She even slept for a while in the hard bed, but as soon as she woke up again her eyes were scanning the windows, looking for Mestraal.

Miss Tavani, the school nurse, noted how distracted Freya was.

'What's your next lesson?' she asked.

'History.' Freya shrank back as a dark bird flew past the window. 'Then . . . English, first period after lunch.'

'Do you feel well enough to attend?'

No, Freya thought. Even if she felt better soon, there was no way she was taking a chance of entering an English class containing Stephanie Rice – not today, not feeling like this. Freya felt ashamed of herself for thinking that, but she meant it all the same.

'What's the matter?' Miss Tavani asked gently. 'You look as if you're still in pain. Are you?'

'No, I'm just weak,' Freya said. 'I am a . . . a weak person.'

'Weak?'

Freya thought about dark angels. Were they evil? Mestraal had looked malevolent, but in their last exchanges Freya had sensed the complexities he was hiding. Beneath his threats she'd detected a profound sadness. Even so, before she left the sick room, Freya scratched out a note and handed it to Miss Tavani. 'Is it possible to make sure one of the Year 10 students gets this?' she asked. 'Stephanie Rice.'

'Can't you give it to her yourself?'

'I don't know what lesson she's in next,' Freya lied. 'But it's important she receives it. It's private,' she added, when Miss Tavani went to read it.

Miss Tavani raised her eyebrows. 'OK, I'll give it to your head of year. If it's private you might think about putting it in an envelope.' Freya nodded and Miss Tavani assessed her again. 'I think the best thing is for you to go home, at least for now.'

A weight started lifting from Freya's shoulders as she realized that Miss Tavani was giving her permission to leave for the rest of the day.

Thanking her, Freya made sure the corridors were clear of students and sneaked out of the main doors. As she passed through the school gates a motion caught her eye.

It was Mestraal, standing on the grass of the eastern soccer field.

He was laughing at her.

Freya ran home.

15

That lunchtime Sam Davenport was gazing closely at a bunch of older boys loitering near Ashcroft High.

'It's OK,' Luke said, walking beside him. 'They're nothing to do with Tate.'

'How can you be sure?'

'I know them.'

'Yeah?' Sam glanced back, unconvinced.

Ever since Tate had issued his death-threat, Sam had been scared about getting too close to strangers. It made no difference how many times Luke told him that Tate didn't mean the death threat literally.

Sam was especially nervous this morning, and for good reason. Overnight, Tate had paid a visit to his favourite Year 7, chalking the words *dead boy* on the pavement near his house. It was just Tate's equivalent of a few minor slaps and punches, Luke realized, but it proved he knew where Sam lived and wasn't scared to take his revenge there. Just sending us a little message, Luke thought. Showing he can get to Sam if he chooses, even at home.

Tate's act of retribution had come fast. Hardly surprising given that every hour Tate spent at school with a broken nose diminished his reputation. I'll be next, Luke realized. And it won't be words drawn on the pavement, either.

As they walked along Sam stayed close, virtually pinned to Luke's side.

'Let's eat,' Luke said, indicating the KFC opposite the main school buildings. He'd decided against escorting Sam home for lunch today. Too risky. It made better sense to stay close to the school, so they could duck inside for protection if necessary. Luke suspected he wouldn't have to keep up this close level of vigilance for long. Tate was obviously just biding his time, playing games with Sam's mind until he could get to him.

'What are we going to do?' Sam muttered, once they had their food. 'Just wait? Just sit around until he gets his gang together again?'

'Let me worry about that,' Luke said, trying to keep a lid on Sam's anxiety levels. 'Besides, Tate's not having it all his own way. Did you see his nose this morning?'

'No.'

'You missed out then. It was a beautiful thing.'

'Yeah?' Sam chewed happily on a chicken wing.

'Yep. His mummy must have been up all night fitting that bandage. Must've taken her hours.'

Sam nodded approvingly, then insisted on getting Luke on his feet and moving them both to a clearer patch. He wanted to see exactly who was coming and going. 'He'll get me *inside* school from now on,' Sam whispered. 'That's what's next. You can't be with me all the time.'

True, Luke thought. In a big school like Ashcroft High there were plenty of opportunities to quietly stick the boot in away from prying eyes. There was no way he was going to be able to protect Sam. The only way to do that was to confront Tate in a once-and-for-all showdown. But the prospect of doing so filled Luke with dread. He knew he was unlikely to find Tate alone now. And even if he did, what would he do? Break his arms? Would he have to go to that kind of extreme? The punch he'd thrown earlier to crush Tate's nose had been fuelled by days of self-hatred at letting Sam down. He didn't know if he could resurrect that mood, let alone do anything worse.

'We'd better get back to the school,' Sam said, heading that way. 'It's too exposed out here.'

'We're OK.'

'No, let's go. Come on. I've got a bad feeling.'

'Everything's fine. Stop worrying.'

'Not about me. It's you Tate's really after, isn't it?'

Luke stopped to look at Sam.

'Don't stop! Don't stop!' Sam quickened his step. 'We've got to keep on the move. A moving target is harder to locate. I've been reading a self-defence book about it. Come on, keep walking.'

Luke did. 'So what else does your book say we should be doing?'

'Keeping a low profile,' Sam said with deadly earnest. 'And finding out the nature of our opponent's weakness.'

'Good advice.'

'You're not taking this seriously,' Sam said. 'Don't you realize Tate's going to really hurt you if he can? In the book it says that if you face a superior opponent you must finish off the task without mercy if you get the chance.'

They were inside the school gates now. Some Year 8s were running about in the playground in front of them. There didn't look to be any older kids who might be a danger. Would they dare attack us here? Luke wondered. In the playground itself? He glanced around. A couple of his friends were within range, discreetly following him, keeping an eye out. Luke was grateful for that, but he didn't want to get them directly involved if he could avoid it. A few of them had made it clear they'd get their hands dirty in a showdown with Tate if he wanted them to, but that would only escalate the fight. In fact, it was just the notch upward in status Tate craved. My gang against yours. Luke knew that Tate could definitely get up the bigger group. He'd win a show of force. Half of Luke's friends had never fought anyone for real in their lives. It was better if he could keep this personal.

Sam found a wall and put his back firmly up against it. 'Using available natural defenses,' he said, without a flicker of humour. 'Plus we can see the rest of the school grounds from here. What are you going to do about Tate?'

'He's mostly talk,' Luke said. 'Don't worry, I can take care of myself.'

'Can you?'

'Sure.'

But Luke didn't really think so. Not if Tate put his mind to the task. And after the mess made of his nose, witnessed by so many, Tate needed to do something really brutal to reaffirm his status. Luke didn't know when the retribution would come, but he knew it would be soon.

The bell sounded.

Glancing one more time around the school grounds, he led Sam inside.

Miss Volhard was better prepared than the first time Stephanie had entered her English class. After yesterday's meltdown, she'd taken the precaution at the start of the lesson to give the class a five minute lecture on behaviour before asking Stephanie to join them.

It made little difference. Everyone twisted in their chairs as Stephanie entered the class. They couldn't believe she was back so soon after yesterday's disaster. Was she crazy? And what would she be wearing under that big old duffle coat today? A few hoped for a sparkly angel dress to brighten up the afternoon.

Stephanie disappointed them – just a pair of jeans and a plain beige top.

Mrs Baldwin, the Headmistress, ushered Stephanie in again, bleakly holding onto her narrow shoulders.

Stephanie's gaze flitted quickly between the desks, searching for Freya. When she saw that she wasn't in the class part of her felt relief, because that meant there was no way she could do anything to embarrass her. But it also meant she was on her own.

They'll expect me to come crawling into the room like a

wounded insect, she thought. So I won't. I'll get them to like me instead. She had a plan for this – written out early that morning, and memorized. Before making a start on it, she touched her heart momentarily to remind herself that there was at least one presence in the room on her side. Then, thanking Mrs Baldwin, she strode across the floor. She managed a definite, if not confident, stride and fixed all the students with a smile.

No one was sitting in the rear set of desks today. Even those students who normally preferred it there had out of an instinct of social self-preservation shuffled down to the next row.

Head erect, Stephanie took an empty seat at the back of the class as if she couldn't have found a better place. 'I'm fine here on my own, thank you,' she said, before Miss Volhard forced someone to sit with her. Taking a couple of textbooks from her bag, she faced forward, looking straight at the whiteboard.

The class, having been warned by Miss Volhard, muttered various things under their breath, then turned round to face the front as well. Flipping to a page of Chaucer, Miss Volhard watched them closely, especially Amy. Amy gazed sweetly back.

For a few minutes the lesson proceeded more or less normally. Miss Volhard was just getting into her stride, questioning the class on the knight's tale, when everyone heard a sudden scraping noise behind them.

It was Stephanie, scrambling from her chair to stand up.

She stood there calmly, or looking calm anyhow, her hands folded across her stomach. Everyone gazed wide-eyed at her, having no idea what she'd do or say. There was something both incredibly exciting and appalling about it.

Miss Volhard motioned her down, but Stephanie cut through her feebly waving hand.

'No, I'm not ready to sit yet, thank you.' Her voice was clear and strong. 'I wish to say a few words about yesterday. Please allow me that.'

Miss Volhard, looking defeated, nodded.

Everyone held their breath as Stephanie cleared her throat.

'First, I want to apologize for my behaviour in class before,' she said. 'I know I came across strangely. I . . . didn't mean to. This is almost my first time at a real school, so I'm not sure how to behave. I do believe in angels. I make no apology about that.' This raised a few snickers, but Stephanie's tone was so sure of itself that others were exchanging surprised, half-impressed, glances.

'I just want to mention that for me angels are a special source of comfort,' Stephanie went on. 'Please let me lodge one thought in your minds before you dismiss them as silly made-up things. It is this: that you cannot go a day, not one single day of your life, without seeing an image of an angel, or reading the word "angel", or hearing it used by someone. Really, you can't. That is how urgently our guardian angels wish to communicate and show each of us that they love us.'

Amy laughed out loud, carrying several others with her.

Stephanie swallowed, aware that she'd departed from her prepared speech. Was mentioning love a bit too strong?

'Anyway, that's all I have to say,' she faltered. 'I hope we can start on a new footing, and that you'll all . . . be my friends.'

She dropped like a stone onto her seat again.

'Thank you, Stephanie,' Miss Volhard said. 'You are of course welcome in this class. Now, where were we?'

She turned back to the knight's tale.

'So you talk to angels then, do you?' said a quiet voice.

Amy.

Miss Volhard gave her a warning glance, but Amy pretended not to see it.

'Sometimes,' Stephanie said warily.

'That's interesting. Really interesting. Chatting to angels. How nice.'

A few snickers followed. Stephanie stood and looked directly at those students who were not laughing. 'There is nothing to be ashamed about if the subject of angels interests you,' she said. 'They're here to help us.'

'Thank you,' Miss Volhard said curtly, turning back to the text. 'Please sit down, Stephanie.'

Stephanie sat.

'What about bad people?' Amy said airily. 'Nasty people? Do they have guardian angels helping them, too?'

'You mean people like you?' Stephanie replied.

Laughter erupted. The insult was deliberate and so unexpected coming from Stephanie that they all cracked up. Amy broke into a smile, too, mostly chagrin, blushing slightly. 'Yeah, people like me,' she said. 'Or worse.'

'You can't get worse!' one of the boys called out, to more laughter. Everyone gazed back at Stephanie, primed for her next remark. They were fascinated by where she might go next.

'Even you,' Stephanie said – eliciting more laughter. She gave an imitation of one of Amy's sweet smiles.

'Maybe Amy's angel is rubbish,' a boy called out.

'Or given up on her,' someone else said.

'Yeah, yeah,' Amy said, reddening.

Everyone was laughing now. It wasn't often that the class got a chance to snipe at Amy. Even Miss Volhard seemed to be enjoying it.

'You need to get her a new angel, Stephanie,' a girl in the middle row ventured.

'It won't be easy,' Stephanie said, feeling the whole class were with her. 'The guardian angels work best when they are cooperating with the natural forces of harmony in the Universe. When they face a hopeless challenge they do what they can, of course, with love.'

Stephanie hadn't quite meant for this to come out as an insult, but the class thought it was brilliant. Even Gemma and Vicky had to stifle their laughter.

'That's nice to know,' Amy said.

'Isn't it,' Stephanie replied. More laughter.

For the first time Amy looked seriously rattled. She gnawed her lip, trying to think of a suitably barbed reply.

Stephanie glanced around the room. She sensed Nadiel's presence with her. It had to be him helping her. She couldn't win against Amy in this situation – it was impossible – but she was doing it.

'What's your guardian angel's name?' Amy asked.

'Nadiel.' Stephanie said it without thinking.

Amy threw her head back and laughed. 'Nadiel,' she purred in a sing-song voice. 'What kind of name's that?'

Stephanie hesitated. 'I . . . got it from a portrait, but –'

'A portrait?' Amy held her hand over her mouth. 'Oh, lovely. From a pretty picture. What a surprise. Do you have his address as well? He sounds cute. Can I have his mobile number?'

Stephanie said angrily, 'I'm really sick of listening to you. You're just . . .'

'I'm just what, you freak?'

'That's quite enough!' shouted Miss Volhard.

Stephanie was furious. What could she do to hurt Amy, cut her down to size?

'I could read your angelic destiny for you, if you like,' she said, smiling tightly.

'My what?' Amy asked.

'A shuffled deck of cards, whereby angels transmit accurate messages to us. You sing the answers. Or are you too scared about what they might reveal?'

As soon as she said it, Stephanie knew she'd made a mistake. Singing with angel cards? The idea was too bizarre for the class. She didn't even use them herself.

'I . . .' She couldn't work out how to recover. She'd overreached herself. Confidence crumbling, she sat down and lowered her eyes.

The class started looking at her again as if they weren't sure what to make of her.

Amy saw her chance.

'You poor sad little girl,' she said slowly. 'Look at you. Better go home to Mummy. Let her sing you a nice little song.'

The words hung in the air like a dagger, so awful that most of the class were embarrassed for Stephanie. A spirited riposte might have rescued her. But when she had no response the class lost any respect they had developed. They'd given her a chance, and she'd embarrassed them. They wouldn't easily forgive her for that.

Stephanie stayed a few seconds more, then, holding back a sob, grabbed her bag and ran from the class.

'Stephanie!' Miss Volhard tried to follow.

As she ran down the corridor, Stephanie yelled out, 'Nadiel! Help me! Help me!'

Miss Volhard tried to catch hold of her, but Stephanie hid in a cloakroom until her footsteps disappeared, then tearfully made her way to the main doors of the school.

Freya, she silently screamed, where were you?

As she was hurrying out of the entrance, the school receptionist called her back. She held out a note. 'Are you Stephanie Rice?'

Stephanie straightened up. 'Yes.'

'I have something for you.'

Stephanie blinked at her, not understanding.

'It's a personal note. I don't know who it's from. Oh, here, it says on the envelope. Freya Harris, is it? I can't quite read . . .'

'Thank you,' Stephanie said, controlling her breathing. 'I'll take it.' She thrust out her hand.

'Are you all right?' the receptionist asked.

'I'm fine, thank you,' Stephanie replied stiffly.

She took the envelope, left the school and rushed out of the grounds before Miss Volhard or any of the other teachers could come after her.

She didn't touch the note. It lay unopened in the pocket of her jeans, like a nasty little growth. She wanted to read it, but what if it said something horrible? After last night's argument with Freya it might be telling her to leave her alone forever. Stephanie couldn't bear it if it did. She took it out, then put it back in her pocket again.

Her mother was out when she got home, but the phone was ringing. Their phone rarely rang during the day. It's the school, Stephanie realized. Ignoring it, she made herself some hot milk and went up to her room. Shutting the door, she took off her tight jeans and stretched into some slacks and a comfortable top.

She placed Freya's note on her dressing table. It lay there like a small unexploded missile. Stephanie delayed opening it for a long time. At one point she threw it in her waste basket, then took it out again and for some reason kissed it. Her faith in Nadiel was not at its strongest today, but she reminded herself that the true test of faith came at times like this.

Dreading it, Stephanie snatched up the note and in one brisk motion opened the envelope with the edge of her thumb. It was a short note. Just a couple of lines. She'd know soon enough what it said. She forced her fingers to open the folded, lined paper. The note read:

Stephanie, I'm in trouble and couldn't think who else to

*turn to. A dark angel, completely black feathers, face,
everything, visited me last night. I don't know if I'm going
mad or not. Please help me.*

Freya

Stephanie re-read the note several times. Then she broke down
in relief. Not a letter telling her to leave her alone, but a cry for
attention! Freya asking for *her* help! Was that why Nadiel had
let events at school today go so badly wrong – so that she could
respond more quickly to Freya's need? Of course! It had to be.
Why else would he have allowed it?

She sat down to think. She didn't know where Freya lived,
or she could have gone over right away. Never mind. She'd find
her at school first thing tomorrow morning. In the meantime
she'd consult her angel books for everything she could glean
about dark angels. She'd once been fascinated by the descriptions of fallen or destructive angels in various texts. Was that
an accident, or had she become fascinated so that now, in a
friend's moment of need, she could reach out to Freya?
Stephanie didn't believe in coincidences. She would stay up all
night if she had to.

'I'll help you, Freya Harrison,' she whispered out loud.
'Don't think you're alone.'

Freya lay in her bedroom, keeping her eyes shut. It was the only way to avoid seeing Mestraal. He *was* real, she was sure of it now. Something about the way he'd laughed on the football field made her certain.

In the early afternoon she cringed at the sound of the front door being opened, not wanting company. From the quiet way it was done she knew it was Dad. Part of her wanted to rush downstairs to tell him everything. 'I'm not making them up any more,' she saw herself saying. 'It's real this time.' But how could she tell him that without breaking his heart? And after she broke his heart, he'd phone the hospital anyway. She couldn't risk that. The hospital was the one place where *nobody* would believe her.

Dad rapped on her door, waited a decent interval, then opened it cautiously. Freya quickly reached for a book and pulled the covers around her, intent on keeping a straight face.

'How's my favourite daughter, then?'

Freya smiled, but didn't meet his eyes. 'She's OK.'

He stepped into the room. 'The school phoned to say you weren't well.'

Freya's right hand, above the bedclothes, visibly trembled.

Dad's gaze was drawn straight to it.

'Oh, look at that,' Freya said, trying to laugh the trembling off, but he knew her too well. She sat there, her face in the book. 'I'm all right, Dad. It's nothing, really . . .'

He approached the bed. 'Freya . . .'

She put out a frail arm to keep him at a distance.

'Dad, please . . .'

He glanced at her, saw she was not ready to talk about whatever it was – angels, he knew, his heart sinking, but he didn't show it.

'All right,' he murmured. 'It's OK. You get some sleep. We can talk later if you like.' He went to leave, stopped at the door. 'By the way, I'm going over to Auntie Janice's for a couple of days. She's on a course, and needs someone to look after the kids. Is that OK?'

Freya nodded, the whole of her will bent on keeping her emotions in check until he went away.

Dad left her room and walked slowly down the carpeted staircase. He'd seen this pattern of behaviour from Freya before – the long periods staying in bed, the suppressed strong emotion, that dreaded holding-on-for-dear-life expression. But there was something subtly different this time, a reaction even more intense.

He couldn't put off the telephone call to the hospital for long if she was sinking this fast. Did I give her too much independence too soon? he wondered. Is it the pressure of school that's sent her over the edge again – all those new friends she's trying so hard to please?

He tried to pretend for a moment that Freya was suffering from some other, lesser problem, not the angels again, but there was no mistaking the signs. Freya always acquired a certain look when angels were on her mind. He knew it well. A haunted look. Sometimes a blissful one as well, though that was hardly what he'd seen recently.

This is what happens when you become ill, he thought. You can't do what a father's supposed to. You can't protect your own daughter.

Events were taking place in his own life he needed to explain to her, but he was glad he'd held off telling her now.

Making his way into the living room, he pressed his face against a wall. What's happening to you, Freya? he wondered. What's happening inside that lovely scared head of yours? Don't you think I can make it better any more? I can.

But inside he realized that might not be so. He looked within himself and tried to measure his strength. Enough left to get Freya through this difficult patch? He didn't know. Do you ever know? How can you know something like that? Steadying himself, he leaned his weight against the wall.

He'd visited Freya's last hospital so often in the past that he knew the number of the doctor's secretary he needed to contact without having to look it up. Picking up the phone, he started dialling. Then he clicked the phone off again.

Not without checking with Freya first, he decided. She's not a little girl any more. She deserves to be part of the decision. But what if she begged him not to, and he *still* thought he had to make the call? What if it came to that? Her silence made it hard to know what to do. If only she'd open up more, he thought, the way she used to.

'Don't wait too long to talk to me,' he murmured. 'Let me in, Freya. While you can. While I'm still here.'

The next morning, at dawn, a second, brighter, angel arrived in Freya's bedroom. He timed his visit for early morning, while the town was still asleep. Maybe it was the promise of the sun that drew him. Or perhaps he simply wanted empty streets and silence because they could more easily be filled with his vision. Who can know an angel's mind? Perhaps it was just to allow Freya a final night of uninterrupted sleep before he ruined that for ever. In any case he came at a time of crisis – for at what other time should an angel arrive? – and met her as the sun rose.

Freya's window was closed to him, and to all angels, but that didn't stop him; he had ways of entering rooms.

His light, splashing off the walls, illuminated Freya. She was blinded by it, but when she woke she recognized him at once. How could she not? The golden halo was the same. The face was the same, so beautiful it was almost a threat. She should have been angry after all the years of waiting, but there are stronger emotions than anger, and her hands couldn't help themselves, fumbling towards his wings like the naïve child of old. And when her fingers touched the innermost feathers they were just as she remembered them being: like a sheen, a yielding layer of some rare creature's inner sanctum of fur, if you could meet such a beast, if you come so close.

His last visit had been six years ago. But Freya sensed now that he had known her for far longer. How long exactly?

'Since you were just a movement,' he answered. 'A movement without a face inside a womb.'

'Hestron.' Like a fragrance, she breathed him in. She wanted to hold him, but was afraid to even come close. 'You left me,' she murmured. 'I didn't know you were real.'

'I am.' That high voice again, the eagle singing.

'You never came back.'

'I had others to look out for; those I guard. And – you were not ready.'

'Am I now?' She thought of Mestraal's contempt for her.

'You judge him harshly,' Hestron said. 'Yet above all other angels he took on this world's problems.'

Freya gazed up questioningly.

'Millions of you are perpetually crying out,' Hestron said. 'You think not being able to satisfy all that need does not wound us?' He shook out his wings. Freya sat up in her bed, trembling with awe. She wondered what Hestron wanted from her now, but was afraid to ask. Why were his wings bending so close to her?

'They have never forgotten your touch,' Hestron said. 'Will you fly with me?'

Freya did not need to give an answer for him to know it.

The outer feathers of one vast wing drew her against his chest. Then Hestron faced the window, opening it fully.

'Are you ready?'

Yes, she thought.

Two huge swoops was all it required for Hestron to carry Freya to the town centre. They flew over a factory outlet, gliding between two run-down tower blocks of council flats. A sad-looking woman stood on a tiny concrete balcony there, a cigarette and half-finished mug of tea in her hand, dimly following their flight with her eyes.

'No,' Hestron said. 'She cannot truly see me. Only you can do that. You alone, of all humans.'

'I don't understand.'

'It is your gift.'

'To be able to see angels?'

Hestron laughed. 'No, your gift is far greater than that, Freya Harrison.' Suddenly his face was alive with surplus love, and this time, as Freya looked down, it seemed to her that beneath them every living thing on the earth followed their path.

She found herself clutching Hestron's feathers, wanting to be closer to him. She put her face up against his heart. It wasn't like a human heart. It beat more slowly than ours. Freya felt her own pulse reduce to match it, until between them there was nearly, but not quite, a single beat.

'Look!' Hestron cried, gesturing at the horizons speeding past.

'I can't,' Freya complained. 'You're travelling too fast.'

But that wasn't true. Her vision was already adjusting to his velocity. Then Freya sensed something else – the people Hestron was guardian to – flashing past below them.

'We call them our wards,' Hestron told her. 'Those we are responsible for.'

Freya sensed that Hestron's wards were dotted at irregular intervals across towns and cities. Stunned, she said, 'You're responsible for *more* than one person?'

'Yes.'

A surge of pure jealousy jabbed through her, that she had to share Hestron with anyone, but it was quickly drowned out by the shock at how many wards he was responsible for.

There were *thousands* of them out there.

Seeing through Hestron's eyes, she sensed their hope, uncertainty, despair, love, bitterness, joy, all emotions. She also felt pain.

'There is always pain,' Hestron said.

'Can't you stop it?'

'Not all of it.'

Freya felt the blood surging inside his wing. 'How high can you fly?' she called over the wind.

In answer, Hestron left the clouds behind. He flew higher than any living thing, effortlessly up and up, until they were beyond the circumference of the Earth. Only there, soaring in the vastness of space, did Freya at last see the real extent of an angel's wings, for they only truly unfurled when naked starlight shone upon them.

Hestron raised his eyes longingly towards the distant points of light.

'You belong . . . in this place, don't you?' Freya realized. 'Not with us. But out here. Among the stars.'

Hestron nodded. 'We were migrating between them when we came across your world. Then we saw your wars, witnessed hunger, loneliness, the way you deny each other love – all the terrifying things you do to one another. How could we leave then?' He stared at her, his expression haunted. 'Why do you do such things? Why do so many of you care so little?'

Without waiting for Freya's answer, as if he knew she had none, Hestron renewed his strength in the light of the sun. Then he dipped back into our winds, a golden nimbus to light his way, only his strong will bringing him back to earth.

Freya gazed up at him, afraid to ask any more questions. Eventually she murmured, 'Show me what you do.'

'Are you sure?' His voice was edged with danger. 'You're certain you want to know?'

'Yes.'

Hestron altered course, approaching a northerly latitude. He swept down a precipice in western Finland, where a lone rock-climber was losing her final foothold on an outcrop. The woman reached out desperately with a gloved hand, but her fingers only found air and then she fell headlong, over a hundred feet, her body striking jagged splinters of rock all the way down.

There was no way she could have survived except that an angel – not Hestron – took the main blow at the bottom of the mountain slope. Interposing its own body between the woman and the ground, the angel took enough of the impact so that she was left with only miraculously minor injuries.

Freya gazed at the feathered body wedged against the rocks.

The angel did not arise and go smoothly on its way. Its bright body dimmed for a few seconds, wings dragging against the ground.

'It's injured,' Freya whispered.

'Of course,' Hestron said. 'Our bodies are more durable than yours, but they still suffer.' He turned to acknowledge the damaged angel, and for the first time Freya clearly saw its face. It was the same androgynous male-female combination she'd seen in Hestron. This time, however, its countenance was distinctly more female than male.

'We fashion ourselves in the image of those we love,' Hestron said. 'We can never make up our minds what face among our wards to use, whose features we should cherish most.'

Freya thought of Mestraal.

Then she watched the other angel flying away, still nursing its injuries. Hesitating, she asked Hestron, 'Do you die?'

'Eventually. We are not eternal beings. Our presence on your world reduces our lifespan. Physical interventions reduce it further. There is little enough that we can do for you in the end. We give hope where we can. We comfort, where that is needed. Sometimes we whisper words to influence an action, where that action may lead to harm. We warn of danger; we prevent it where possible. That is all.'

'Why can't other people see you?'

'Manifestation on your world is extremely difficult for us. Only some angels have the power to appear directly to mortals. I can do so. Mestraal, obviously. Many cannot. '

'But I can see you, and I can *feel* you.'

'Because, Freya, you are not entirely human.'

Freya trembled. She almost fought against an understanding, knowing her life would never be the same once she knew.

'I'm . . . I'm just a girl,' she said. 'I'm not an angel.'

'No. Not an angel. Rarer than that. Your kind is so exceptional that among the angels we do not even have a name for the spectacular thing you are.'

A desert flashed past below them, a forest, a great city – morning across half the world.

'What am I?' Freya breathed.

'You are both human and angel,' Hestron said. 'Not more powerful than an angel, but capable of coexisting on both planes. Only three others in human history have been able to do so. One was the man called Elijah, who became Sandolphon. Another was Enoch, who became Metatron.'

Freya thought of her dad, of Luke.

'No, the gift is not hereditary. Nor do we know why your kind is so rare.'

Freya shook her head, touched her face. 'I don't feel any different.'

'Yet you've always been at odds with the world.'

'I can't fly.'

'But what have you ever desired except flight? Part of you has always wanted to be among us.'

'I thought . . .'

'I know. That it was a child's mistaken obsession.' He stared at her. 'But what do you feel now? Mestraal opened up your gift when he came to visit you. He may not have meant to, but his power is so great that he cannot help himself.'

'I'm just a girl,' Freya protested.

But she knew she was only saying those words out of fear. No human could have withstood the speed of the winds buffeting her. Clinging to Hestron, Freya suddenly longed to do things she had never done before: to breathe in new ways; to love differently.

Hestron said, 'As a child, I left you a half-fledged thing I could not fully set free. Forgive that, if you can.'

Freya gazed into his eyes. 'But what about you? If angels lead this life of service, how do you find happiness?'

'What is happiness but the easing of the lives of others?' Hestron answered. 'There is nothing more important than our wards. To protect and honour them has become our way now. It is so long since we have known any other.'

'What if an angel abandons its wards?'

'There is no worse crime.'

She thought of Mestraal.

'Yes,' Hestron murmured. 'He no longer intervenes to help his wards. Chaos ensues.'

'Doesn't he care in the same way as you?'

'No, you do not understand. He cared too much, and for too many. He took too much upon himself. And now our beloved is lost to us.'

Hestron closed his eyes – a sudden jarring – and for a moment Freya felt something insistent. It was a cry that could not be ignored.

She knew at once it was one of Hestron's wards calling out in desperate need to him.

She also felt personally drawn to the ward.

'And they to you,' Hestron whispered.

'But they don't know me.'

'Yet they sense what you are. Have others not been drawn to you all your life?'

She felt a painful tug from the ward below.

'Is this what it's always like?' she gasped. 'For every angel?'

'Yes. It is a cry for human help,' Hestron answered quietly. 'Rarely does anyone respond. Why don't any of you listen?'

'Take me there,' Freya said.

Hestron lowered his wings. He flew to an old woman, riddled with disease, in an African hut. Unseen by her, Hestron took her emaciated body in his arms, temporarily easing her pain. They were immediately on the move again, no time to dwell in any one place, and this time Hestron alighted beside a Taiwanese man searching under the wreck of a collapsed building that had already taken too many lives. Freya gazed up into Hestron's eyes as he worked to help the man accept what had happened, but she wasn't sure she was seeing Hestron clearly; her eyes didn't yet work so well, squinting into his kind of light.

And then, as if Hestron knew Freya's education must be swift, he took her to a hospital room where a five-year-old child lay dying.

The child's father sat at the bottom of the bed. An angel was with him. She held the father dearly – human arms have never held so well – and, though Freya and Hestron stood close, the angel did not see them. In that moment the angel had no consciousness of anything except the requirements of the man in her arms, her ward, a total love only for him.

'Why is there no angel with the boy?' Freya murmured.

'He is already beyond our reach.'

'You can't save him?'

'We have a clearer understanding of the physical properties of things than humans, but we cannot rid bodies of disease, enter cells, fix bones. We are as powerless as you against those things.'

There was a blip on the electronic board above the boy's head. A steady low alarm. Medics came crashing into the room, and jolted the boy's chest with cushioned pads. For over five minutes they tried unsuccessfully to revive him, and as the boy finally died Freya saw a new angel enter through a window.

It arrived in a pool of its own radiance, sat by the boy and held his head.

It's come to witness the death, Freya realized.

'Of course,' Hestron said. 'To say goodbye. We have known you all your lives.'

Freya watched. The doctor poignantly stepping back from the boy's bed seemed inconsequential compared with the new angel as it felt under the blanket. It reached there, continuing to cradle the boy's shoulders. Even in death it did not wish to let go, still holding him while a nurse pulled a screen around the bed.

The doctor recorded the time of death. At the same time

Freya saw the boy's angel whisper something over his face.

'He is wishing his ward a better life in the next,' Hestron said. 'If anything comes after.'

'Don't you know?'

'No more than you. But it must be better, mustn't it?' Hestron added, as if in that moment he needed her to affirm an afterlife. 'Some of us believe; some not. In that at least our two species are alike.'

The angel of the boy and the angel of the father both departed, in different directions. Freya distantly sensed other wards calling them – there was no time for them to linger, even now.

There isn't a guardian angel for each of us, she realized.

Hestron gazed at her. 'No, though most humans wish to believe that. Your writings are full of us, as if we were everywhere. "Then I looked and heard the voice of many angels,"' Hestron recited, quoting from the Bible's Book of Revelation; '"and the number of them was myriads of myriads, and thousands upon thousands."' He sighed. 'But it is not so, Freya. There is so much unnecessary suffering among your kind, so much we could prevent, yet even those who believe in angels on your world rarely recognize the truth of why so little is done to help them.'

'*That there are so few of you to guard so many,*' Freya said.

'Yes.' Hestron glanced regretfully at his wings. 'And while these carry us swiftly, we are often too far away to reach our wards in time.'

'Do you choose your wards?'

'Their need chooses us. Whichever angel can reach them first does so, and usually remains with them thereafter.'

Freya breathed deeply, stroking Hestron's feathers, not aware she was doing so.

'The angels are everywhere on your world,' he told her. 'Most are clustered where you would expect us to be, the areas of famine, war, hatred. Your species create misery and carnage wherever you go. There are some individuals we cannot ever leave, their torment is so great. Mestraal was our finest strength. In all the worst places he was present.'

'How could he endure it?'

'He could not.'

Hestron gazed at Freya. Then he suddenly smiled and shook out his feathers. 'But the life of an angel is not all misery and death. Far from it.'

And with that, accompanied by Freya, Hestron took to the air again. He searched out his wards seemingly at random, and wherever he was near them their problems were wondrously alleviated. Freya sensed that for a time Hestron almost forgot her, he was so locked into his duty, letting himself be guided by their needs.

And it was no accident that they found themselves at a train station between a mother sodden with cold and a chronically arthritic elderly man. And this much is true, is certain – that the woman walked onto the train infinitely more at ease, and the elderly man a little more healthy, a little lighter in his step.

Hestron spread his wings, and laughed. Freya saw them

glinting, more sun and air than feather. *I like to travel in sun-light*, he said. But Freya knew that. She was already drenched and glowing in the light he travelled by.

19

Freya didn't go in to school that morning. After Hestron brought her home she stayed in her room, utterly absorbed by what he'd told her about her gift – a gift so rare that even the angels had no name for it. Coming out of her reveries at last, she was vaguely aware of normal morning activity starting up in the house: the central heating creaking on, Dad leaving for work, Luke departing early again.

Exhausted after two nights with very little rest, Freya slept.

It was late afternoon, and getting dark, before she awoke. And the second she did, the room felt different. No, not the room, she realized. The difference had nothing to do with the room. She was simply different. Colours were suddenly sharper to her vision, distances closer, edges more precise.

To have flown with angels! To have known such magnificence! And wasn't she one of them now as well, or something like it? A hybrid: part human, part angel. But what did that mean? That she could do what angels do? That she could fly with them? Freya felt her pulse race at the prospect, and tried to calm down. How could she possibly soar like Hestron? But the idea burned tantalizingly in her mind. She couldn't stop thinking about it. And she couldn't stop thinking about

Hestron, either. Only a short time with him, and already Freya was more than half in love. She even knew why. It was impossible not to love something that gave so much and so willingly.

Turning her head, Freya settled back into the warmth of her pillow again. Achingly tired, luxuriating in her newly-found awareness, she fell into a deep, comfortable asleep.

Stephanie spent half the night consulting her angel texts and feverishly trying to recall everything she had ever read about dark angels. She couldn't sleep, couldn't keep frightening images away. Was a dark angel with Freya even now, whispering gusts of hate into her soul? If only she knew where Freya lived, she could have run over to her house and at least warned her. Since that wasn't possible she'd have to wait until Ashcroft High opened tomorrow. But there *had* to be something she could do before then.

Perhaps there was.

Hastily, Stephanie cleared a wide circular space on the bedroom carpet. Then, lighting seven of her finest candles, she got down on her knees and imagined their combined radiance forming a shield around Freya. She stayed for hours in that cramped position, ignoring the increasing pain in her joints. It was only as the final candle guttered, spreading a dark patch across Nadiel's face, that a startling question flashed out of nowhere into her mind.

Did Nadiel have the power to stop a dark angel?

Stephanie had no idea why such a question stole into her

thoughts, but it terrified her. She rejected it at once. It wasn't doubt Freya needed at this moment. It was the opposite: trust. She had to trust in Nadiel completely, now more than at any time before.

Touching the tips of her fingers to Nadiel's portrait in apology, Stephanie emptied her mind of everything except Freya. Then she shakily fetched pen and paper, and wrote:

I will hold on to you, Freya Harrison.
Take bold steps, for I will walk in front of you
and behind you and watch your feet.
If you stumble, I'll pick you up.
I won't let anything hurt you.
When everyone else has gone, I'll wait for you.
Angels are reaching out in the darkness,
Hands and wings to hold your heart.

She read the words out loud several times, asking Nadiel to send them like doves from her soul to help build a fortress around Freya. Then she tidied the waxy remains of the candles away and lay back on her bed. The night hours elapsed slowly, and Stephanie didn't even try to sleep. Instead, she concentrated on Freya, preparing what she would tell her about dark angels, and waited patiently for school to open.

At Ashcroft High the next morning, Stephanie was one of the first students to arrive. She didn't care who saw or sneered at her today as long as she found Freya. Ready for anything, she took up a position beside the main gates, so she would see Freya the moment she came in.

Amy Carr, arriving at her usual time, could hardly believe her luck. It was almost too good to be true that Stephanie was standing there, a great big target in that oversized duffle coat of hers. She quickly passed word around the school grounds that the weirdo was back, then returned to the main entrance to begin the fun.

Stephanie ignored the gathering crowd. She stood like a sentry beside the gates, clutching her bag, waiting for Freya.

Amy circled her. Seeing the other students milling around Stephanie, but not saying anything, she ordered Vicky and Gemma to orchestrate the first round of insults to warm them up.

Vicky's attempts were feeble, so she and Gemma went at it together.

'Is that a halo I can see around your head?'

'Where're your wings, girl?'

'Why don't you just fly out of here?'

'No? What about calling on that cute guardian angel to save you, then? Where is he? Abandoned you, has he?'

Stephanie endured it, never taking her eyes off the gates.

The bell went at last, and she hung on for as long as she could, willing Freya to come, before a teacher chased her inside.

The first three periods – Physics, French, Geography – gave Stephanie some respite from the scorn. The arrival of mid-morning break, though, offered Amy a chance to gather her forces again, and after a teacher on playground duty had passed by she resumed the insults.

This time, when Stephanie refused to respond to any of her jibes, Amy told Gemma to pop out for a bag of chips.

The chips arrived dripping with grease, with a ketchup dip.

Amy selected a large chip, dunked it in the ketchup, and threw it at Stephanie. A couple of kids objected, but several more laughed, and after that the objectors stayed silent.

The chip bounced off Stephanie's coat, leaving a small smear. Amy changed her aim and flung another. This time the chip lodged between the collar of Stephanie's coat and her neck.

'Just get lost,' she snapped, flicking it off. 'Leave me alone.'

'Ooh, she's talking now.' Amy laughed. 'Not completely in awe of me, then.'

'Go away!'

'I'll do what I damn well like, you ugly scumbag.'

'*You're* the scumbag.'

Amy immediately stepped up and slapped Stephanie across the cheek.

Stephanie stood there, her face stinging for a moment – then threw herself at Amy.

It caught Amy by surprise. She hadn't expected Stephanie to do anything at all, and they fell together onto the damp tarmac of the school playground, writhing about ineffectually until Stephanie managed to get a scratchy punch directly on Amy's chin.

Vicky and Gemma stood by, not sure how to react. They'd

never seen Amy in a real fight before. A crowd of boys gathered round, enjoying the scene.

After an untidy scuffle, Stephanie managed to grab Amy's fringe and haul her upright. Amy fought her off, and stood there breathing heavily, her lip and chin cut, her skirt caked in mud and ketchup where she'd fallen onto the bag of chips. A significant tuft of her blonde hair was also in one of Stephanie's hands. Amy stared at it in disbelief, feeling her head to see how much was missing.

Shivering with disgust, Stephanie let the hairs drift away on the wind. Vicky glanced nervously at the disappearing locks, wondering if she should try to catch them.

While Amy recovered, Stephanie positioned herself in exactly the same spot by the school gates again. She doubted Freya would be coming in this late, but if she did this was almost certainly the gate she'd use.

She was just wiping the last smear of ketchup off her coat when Amy hit her with a heavy bag of textbooks. The blow was a crushing one and came without warning from behind, striking Stephanie on the side of the head and knocking her over. Amy jumped on her while she was down, kicking her twice with the point of her shoe in the stomach.

Stephanie, still dazed, reacted instinctively to protect herself. Catching hold of Amy's leg, she dragged her to the ground.

This time Miss Tavani, seeing the confrontation from the sick room, ran out to break it up.

'Both of you, right now, follow me!' she roared. 'Two Year 10 girls fighting like this – I've never seen anything like it!'

Amy hesitated, then bowed to the inevitable and followed Miss Tavani in the direction of the main entrance.

Stephanie held back.

'Come on!' Miss Tavani insisted.

'No,' Stephanie replied.

'What?'

'I can't leave this place.'

'Stephanie Rice, you're in enough trouble already. Don't make things worse.'

Stephanie stayed where she was.

Miss Tavani bent close to her and whispered. 'Look, I've heard about Amy's games yesterday. I'll do what I can, but you've got to come with me now.'

'I'm waiting for someone,' Stephanie said.

'Who, for goodness' sake?'

'Freya Harrison.'

'She's not in today. She rang in sick.'

Alarm raced across Stephanie's face.

'Sick? What's wrong with her?'

'I don't know. Flu, I think she said.'

'But she *has* to come in today!' Stephanie yelled. 'She has to! If she's sick it could be the dark angel's fault. Don't you understand? Where does she live? I have to know where she lives. Tell me.'

'What's the matter?' Miss Tavani said. 'If it's really urgent the school office will have a record of her address, but –'

'Get it for me! Get it now!'

'Stephanie, just calm down.'

But Stephanie wouldn't listen. She turned to Amy, demanding Freya's address. 'No idea,' Amy lied, and Vicky and Gemma, hovering nearby, didn't dare contradict her.

Miss Tavani could see that the girls were holding back, but Stephanie was enough of a handful right now without having to deal with them as well. While she reasoned with Stephanie she told Vicky to go to the school office and get the receptionist to call Stephanie's mother immediately. Vicky glanced at Amy, waiting for her permission.

'Get a move on!' growled Miss Tavani.

20

'What's that?' Sam heard something and edged closer to Luke.

Luke thought: this close to Sam's home, it can only be an ambush.

They'd taken a complicated route back after school this time, the final part of which led across a kiddies' play area. They were just cutting through it, about to take a back entrance into Sam's street, when they saw what was waiting for them.

Tate was in the play area. No more than thirty feet away, he was gazing intently at the other end of the street where he expected Sam and Luke to emerge.

Luke immediately dropped onto his haunches, pulling Sam down with him. For a moment they were exposed, then Sam flashed his eyes at a broad oak tree and they retraced their steps to find cover behind it.

'Who the hell is with him?' Sam asked, frightened to death.

Four big lads were crowded like uncomfortable giants on a thin toddler's bench next to Tate. Luke knew only two of them. Tate had obviously been widening his scope to include some extra, more reliable muscle from outside Ashcroft High. One of the new kids had a shaved, lozenge-shaped head covered with death-skull tattoos. At another time Luke might have found the intricate artwork interesting.

He kept a firm grip on Sam's hand, worried that he would bolt and give them both away.

'What do we do?' Sam whispered. 'Just stay here? I can keep still if I have to.'

Luke was tempted to do just that. The trouble was, Tate's crew were likely to head back through the playing area when they left, in which case they'd spot them straight away. Anyhow, how long could Sam stay still? Not that long, Luke decided, resting awkwardly on his ankles the way he was.

Every few seconds the lozenge-headed boy kicked out at a hawthorn hedge, giving Tate a bored glance. Luke listened in.

'You can handle Sam Davenport on your own then, boss?' Lozenge-boy was saying. 'I hear he's a big guy for a Year 7. You sure you don't need my help to hold him down?'

Tate merely shook his head irritably.

Luke took some pleasure in hearing this. Within his own gang, Tate's reputation was obviously suffering – which might explain why he'd had to go outside for help. Of course, it also meant he'd be even more determined to complete the job at hand quickly.

'You should have head-butted him,' Lozenge-boy was saying. 'Broken his nose, like he did yours.' He laughed and clapped Tate's shoulder. 'You ready then? Ready to take Luke on like a man?'

'I'm ready,' Tate replied. 'Just shut up and keep watch.'

A few minutes passed in silence, except for the occasional

booting of the wrecked hawthorn bush.

Luke tried to decide what to do. Run for it? But Sam couldn't outrun anyone. I can't carry him, he realized. If I do, we've both had it. The only choice was to stay put and hope that Tate left soon and took his boys in the opposite direction. Luke glanced down, suddenly aware of Sam twisting uncomfortably.

'What is it?'

'Nothing,' Sam said.

A couple more minutes passed, then Sam bit his lip hard.

'I need to go to the toilet,' he said.

'Can't you hold it?'

Sam shook his head dolefully. 'Luke, I'm sorry . . . I . . .' He shifted position slightly.

That shifting footfall was enough. Tate twisted his head. For a couple of seconds he and the rest of the gang listened, while Sam screwed up his face, holding still. Then Tate lost interest again and turned back to scrutinize the street.

Luke realized that there was no way they could stay hidden for much longer.

'Here's what we do,' he whispered. 'We're going to walk in single file back the way we came. Straight out of the park. We'll keep this tree between us and them. It's wide enough if we're careful. Hold your arms by your side and they won't see us. You understand?'

Sam nodded.

'You sure?'

Another nod.

'All right. Just follow in my footsteps.'

Luke stood up carefully, keeping all parts of his body within the scope of the tree trunk. Then, making sure Sam stayed close, he set off, plotting a direct line away from the tree.

Five feet and no sound of pursuit. Twenty feet. Twenty-five, and they were nearing the end of the play area. Once they reached it a stand of alder trees would completely conceal them.

Luke stopped, checked behind.

Sam was picking each foot up with infinite care and placing it down as daintily as a ballet dancer.

'Stay close,' Luke whispered.

Then he – not Sam – stumbled over a glass bottle hidden in the grass. He suppressed a curse, and both of them stood absolutely still, listening.

Motion behind them.

Luke glanced over his shoulder to see Tate's long legs pelting across the tarmac of the playground.

'Get going!' he yelled at Sam.

Sam fled out of the play area, leaping along a muddy exit path.

Luke waited long enough to make sure he had Tate's and the other four boys' full attention. Then he ducked into a small gap beside the toddler's swings and started running hard.

Freya was still lying in bed, dreamily re-living last night's adventure with Hestron, when Luke finally made it back to the house. His cursing woke her, and as she rushed downstairs he was pulling off his school blazer and trousers. Both were spattered with blood. His shirt was torn as well, all the upper buttons missing.

'What happened?' she asked, appalled.

'Don't ask.'

She saw the ripe bruise on his forehead, and a nasty cut under his left ear. He touched it gingerly.

'Luke – '

'Don't worry about it.'

'What do you mean, don't worry about it?'

Luke stood in his boxer shorts in the middle of the kitchen, bloodied trousers in one hand, washing powder in the other. Freya took the clothes from him, forcing him to look at her.

'Who did this?'

Wiping some blood off his neck, Luke managed a thin grin. 'I know it's hard to believe, but I got away.'

Freya questioned him further, but Luke waved off her concerns and traipsed upstairs, locking himself for a while in the bathroom. Freya heard the shower running, and more cursing. She waited outside, determined he wouldn't slip into his room to avoid her before answering her questions. When he emerged, she noticed another cut on the left side of his neck.

'Look,' he said, 'I don't want to talk about this, all right? But I don't want Dad worrying about it, either. How about getting out that make-up of yours and doing something useful with it for a change? Like patching me up.'

Freya folded her arms. 'Not unless you tell me what's going on.'

Luke walked down to the kitchen and put the kettle under the cold tap. Fresh blood was seeping from the cut on his ear.

Freya improvised a bandage out of a fresh tea-towel, staunching the bleeding.

'You don't need to do that,' Luke said, wincing.

'It'll get infected. Shut up and let me finish.' She cleaned up the wound and put on a large plaster, then waited for more information.

Instead of providing it, Luke said, 'Do you know a girl called Stephanie something or other?'

'Yes.' Freya waited warily.

'Apparently she went berserk in the playground today. Screaming about dark angels, and that she had to see you. It's all over the school. She even started fighting with one of the teachers, trying to find out where you live. From what I hear, her mum practically had to drag her home. You know what it's all about?'

Freya nodded bleakly. It had to be her note.

Luke dumped himself in front of the TV, obviously not wanting to say anything else about his injuries. Freya wasn't letting him get away with that. 'Come on. How did you get these cuts?'

Luke shrugged. 'It's just a kid at school. Tate's boys have taken to knocking the stuffing out of him for a bit of fun.' He reluctantly explained the details.

'Have you told any of the teachers?'

'What, and make it worse you mean?'

'But why are *you* involved?'

'I'm just making sure he gets safely in and out of school.' Luke laughed grimly. 'Not doing a very good job.'

'You don't get injuries like that by walking someone to school.'

'Things got . . . out of hand.'

'Are you going to tell Dad?'

'Not unless I have to.'

'Why?'

'Mainly because it wouldn't make any difference.'

The wound on Luke's neck was bleeding slightly. Freya held a cold compress against it, searching for other injuries. She was sure there must be some she couldn't see.

'Luke,' she said hesitantly, 'I know this boy needs help, but does it have to be you doing everything for him? Surely someone else –'

'Who else?'

'I don't know, but . . .'

Luke raised his eyes. 'But what? There isn't anyone else.

Look, are you going to help me cover up some of this damage before Dad gets back or not?'

'I can't understand why you won't tell him,' Freya said, frustrated with having to dig for every word to get Luke to say anything. 'He'd want to know. He'd want to help, you know that.'

Luke saw the concerned frown on Freya's face, then shook his head as if he despaired of her.

'Freya, this is not a good time to be bothering Dad with things that aren't that important.'

'What do you mean?'

Luke sighed. 'You haven't even noticed what's going on with him, have you?'

'What do you mean?' Freya repeated, stung.

'Have you seen Dad lately? Have you really looked at him?'

'I know he's been tired.'

'Tired? Oh, so that's what's the matter with him. He's just tired. Jesus, Freya . . .' Ignoring her protests, Luke made his way upstairs.

Freya stood in the living room, her heart beating wildly. What was wrong with Dad? What had she missed? She hung Luke's jacket and trousers over one of the radiators to dry them out, too nervous to go straight up to his room and ask what he meant. Then she composed herself, forced her feet up the stairs and knocked on his door.

'Go away,' Luke protested. 'I didn't mean anything. Forget what I just said.'

Freya took a shuddering breath and strode in.

'Listen, I know . . . I know . . . I've been preoccupied recently,' she said. 'I thought Dad was just working too hard. I asked him about it, but you know how he is. He likes his job, so I thought –'

'Likes his job?' Lying on the bed Luke rolled his eyes. 'Freya, since you were a kid he's never much liked it. It just keeps the money coming in, that's all. He needs plenty right now as well. What with the extra he's spending on you. All the outfits.'

Freya reddened. 'I never asked him for anything!'

'Didn't you?' Luke shook his head, as if unsure whether to say anything else. 'Anyway . . . it's . . . more than just tiredness. You never talk to him any more. You'd know otherwise. Damn, why am I having to tell you this?'

'Go on,' she said, when Luke fell silent.

His jaw was set. 'Dad's doing extra hours at the plant, OK?'

'Why?'

'Because . . . he has to take a lot of time off to go to the hospital.'

'The hospital?'

'He's ill, Freya. He's really ill.' Luke gave her a moment to absorb that before continuing. 'I knew something was wrong about a year ago. But it's only in the last few months I've been able to get him to talk about it. He didn't want to. Felt he was letting us both down. You know what he's like, got to be the perfect Dad and all that – especially . . .' Luke trailed off.

'Especially for me, you mean.'

'Yeah.'

Freya felt herself shaking. 'Luke, what's the matter with him?'

'He'll kill me if I tell you.'

'You'd *better* tell me.'

'It was diagnosed a while ago, all right? Why do you think I've been spending so many nights in with him lately?'

'What is it?'

'It's his kidneys. They're not working properly, and it's getting worse. He's been on dialysis for over a year, but he needs a replacement. And it had better come fast.'

'A year?' Freya shivered. He'd been ill for a *year*?

'Dad deliberately asked me to keep it hidden from you.'

'Why?'

But Freya knew the answer. He could see how well she was doing recently, and didn't want to spoil it. And once he knew she was seeing angels again . . . Freya closed her eyes, preparing herself for the next question.

'Is he going to die, Luke?'

Luke jumped up from his bed. 'No! Damn you! He isn't! No way! What are you talking about? He is definitely *not* going to die! He just needs a new kidney, that's all, and one is going to come soon. He's on a list. He says he's near the top of it. Right near the top.'

Freya stood there, trembling. 'What treatment is he having?'

'Weekly dialysis, plus some other blood stuff. It works, but lately he can't hide how bad he's feeling.'

'Is that why he's over at Janice's? Because he didn't want me to see him looking ill?'

Luke nodded, his shoulders slumping. 'Look, you know what he's like, Freya. He's just happy to see you back at school, doing normal things again. He didn't want anything to hold you back. Don't treat him any differently when he gets home, OK? It's really important. He made me promise not to tell you.'

Freya walked numbly to the door. She couldn't believe this conversation was taking place. She loved her Dad. How could she have failed to notice so much?

'I didn't know,' she said from the entrance. 'I . . . don't need babying any more. I don't. Dad doesn't need to hide things from me. You don't either. You should have told me much earlier, Luke.'

He gave her a sharp glare, then drew a deep breath. 'Look, I'll tell you what's going on from now on, OK. The important stuff, at least. I promise.'

'Dad talks to you, does he?'

'Sometimes. If I catch him at the right moment.'

Freya held back a lump in her throat.

Closing the door behind her, she stumbled to her own room.

Dad, she thought. Sinking onto her bed, she recalled all the times she'd seen him looking weary lately, pale-faced, lacking his usual energy. Only once had she bothered to ask why, and even then she'd accepted the first unconvincing answer out of his mouth.

Mestraal is right, she thought bitterly. You can't even see what's in front of your face. How can you ever make a decent angel? You never will.

Tears rolled down her cheeks as she walked across her room. Not bothering to wipe them away, Freya stared severely at her reflection in the mirror. The only light in the room was from the ebbing sunset, faintly slanting across her body from behind. In the mirror her face was a silhouette, almost black. More like Mestraal than Hestron, she thought.

'Oh Dad,' she murmured, 'I'm so sorry.'

Can you bring someone towards you by a sheer act of will? Can the depth of your desire alone draw them to you? Freya lay in a cold sweat in her room that evening, thinking about Dad, wanting him home, wanting only that. But she also knew that if she rang Janice's and talked to him tonight she wouldn't be able to hold herself in check. It was only two days before he was due back. Two days would give her time to order her thoughts and prepare exactly what she wanted to tell him. I can last that long, she thought. I can wait two days.

But what about the person she'd forgotten, Stephanie Rice? Freya knew she'd left her at school to fend for herself yesterday while she lay in bed, happy to daydream about flying. Would an angel have done that? Of course not. She tried to imagine what a true angel would have done for Stephanie in the same situation. What, in particular, *Hestron* would have done.

Then, seized by an idea, Freya hurried across to her open window. Hadn't she been told she was a hybrid: human, but linked to angels, her latent powers awakened by Mestraal? If that was so, and she called loudly enough, wouldn't other angels hear her?

Leaning out into the street, Freya held her breath a moment, then whispered Hestron's name.

For a long time the orange-tinted street light showed only a deserted road. Then she heard ardent flight, followed by the sound of wings being folded.

Hestron's feathers trailed across the floor as he entered her room. Their brightness lit up the carpet threads like fire. And looking at them, Freya realized for the first time that the individual feathers were alive. Restless, swaying in a breeze of their own making, they yearned for the skies. Or was it their master who yearned, and they merely his anxious tools, to take him wherever he must go?

Freya looked beyond their glow, out into the quiet night. Something made her think of Mestraal. Why was she always thinking of him, when all she wanted to do was shut him out of her thoughts?

She turned slowly back to Hestron, aware of a difference in him – the new way he was looking at her. Or was it new? Hadn't Freya seen that look once before, when she was a little girl?

The hairs rose on her neck, a trickle of anticipation rippling through her body.

'You . . . you didn't come just because I called, did you?' she realized. 'You're here to *ask* for something. For what you never dared ask that first time.'

Hestron nodded. 'When you were eight, and I came to you, already knowing what you were, I –' He hung his head, as if ashamed. 'There are so few of us,' he murmured. 'Mestraal always had the most in his care. I took on some of those he abandoned. I came to you that night in the hope –'

'That I would take on some of his wards.' A thrill ran through Freya. She checked it.

'Yes,' Hestron admitted. 'Mestraal was the finest of us. Revered by all, a magnanimity of spirit, a greatness, all song, ever what his wards needed him to be. His loss is terrible. Knowing of you, I wondered if you might be capable of taking on some of his wards, perhaps children, since you were a child yourself. But when I saw the way you wanted to play with my wings, I knew it was too soon.' Hestron's heavily-lidded eyes were diffident, as if he barely dared ask, even now.

Freya's heart nearly burst when she saw that look.

She swallowed, glanced at the brilliantly-lit carpet, back at Hestron again. She gazed into the light of his face. When had she started being able to look straight into his purity of light?

'Yes,' she said, so that he would not have to ask. 'I will.'

All her life she had wanted only this. Even before she met Hestron, there was nothing she had ever wanted other than to be an angel. And now the moment had so unexpectedly arrived, she knew she ought to be afraid, but she wasn't.

Hestron saw her expression, and said, 'You are the first not to show fear. Yet you should.'

'I'll make any sacrifice.' Freya was already terrified that Hestron would take the dream away from her. She couldn't bear the possibility that he would change his mind again. 'I'll do it,' she said, aware that she sounded just like the child he'd ignored all those years ago. But she couldn't help herself. Nor could she take her eyes off Hestron's wings.

He fixed her with a solemn gaze. 'They are not for flitting idly around the sky.'

'I know.' But Freya didn't know, not really. She was only half listening. She was too excited about the possibility of becoming a fully-fledged angel to care about the repercussions.

'If you choose this, there is no going back,' Hestron warned her. 'The wards of Mestraal I give you will become your responsibility, and yours alone. Their voices will always be with you. If they suffer, you will know. There will be no shutting them out. Do you understand?'

Freya nodded, her mind racing.

'Listen to me,' Hestron insisted. 'Your powers are also more limited than ours. When we intervene in human life to save someone, our bodies suffer for that, but not as much as yours will. You remain part human, Freya. Your wings will take you as swiftly as any angel, but you retain human frailties. That means your body will still be fragile. It can be injured like a human body. You must never act to physically intervene if someone is in serious danger, even one of your wards. You will probably be killed if you try.'

Freya nodded, blinking, trying to concentrate and let that sink in.

'Apart from Metatron and Sandolphon there was one other of your kind who shared your skills,' Hestron said quietly. 'He was about the same age as you when I saw him last. He ignored the advice I am giving you. He took on too much, and the consequences for him were terrible.'

Freya stared uncertainly at Hestron, for the first time doubting herself. Then the doubt subsided and she felt calmer than she had ever done in her life. Hestron, shaken, backed away from her, seeing that certainty.

'There *is* greatness in you,' he whispered, and her heart flipped.

'Mestraal doesn't think so.'

'Oh, he suspects it. Why do you think he cannot stay away from you? Even better than I, he understands what you may be capable of.'

'He wants me to fail, doesn't he? He wants to watch me fail. That's why he's following me.'

'No, he only thinks he does. He gave everything he had, Freya, and now he hates all of humanity for what he has become.'

Freya stood there, in her nightgown. A light wind from the window cooled her bare arms. She realized that Hestron was waiting for her decision. It was too serious a decision for him to make for her, or even influence greatly. She had to make it alone, in full knowledge of the consequences. Suddenly she was unsure of herself.

'Show me what you really look like,' she said. 'I know you and Mestraal and the other angels have been hiding your true appearance from me. You're not winged humans, are you? You don't look like us at all.'

'Still concerned about appearances?' Hestron said, mildly chiding. 'Do you really need to know before you make your decision?'

'No,' Freya realized.

'Then, if you are ready, Freya Harrison, prepare yourself. For you will know what we look like soon enough.'

She waited, half-expecting wings to burst from her shoulders. Still clinging onto my childhood beliefs, she realized. Mirth rose in Hestron's eyes. He slid one of his own wings out of the window, arched the feathers.

'Here they come,' he whispered.

'Who?'

Hestron put his broad back between her and the view outside, enjoying keeping whatever it was a secret.

Freya heard wing beats, but she had no idea what they meant. Gradually the individual beats became many until they were a mysterious and overwhelming thunder. Finally Hestron allowed her to look, and Freya saw what was beyond the window.

It was a gathering of angels.

A gathering of nearly all of the angels except Mestraal.

They were in every aspect of the sky, here to witness. Most of the angels wore expressions as excited as hers, and Freya suddenly realized that they felt privileged to be here, in awe of her, even – *them, in awe of her!*

But next moment she saw their eyes turning exclusively to Hestron, and when she followed their gaze she understood why.

Hestron's beauty was flowing away.

His face had already lost its brightness; he seemed suddenly – vulnerable.

'Stop!' Freya screamed, realizing that his power was entering her, what a great sacrifice he was making. But he would not, and the other angels merely shook their heads gravely at her until Freya's transformation was complete.

At the end of it, Hestron, unsteady himself, carried her carefully into the centre of the carpet, where there was more space for her to stretch out. For a moment he held her delicately, as if she was a newborn whose abilities could not yet be trusted.

Then Freya felt her back enlarge. A spread of white flowed from them, splashing light across the wall behind her.

She wanted to see her new wings, but she could only look at Hestron. 'What's happened to you?' she whispered, appalled by how weary he looked, how aged.

'We live long, but not eternally,' he murmured. 'My time will be soon anyway. This merely hastens it a little.' He gave her a measured look. 'I did this as willingly as you undertook your duties. I thank you for that. Love and light, as Stephanie would say. Remember you are also human. Do not try to do too much.'

'But what *do* I do?'

'You will know. You are an angel now.'

He made to depart, but Freya clutched onto him. She gazed wildly around. Nearly all the other angels had left. Nothing, she realized, could keep them away from their wards for long.

'I'm frightened,' she said.

'Don't be.'

Hestron held her. Then, as he turned to leave, Freya realized that two angels had remained behind. They supported Hestron as he hauled himself with difficulty out of the window. To Freya he seemed more mortal than angel now. Pausing on a nearby sloped roof, he tested out his wings, as if unsure they would lift him again – but they did. He smiled at Freya. 'See? They obey me still.'

And now, as she gazed at him, she saw the true angel. Not the classic angel, or any of the endless variations of human shape the angels assume to make them more acceptable on the rare occasions they manifest to us, but the real Hestron. He stood before her and he was not human. More arms than a human being, four of them; and more wings than a bird as well, seven pairs, long and broad, and not remotely like a bird's – for how could that structure ever carry an angel as fast as it needed to fly? These wings were more tensile, thinner, with a gossamer lightness. As Freya watched their bristling motion, she saw the leading edges of the feathers forever angling and leaning towards the stars.

'As are yours,' Hestron whispered.

Freya felt a wondrous surge of elation as her wings fully opened. It was a kind of birth – her shoulders unfolding and separating, the huge wing-blades making room for themselves in the musculature of her back. Freya gasped as her shoulders rose, then dipped in a great swell as the wings settled. The feathers themselves took longer to come under control. After all that time in darkness, buried deep inside her back, they swirled with life, all trying to spring out at the same time.

But before she could even consider what to do with them one more thing caught Freya's attention. It was Hestron's eyes. They were multi-faceted and many-lensed, but that was not what she noticed. It was the *sheer number* of them. The eyes were not merely on Hestron's face, but on his torso as well. Thousands of unlidded bright patches.

One, Freya suddenly realized, for each of his wards.

There were so many eyes that they fought for space on him.

Freya should have been appalled, but already she was leaving the narrowness of her human vision behind. She was not, however, the same as Hestron or the other angels. Except for her wings, her body looked unchanged. Nevertheless she could feel subtle changes and strengthenings within her. There was a greater understanding of chemical properties, the switching alive of senses that had been dormant. And she had her wings, of course. Already feeling like a natural extension of her body, they turned restlessly in the room, wanting flight.

'People will only see you as human,' Hestron said from the roof opposite her house. 'And that is how you must be most of the time, purely human. You can only achieve this angelic form for brief periods. Use them wisely.'

Freya didn't want him to go. 'Where will you be?'

'Nearby, when I can, but not always. My wards carry me to many locations, as will yours.' He lifted his eyes, and laughed. 'Well?'

She knew he was urging her skyward, but she was afraid to let go of the solid ground under her feet.

Hestron laughed again, his flashing eyes meeting hers.

'So many of you idealize us,' he whispered. 'Yet an angel would give anything to get as close as you, being human, can get to your wards. We are so limited. We can reassure, we can intervene in small ways, but think what an angel could do if only it was mortal! The advantages you have – to interact without the limitations of the physical planes, to persuade, to touch, properly to do that, to be with each other.'

Launching himself, he headed away into cold night.

Freya breathed in deeply. The air smelt of take-away shops and the local curry house. Laughing, she clambered to the edge of her window ledge. It was awkward pulling her huge wings through, and the feathers complained. Kneeling on the ledge, unsure how to answer them yet, Freya's toes gripped the edge of the sill like a huge and cumbersome bird. Then her wings gradually unfurled: first the lower portion, followed by the heavy mid-section, and finally the keen leading edge of the outer feathers. Of all the feathers the outers were the most alive. Freya sensed them watching the way Hestron flew, following his flight in the darkness for as long as they could, like children learning from a father.

The other two angels still flanked Hestron. They stayed with him as far as the highest clouds. Only when they were sure he was strong enough to fly unaided after his ordeal did Freya see them strip like comets away from him to left and right to be with their own wards somewhere else in the world.

Freya was now alone. Even Hestron was gone. There were no other angels in the sky. The brightest light was the dull orange street lamp.

No. That was not the brightest light.

The sky was empty. Beckoning.

Freya's wings wanted to fill that emptiness.

'Let us,' they whispered.

And she did.

Stephanie pressed her hands together, her face raised in supplication towards the green angel smiling down from her bedroom wall. 'Nadiel, continue to be at my side,' she muttered fervently. 'And show me how to help Freya from inside this locked room. Please show me.'

Her mother hadn't locked her door at first. That only happened after Stephanie spent the evening wandering the streets looking for Freya. Her father had found her running alongside one of the main roads of the town. Stephanie hadn't even known where she was going. She'd just placed blind trust in Nadiel that he would guide her to Freya's house if she was prepared to search for long enough.

Stephanie felt no shame, either about wandering the streets or making a spectacle of herself at school. But her wild attempts to contact Freya meant that neither of her parents would listen seriously to her when she spoke about the dark angel. Their sensible reasoning gradually drove Stephanie to despair. Why wouldn't they *do* something to help her?

Perhaps this was the dark angel's ploy – to keep her away from Freya until it could completely control her life.

Stephanie spent the evening desperately trying to convince her parents to change their minds and find out where Freya lived. By the end of the day, exhausted and hoarse from shouting, she just lay in bed staring in fear at the ceiling. For want of any better ideas, she read the full set of her affirmation cards over and over. Perhaps, if she injected enough passion into them, they could still convey resolve to Freya, despite the gap between them.

'Security and safety,' she said out loud. 'Personal peace.' 'Taking control.' 'Strength and beauty.' 'Inner guidance.' 'Each person uniquely perfect.' 'Clear and ethical choices.'

'I am a good friend,' Stephanie whispered between cards. 'I always reflect perfect confidence in Nadiel, knowing he is by me, working with me.' She swayed from side to side on the bed, her eyes glassy, saying the words again but suddenly feeling they were empty. Was Freya lying in her room right now, with the dark angel hovering like a blade over her face? It was a horrifying thought, and Stephanie fell quiet. She blinked, her breathing coming fast, and peered up at the portrait of Nadiel on her wall. For the second time in two days she wondered if he really had the power to help her, and this time, unable to dismiss that doubt, her world briefly shattered. Turning to her window, she gazed out over the bleak wintry streets and silently screamed.

Freya wanted to go straight to her wards but her wings refused. They resisted her will; they wanted the stars. She knew it was some ancient trace of angelic origins drawing them that way and, not wishing to deny them anything in this their first hour of life, she let them decide where to go themselves. They chose the constellations of space.

There were other angels wheeling in the darkness up there, feeding on the sun's rays. Each of them turned to look at Freya with as much wonder as she looked at them. Below, on the earth itself, she sensed the rest of the angels. They were spread around the globe, but a pitifully small number to meet the human need. Most were forever on the move, flying on to new locations.

Freya suddenly felt a tremendous sense of responsibility. She understood the sacrifice Hestron had made, and wanted to justify his faith in her. It was glorious to fly with a backdrop of stars, but it was time to take on her duties. Already Mestraal's abandoned wards were calling to her. She could sense them out there. A part of Freya recognized that Hestron had only unloaded the easiest of them onto her, but those were challenge enough. She argued with her wings until they returned to the buffeting of air.

All air should be so light; all light so radiant. Freya dropped through the clouds, speeding up, a spear of purpose, and she was not the same. The night was a deeper night, trees made from a richer bark, leafy canopies more sensuous. The moon itself appeared to glow brighter under her wings, showing a clearer path to her wards.

Freya thought of Stephanie, but it was not towards Stephanie that she headed. She found herself soaring over an Israeli town she had never heard of. The man standing there was not the most despondent she would meet this night, but he was the first, so she would never forget him. A financier who had lost everything in a stupid risky business transaction, he was loitering near the edge of a suspension bridge, trying to find the courage to fling himself over the edge.

It was no accident that just as he gathered the resolve to do so, he stopped. It was not a coincidence that he thought of his children, and felt an abrupt sense of vertigo. There was a reason why he was suddenly afraid to lose his life. There was a purpose behind the way the bridge gained a cold, menacing edge, no longer the welcoming sight it had been only a few minutes earlier.

Freya sent the man rushing back to his car, staring around in astonishment, bewildered with joy.

Freya returned to her room just after dawn, weary but satisfied. She'd followed the Israeli businessman home, and watched the delight with which he greeted his family, unable to believe what he had nearly done. Other wards had followed: a small boy lost on a dangerous highway; a man with a disfiguring disease coping alone; an elderly woman who perceived her entire life as a series of failures.

Freya stayed with each of them, offering her strength. And by the end of the night she understood what it was that made the angels ignore the stars and come to our aid over and over again. It was because nothing could feel better than to give so much to someone else in real need. But it was also gruellingly hard work. After only one night of it Freya was so exhausted that when she flew back to Cardigan Street she stumbled as she alighted outside the house. Re-entering her bedroom, she shed her angelic form, folded her wings away, and slept.

She awoke less than an hour later, still exhausted, but knowing she needed to reassure Stephanie about the dark angel.

Time to go back to school.

After her recent spat with Amy, she expected a chilly reception from the old gang, but so what? How could you compare a little abuse from Amy with the company of angels? Freya also realized that she didn't care quite so much what Amy thought any more. It was a realization that lingered pleasantly in her mind, surprising her.

She had a shower, and washed her hair. Her dark roots were beginning to show under the blonde dye, and it made her smile, seeing her old self peeping through that way.

Back in her bedroom, she put on her school uniform and sat down to apply a little make-up. She found herself deliberately choosing a new look – lighter lip-gloss for a start, and almost no mascara – a combination bound to irritate Amy Carr. In fact, Freya realized, she chose it exactly for that reason.

She was later setting off than usual. No sign of Gemma or Vicky, but then, as she swung into Robert's Road, Freya saw something that completely wrecked all her newly-discovered confidence.

It was Adam, making his way alone into school.

Before she could think about what she was doing, Freya waved at him. Even remembering the way he'd betrayed their time together didn't stop her; she couldn't prevent her hand from taking on a life of its own, rising and waggling hopefully.

He saw her – awkwardly turned his face away – then carried on as if she wasn't there. Despite the events of last night, Freya came to a halt on the path, stunned by the snub. She swallowed, waited for Adam to get a long way ahead, then continued down the last of the streets heading towards school.

When she arrived, Gemma and Vicky were already inside the main gate, keeping Amy's usual spot for her. Gemma was checking out the boys. Vicky was stamping her feet against the cold, her breath a plume in the frosty air. Adam stood close by, leaning against the school railings, looking in Freya's direction. For a moment Freya thought he was looking straight at her, and her heart turned over, even though she thought she'd conditioned it not to. But he wasn't looking at Freya. He was following someone quickening in pace behind her.

Without even a suggestion that Freya existed, Amy breezed past. She didn't say anything. Instead, giving a brisk nod of acknowledgement to Vicky and Gemma, she walked straight up to Adam, wrapped her arms around his neck and kissed him fully on the lips.

Adam didn't act overly surprised. He was obviously embarrassed to be jumped on in such a manner in front of everyone watching, but it was patently not a stunt Amy had staged out of the blue. Freya could tell he'd known it was going to happen, if not here and now, then at some point during the day, timed for when she appeared.

Part of Freya hated him for that, for allowing Amy to use him that way. Another part, the one Amy was after, felt stabbed with pure jealousy. Her angelic aspect was no protection against that. Amy finished the kiss, put her arm tightly around Adam's waist, smiled and turned to speak to Freya.

'I've taken him back again,' she whispered. 'Hope you don't mind.'

Freya tried to think of something – anything – to hurt her,

but couldn't. Instead, she strode away behind the science block, where she could get away from Amy and keep an eye on the front gates.

Freya waited until a few minutes after the bell went for Stephanie to appear, then made her way to reception. She was told that Stephanie's mother had phoned in to report her too unwell to attend today. Freya walked straight to the staff room and asked for Miss Volhard.

'For the foreseeable future, I understand Stephanie's mother has taken her out of the school system,' Miss Volhard told her, explaining what had happened yesterday. 'As far as I know –'

Freya cut her off. 'I need to find out where she lives.'

'I don't think that's wise.'

'I have to speak to her. It's my fault she's like this.'

'Your fault?'

'I can't explain, but yes, it is.'

'The school office won't give you her home address, not without checking with Stephanie's parents first.'

'Please, it's important. I won't make it worse for Stephanie. Will you help me?'

Miss Volhard gave her an uncertain look, but agreed to speak to the Headmistress between periods. The message Freya got back during the first break of the morning was that Stephanie's mother was furious with her, and on no account wanted her near the house.

But I can't not go, Freya thought. I have to see her. She sat down and wrote a note:

Dear Mrs Rice,

I'm really sorry to have caused you and Stephanie so much anxiety about the dark angel. It wasn't what I thought. I'd really like to be Stephanie's friend if I can. I hope she'll let me.

Freya paused, wondering whether she should say anything more about the dark angel. No. That would only make Stephanie's mother even more nervous about contact with her. Scribbling her home address at the bottom of the note, Freya walked along a short corridor until she was outside the door of Mrs Baldwin, the Headmistress.

Mrs Baldwin expressed surprise at seeing Freya, then gestured for her to sit when the name Stephanie Rice was mentioned.

Freya told her she'd let Stephanie down, showed her the note, and begged her to contact Mrs Rice.

'Perhaps if you'd showed such loyalty earlier, things might be different,' Mrs Baldwin said irritably. 'As it is, events are out of my hands now. It was hard enough to persuade the staff to take Stephanie into their classes in the first place, given her behaviour. After yesterday's fiasco, I'll never convince them she can be anything but a disruption.'

'I'll help you convince them,' Freya said calmly. 'I'll help Stephanie adjust as well.'

'I don't think she can adjust.'

'*I* did,' Freya reminded her.

Mrs Baldwin frowned, folding her arms. For a moment they stared at one another quietly across the room.

'I'll persuade every single one of Stephanie's teachers to take her back,' Freya said. 'If Stephanie gives you any more trouble after that you can ask her to leave.'

'Well, thank you for giving me permission to make that choice,' Mrs Baldwin snorted. But then she sat back in her big brown leather chair, sighed and prodded her glasses onto the bridge of her nose. 'You'd be prepared to talk to every one of her teachers?'

'Yes.'

'What if one of them says no?'

'Then Stephanie has to leave.'

A disorientated expression appeared on Mrs Baldwin's face. The matter was settled, there was no question of taking Stephanie back given her mother's objections, but even so . . . she looked at Freya, and had a strange urge to reach out towards her. Flustered, suddenly needing to occupy her hands, Mrs Baldwin fiddled with the paperwork on her desk. Then she stopped fiddling and drew her hair in one long sweep behind her ears. She slowly took off her glasses. Her throat felt dry as she gazed at Freya.

'None of the teachers are going to say no after you've spoken to them, are they?'

There was a hush in Mrs Baldwin's voice. She felt other things as she gazed at Freya: safer; wanting to be outside, in open air; wanting to confide secrets. Confused and embarrassed, she picked up her glasses and cleaned them vigorously.

'I'll have a word with Stephanie's mother,' she said.

'Thank you.'

· 200 ·

Freya stood up to leave.

Mrs Baldwin stood up at the same time, not knowing why. She quickly made herself sit down again, straightened out her skirt.

'Goodness knows,' she whispered, her eyes misting over, 'if any girl needs a friend it's Stephanie Rice.' It was the first time she had ever shown strong emotion in front of a student, and she quickly hardened her expression. 'I'll post your letter to Stephanie's home,' she said. 'And I'll have a word with the teachers about giving her another chance. If, that is, you meant what you said about being a real friend to Stephanie. Or was that an idle claim you made just now?'

'No,' Freya said. 'It wasn't.'

She thanked the Headmistress and left.

Mrs Baldwin almost tried to keep her in the room. As the door shut she reached out a hand for Freya, then hurriedly retracted it. Afterwards, she looked at her hand. She twirled the fingers, as if they belonged to someone else. What was wrong with her? Her emotions weren't ones she recognized. She felt like running – or weeping. She only knew one thing for sure: that if Freya had stayed a moment longer in the room she would have had difficulty letting her leave.

Freya walked away from the Headmistress's office. Morning break wasn't yet over, so she wandered out into the playground, in case Stephanie arrived late. She was standing near the school canteen, engaging one of the Year 10 boys in conversation, when Amy and the others caught up with her.

Amy had obviously made a point of finding Adam before she turned up. He was virtually attached to her arm when Amy 'accidentally' bumped into Freya.

At Amy's signal, Vicky and Gemma both turned their backs and started up an animated conversation among themselves. Adam, left on the outside of the circle, looked guiltily away.

No more kisses then, Freya realized.

'Oh, it's her!' Gemma blurted in mock amazement, twisting melodramatically around in an act clearly rehearsed with Amy. 'The freak who likes the angel girl.'

Freya ignored her.

'Where exactly is your girlfriend?' Amy said. 'Never mind. I'm sure she'll be here soon. Then you'll have someone equally hopeless to talk to, won't you.'

Adam looked distinctly uncomfortable, and Freya took some pleasure in that at least. Amy pointedly draped herself across his shoulder and batted her eyelids. 'He's rejected you,' she said sweetly to Freya. 'He's rejected you for me.'

'That's fine,' Freya shot back. 'You can keep him for good this time.' But the words weren't delivered with any confidence. She couldn't keep the heartache out of her voice.

'Adam tells me you're only an average kisser,' Amy said. 'But I told him that wasn't fair, since you'd never kissed anyone before, had you?'

'Hey, leave me out of this,' Adam groaned – but weakly, more embarrassed for himself than thinking of Freya.

Vicky looked uncomfortable about the whole scene.

Amy couldn't let her get away with that. From Vicky she

expected instant and outright deference. 'Oh, what's going on here then?' she said, casting her eyes between Vicky and Freya. 'You two been chatting behind everyone's backs, have you? Getting all friendly?'

'No,' Vicky spluttered, panic in her eyes.

'You sure?'

Vicky nodded pathetically.

'Oh, just leave her alone,' Freya said.

'Leave her alone?' Amy mimicked. 'Fighting talk on your behalf there, Vicky. You haven't been befriending the little Rice girl on the quiet as well, have you?'

Vicky had no idea what to say.

'Shut up,' Freya said forcefully to Amy.

'What?' Amy gaped.

'You heard me. I said shut that foul, ugly mouth of yours.'

It was a naked insult, just the sort Amy loved to dole out publicly herself. Freya had chosen her words carefully. She wished, in fact, that Stephanie was here to see Amy's face collapse.

Amy was speechless for a moment. Then, recovering, she gave Vicky a spiteful glance and turned back to Freya, searching for a new way to needle her.

'Nice change of make-up,' she said to Freya. 'Trying a better way to cover up those spots you're just starting to get, I suppose. Maybe, once you're over them, even without my help a remedial boy like Darren would still fancy you.'

This time even Gemma didn't laugh. Vicky took a second to take in what had just been said, and turned pale. Belatedly,

Gemma twisted round to whisper something placatory to her. Vicky shrugged her off, staring fixedly ahead. Amy focused back on Freya.

'Maybe it's your new hairstyle that's making you look so different,' she said. 'Tell us the secret, Freya. You letting those roots grow right out this time, are you? Going back to the dull thing you were before.'

It would have been possible in that moment for Freya to have walked towards Amy and shown her a glimpse of her angelic aspect; maybe Mestraal's face; have her grovelling on the floor to get away from it; have her weep.

Instead, she laughed. 'What about *your* hair, Amy?'

'What about it?'

'Well, it's not real, is it? All those natural blonde locks you're always boasting about. You're as mousy as they come.' Freya's eyes could see it now. Amy maintained the roots industriously, but not well enough to escape Freya's improved vision.

'I'm not mousy,' Amy said.

'Yes, she is.'

It was Vicky. She'd turned to face Amy. 'I saw her once, when I was over her house, dyeing it.'

One girl in the playground started to laugh. Others were silently enjoying the smacked look Amy had on her face.

Amy ignored them.

'You little bitch, Freya Harrison,' she hissed murderously. 'You're out. You're all the way out. No more Adam for you, or any other boys if I can help it. I mean it.' She shook her head, in disbelief at being challenged. 'To think, I bothered to talk to you, set you up with Adam, and all the time you wanted to be with that little Rice tramp.'

'She's not a tramp,' Freya said. 'You are. Even Adam knows it.'

Adam's eyes widened in alarm.

'How dare you!' Amy turned bright red.

'Why shouldn't I say it? It's true.' Freya waited to see if Amy would come up with a biting reply. She didn't. 'There,' Freya said. 'Even *you* know it.'

That night Freya knelt beside her bedroom window, thinking of Dad. He was due back tomorrow. Only one more day to go. She'd phoned him at Janice's earlier that evening to make sure, without letting on that anything was wrong, and was already planning the meal she'd make for him.

As for Stephanie, Mrs Baldwin's note should reach her in the morning. And I won't talk to her from behind some corner the next time we're at school together, Freya thought. I'll do it in public. In front of as many others as I can find. In front of Amy.

As she gazed out into the hushed night-time darkness, Freya could sense the restlessness of her wings. They were eager, impatient to be set free again. The furniture, the ceiling, the room itself, was too restrictive for them now. The feathers twitched, resisting the confinement. Even so, Freya felt curiously at ease. For some reason nothing seemed to be able to dent her mood this evening. Her heart felt light, unburdened, almost happy. She couldn't put her finger on the reason, until she realized it was her wards. They were out there in the world, doing mysterious and potent things to her mind.

Freya couldn't wait to be with them again. They would be

easier to locate than the first night as well, because she was more attuned to them now. She'd been resting since she came home, determined to retain her angelic form for longer this time.

None will go without tonight, she thought. I'll make Hestron proud.

What would the needs of her wards be? Freya had no idea, but she'd know as soon as she was with them. The truth of that sent a rush of exhilaration through her.

She was just beginning to anticipate the night ahead, preparing her wings, when she heard slow hand-clapping.

It was Mestraal, standing near her window.

His face was as black as ever, his expression blacker.

'Feeling comfortable?' he asked, his voice laced with sarcasm. 'How convenient. But I've noticed how well trained you have that conscience of yours, Freya. It rarely stirs itself for long, does it?'

In the darkness his face seemed demonic. His eyes thronged his body like a terrifying accusation.

Freya turned away, the sight of him making her feel ill.

'I'm helping Stephanie now,' she said.

'By sending a little note? How brave. When it really matters, I doubt you'll help her.'

Freya stared at Mestraal's distorted body, at his neglected wings, his repulsive face. She knew now that he'd deliberately chosen the features of that face from the most pitiful members of humanity.

'You'd prefer to believe I'm really a bad angel, wouldn't

you?' Mestraal said quietly. 'Something evil. Like so many others, you'd love to think that the evil in the world is caused by fallen angels or creatures you've invented like them. That's easier to accept than the truth, isn't it? That ordinary people like you are doing all the damage.'

He regarded her scornfully. 'I gave you yesterday's night of childish dabbling. I allowed you that. Hestron made me promise. Now it's time to bear witness to what a real angel must.'

The next moment Mestraal gripped her roughly against his flank, and they were through the window and out into the cold night.

He flew her to a large house in her own town. They entered the basement. A golden retriever dog was inside it, being wilfully mistreated by its owner. Mestraal forced Freya to watch as the man struck the dog every minute or so, not that hard, but enough to hurt.

The dog didn't crawl away into a corner. It whimpered slightly, but kept coming back to its master, the pain of his rejection worse than the kicks.

Freya was appalled.

'This bothers you?' Mestraal said. 'You think this is the worst thing a human being is doing now in the world?'

'Stop him!' Freya begged. 'Don't let the man do it!'

'But what about all my other wards? I can't be with them at the same time as this man. Do you think that none among them is suffering greater indignity than this dog?'

'Please . . .' Freya couldn't bear to watch.

'You wish to be an angel?' Mestraal asked.

'You know I do.'

'Of course. But not *my* kind of angel. You want to be like Hestron: all beauty, all love.'

Freya stared at him fiercely. 'Yes.'

Mestraal clasped her face, twisted it back to the retriever. 'You really think Hestron does not permit such things all the time, every day? This is a *dog*, Freya. It loves its master, despite this. His behaviour, not always so cruel, is all it knows.' Mestraal's dark shadow spread across her face. 'Don't you understand? Hestron has shown you how few angels there are. If I whisper words to persuade this man not to harm his dog, that is precious time which could be used elsewhere.'

'If he's your ward, stop him doing this!'

'That would certainly be easier than some duties.'

'Then what are you waiting for?'

'Is that what you would do, Freya? Assist the ward that is *easiest* to help?' He squeezed her arm companionably. 'Yes, I think you would. Because that's the choice you've made all your life, isn't it? You're always making it; all humans are. You think one day of being adorned with an angel's wings has changed that?'

The dog was still being kicked in front of Freya. She could no longer watch.

'No, live with it,' Mestraal said. 'An angel has to. Every moment of our lives among you we are faced with the decision to help one out of many.'

'I wouldn't let someone suffer if I could help them.'

'You do it all the time.'

'I don't . . .'. Freya struggled with her confusion. Then she gazed at Mestraal. He wasn't watching the dog being hurt. All the time they had been in the basement, he had not been watching.

Freya stopped thinking about the dog.

She faced Mestraal.

She touched his deformed face, made him look at her.

'Did you get the people other angels couldn't bear to be with?' she asked quietly. Seeing his eyes widen, she knew she was right. 'Oh, you did, didn't you? You got the worst of humanity.' She saw Mestraal's mask of hatred collapse, but it was back in a moment. Looking at him, touching him, with horror Freya realized something else. 'Hestron's not my guardian angel, is he?' she whispered. 'It's not him at all. I just assumed it was. It's *you*, isn't it? That's why you're always in my thoughts.'

Mestraal's lips briefly parted, then closed again.

'Help the dog,' Freya demanded.

When Mestraal refused, Freya walked towards the man. Steeling herself, she took his head firmly in both her hands. He could not see her, but he felt – something.

Freya stood next to him, and held him for a long time, all her thoughts focused on the dog. Silently, surrounding the man's body entirely with her wings, she waited until the kicking stopped.

Mestraal said, 'You think you're making a real difference?'

'At least, unlike you, I'm trying.'

'Are you a decent person, Freya Harrison?' Mestraal was deeply roused now. 'A good person? Do you think you could assuage a soul in real torment?'

For a fraction of a second he opened up the pain of his wards to Freya. She experienced each one – not the few easier ones Hestron had given her to oversee, but *all* Mestraal's wards. Their despairing cries made the dog's whimpers seem like nothing.

Freya was unable to believe the extent of the suffering.

'You abandoned them all,' she whispered in revulsion. 'Hestron would never have done that.'

'Because Hestron always sees the best in each of you.'

'And you don't any more.'

'You think you would make a better angel than me?'

'That's why you're so bitter, isn't it?' she said, standing closer to him. 'You gave up, and now your wards are in disarray. But you can't bear what you've become. You can't stand the thought that you'll always be like this.'

For a second she thought Mestraal was going to strike her.

Then the mask of indifference was back.

He snatched Freya up. 'I'll give you a ward then. Since you're so sure of your superiority. Someone you've managed to forget.'

He transferred her to a place near the town centre.

There was a young woman in front of her, shivering in a corner of an underpass. It was the same woman Freya had seen begging for sweets near the school weeks ago. A soiled towel was now wrapped ineffectually around her as she tried to keep out of the wind, and her face was riddled with pain. The last time Freya had seen her she hadn't looked like this.

'Why the shock?' Mestraal said. 'It only takes a few nights on a cold street to rob someone of the will to live. Didn't you know she was here? Surely a good girl like you has been looking out for her, wondering how she's been getting along?'

Freya stared at the woman, trying to recall her name.

'Davina,' Mestraal said. 'You couldn't even remember that.'

The pain pouring out of Davina represented a more deep-seated need than anything Freya had experienced so far. She hesitated, then bent towards her. Crouching on the wet pavement next to Davina, she ignored the awful smell of stale sweat and asked her wings to encircle her.

They did, and for a moment Freya made a difference. Davina stopped shivering. But not for long. Refusing to give in, Freya offered more of her strength. It hurt to give so much – Freya could not believe how much Davina was draining from her – but she enclosed her more tightly, attempting to reach through the woman's agony and confusion. And finally Davina's eyes flickered open, and something that was not entirely fear shone in her eyes. Yet almost as soon as they were open they closed again. Freya made herself try once more, but this time Davina simply pressed her face into the pavement, lost in her sorrow.

'I can't do it,' Freya whispered, stepping tearfully away. 'I can't. She needs . . . too . . . too much.'

Glancing at Mestraal, she expected the usual contempt in his eyes, but that was not what she saw this time.

More than I expected of you, his look said.

'Show me, then,' she dared him. 'If I'm so useless, show me what a real angel can do.'

Mestraal stirred momentarily, then shook his head, no. Whether there is suffering or not makes no difference to me, his look said.

No, his look was blank. Freya realized that for the first time she had read his thoughts directly.

'If that's true,' she whispered, 'if it matters so little whether you choose to do something or not, then prove it. Help her.'

At first Mestraal stayed still. Then he gradually stood upright and moved across to Davina. He hesitated, then draped both his heavy black wings over her shoulders. Freya instantly felt the power, the authority, exuding from him. It was beyond anything she could understand. Less than a minute of it left Davina shaking and weeping for joy, and afterwards Mestraal's body was briefly not quite so dark.

Nothing, Freya realized – not even Hestron – could give comfort as Mestraal could.

Davina was now up and stumbling. She kept turning in circles, hands outstretched, seeking something.

'What's the matter with her?' Freya asked.

'Don't you understand yet?' Mestraal murmured, turning away from Davina. 'It isn't enough. The more I give the more they always want. It is *never* enough. Ah, brother,' he said to the air, 'is that what you're doing, using a child to remind me who I once was? Too late for that, no matter how remarkable the child.'

Freya, seeing Mestraal sob, found herself placing a supportive wing on his shoulder.

A human comforting an angel.

It brought a powerful reaction from him – shame, gratitude,
all the emotions he did not want to face. And the next moment
he turned to look at her, straight into her eyes – straight
through to her soul. And in that moment Freya knew he understood everything about her – her plans, her doubts, everything
she loved, and despised, and dreamed about. He knew that
Freya was desperate to become an angel that Hestron could
admire, but was scared of what it would demand of her. He saw
how much she was prepared to give, but that she doubted her
capacity to give, partly because of him. Most of all he saw her
fear of him.

Freya forgot about everything else in that moment. Davina,
the underpass, the abused dog, receded. She only saw the dark
hollows of Mestraal's face and, behind it, the incandescent
mind observing her, probing all her secrets, loving her. She felt
the love. Even now, having abandoned her along with his other
wards, there was that love. There was no way she could hide
anything from him. But equally he could not hide himself from
her.

A moment ago she had hated him. Now she fell to her
knees.

'People question why their angels rarely reveal themselves,'
Mestraal said. 'The truth is that we would like nothing more
than to tell you that you are not alone. But we cannot.'

He stared at her fiercely. 'Because do you know what happens when we do? Do you think they are content? No, instead they come to depend on us *even more*. After we reveal ourselves a few even put themselves deliberately in danger to test us. Others worry less about neglecting people, because haven't those people a guardian angel who will look after them? We know your species well now. What would the worst of you be like if you knew for sure we existed?'

'But it's so wonderful to be able to give what you give,' Freya whispered.

'Yes. It is wonderful to give freely and openly, as you did, as we both have done for Davina, an angel opening up to its nature. But what if you have other wards who need as much as Davina?' Mestraal gazed at Freya solemnly. 'Our wards die because we cannot reach them in time. On other occasions we have more than one ward in danger – and we have to choose who to help. To choose between those we love. We *once* loved,' he corrected himself.

'What would you do?' Mestraal asked. 'What would you do if you were responsible for so many that you could only assist those wards who send out a *cry from the very depths of their souls*?' Mestraal drew his wings in against his body. 'You grow to love them all, Freya. Once you are inside their heads, you cannot help it. But you have to choose, often between good people, leaving one to suffer. How do you make such a choice? Which do you protect?' He gave her a challenging glance. 'And could you make that choice over and over again? Or even once? Could you do that and come through it with your mind intact?'

Freya stared at him, unsure. 'That's what happened to you,

isn't it?' she murmured. 'You had to choose too many times. That's why you're like this.'

Mestraal's eyes were like stone, giving nothing away. Then his old sarcasm reasserted itself. 'Could you sacrifice your own life for one of your wards?' he whispered. 'If you had to, could you do that? Any angel would. That is what it means to be an angel. To be able to give up your life unquestioningly. Unflinchingly.'

Freya hesitated. 'Hestron told me not to. He warned me.'

'Why do you think he did that?'

'I don't know. He cares about me. He's . . . scared I'll be hurt.'

'Yes, but there is another reason as well. He senses you are not strong enough to make such a sacrifice. He said what he did to protect you, because he was afraid you would fail. And he knew that such a failure would crush you.'

With that Mestraal transported Freya back to her bedroom. He carried her through the window, and placed her gently onto the bed. He even covered her shoulders.

Freya lay there in shock, staring at the sheets.

Outside, dawn was breaking.

Freya did not sleep. Instead she lay in bed, letting the meaning of Mestraal's words eat into her soul like a poison. Was he right? Wasn't she brave enough to sacrifice her life for a ward if she had to? Somehow it hurt far more that it was Hestron who thought so. She wanted him to believe only the best of her. She couldn't stop turning that over and over in her mind, ashamed that it was otherwise.

She didn't go to school. She saw Luke off, then phoned the school office with an excuse and went back to bed. She wanted to close her eyes and forget about what Mestraal had said. Shutting the window of her room, she crept under the covers of the bed and eventually fell asleep.

It was late afternoon by the time she woke again, and the first thought that came into her mind was not about Davina weeping joyfully in a wind-swept underpass. It wasn't even about Stephanie or Dad. It was about a boy with an annoying lock of blond hair that kept falling over his face.

Freya sat up in bed, her breath quick, not knowing why.

For once Sam Davenport was without company as he walked away from school. Luke had an extra chemistry class after regular lessons were over, and had told him to wait inside the grounds.

Sam, after much soul searching, had decided not to. He wasn't sure why. Maybe it had something to do with the fact that other kids in his year were mocking him over the way he hung around with Luke all the time. Maybe it was just the need to show an ounce of independent spirit. All the self-help books he'd been consulting talked about it – willpower, demonstrating some mettle. Sam didn't think he'd shown much of that.

So he'd decided to go home on his own this once – just to prove he could.

Even so, he was cautious. He waited over half an hour to make sure Tate and others were gone. Only then, and surrounded by the gathering darkness, did he take a side gate and set off home.

The first indication that he'd been followed came when an arm yanked him into a doorway. The door was immediately shut, and Sam blinked, catching his breath. He couldn't see anything yet, but he knew who was there.

'No one to save you this time,' Tate murmured.

The derelict warehouse Sam had been dragged into was virtually soundproof once the big door was shut. It was also wonderfully echoey and damp, perfect for Tate's intentions.

Tate stood there, staring cheerfully at Sam. Then he switched on a torch and indicated his shoe. 'Still dirty,' he said. 'You never did lick it clean last time.' He flashed the torch around the warehouse. 'I hate mess, don't you, Sam? Best clean this filthy place up before you do the shoe. Start with the floor.'

Tate laughed, realizing how impossible that would be. But he also knew Sam would try, and that should be amusing to watch. 'Give me your mobile,' he said. He kicked Sam twice in the shin when he fumbled to get the phone out of his trousers quickly enough.

Inputting Luke's number into his own mobile – just in case he needed it later – Tate sent a message using Sam's phone. He'd carefully prepared the message for Luke last night, and now he took his time over the wording, to be sure there was no possibility of misunderstanding.

Once that was done he reminded Sam to lick his shoe clean. Followed by a tad more floor mopping using the jacket. 'Give it a good and thorough polish over there,' he said expansively. 'We can have some fun, be here for hours if we like, until we're satisfied it's all done.'

Tate was in a mood to do some real damage to Sam, but Luke was his main target and he didn't want to risk any awkward repercussions at school. Even so, by the time Tate finished with him, Sam was so terrified that he simply stood there in the middle of the warehouse, holding his blazer in his shaking hands.

'Put your jacket back on,' Tate ordered.

Sam was shaking too much to do the buttons up, so Tate helped him, then ripped the top one off and pulled Sam close to his face.

'You can go now,' he said, smiling. He opened the warehouse door, but as Sam was preparing to run Tate held his arm. 'First, what do you say?'

Sam blinked at him uncertainly.

'Aren't you going to thank me?'

Sam lowered his face. 'Thank you,' he whispered.

'Sorry, I didn't hear that.'

'I said thank you, Mr Tate.'

Tate grinned from ear to ear, finding the use of his surname hilarious. 'Good boy,' he said, almost fondly. 'Now run off to find Luke and tell him all about it. Off you go now.'

One more shove and Sam was staggering from the entrance, wobbling his way up the footpath.

Sam's voice, asking for Luke's help on the mobile, was no more than a petrified whisper. Luke could barely make out what he was saying at all, and got to the warehouse as fast as he could.

On the way he listened to Tate's jaunty message.

'Hi, Lukey! Its been an exciting evening for Sam. I'm sure he'll tell you all about it. But as long as he makes something up for mummy's benefit, I'll be generous and leave him alone from now on. As for you, let's meet at five p.m. tomorrow after school. On Inkerman Street, near the pet shop. There won't be anyone else around. Just me and you. If you don't turn up, I'll do much worse stuff to Sam. Stuff that'll give mummy night-mares. You know I mean it. What I did to him tonight is just a taster.'

Luke found Sam huddled inside a shadowed doorway near the warehouse. He was still too scared to say anything, so Luke just brushed down his uniform, cleaning him up. When he could get a few words out at last, Sam mumbled that he was fine, no problem, nothing to worry about. Seeing the pitiful way he couldn't stop shaking, Luke knew that he had to bring this conflict with Tate to an end. He couldn't risk him getting hold of Sam again.

'That message from Tate,' Sam said, holding back his tears. 'Just you and him. Do you . . . do you believe that?'

'No. It's bound to be a trap.'

'You're not g-going to try taking him on, are you?'

'Of course not.'

Sam gave him an anxious look.

'Look, I'll be OK.' Luke rubbed some warmth back into Sam's shoulders. 'I'm hardly going to just walk into Inkerman Street and let him set me up, am I? But do me a favour. Find a way to stay off school tomorrow. Tate might try nabbing you if you don't.'

Sam nodded, looking right into Luke's eyes.

'I mean it,' Luke said. 'Don't come in. Tate will only find a way to use you against me.'

After tidying Sam up enough to get him home in some kind of half-decent state, Luke set off back to Cardigan Street. He felt faintly nauseous at the thought of the violence that was almost certainly coming, but he couldn't see any other way out of it now.

A wind sprang up from the north, blowing his hair back. Pausing for a moment, Luke raised his fists, imagining what he might have to do with them. Then, pulling up the collar of his coat, he set off in the direction of home.

Freya knew that something was up with Luke as soon as he walked through the door. But he wouldn't talk about it, no matter how much she pressed him, and finally she needed to get the dinner ready for Dad's return. She'd prepared a spaghetti bolognese sauce earlier in the day and was just putting the finishing touches to it when a scream reached her.

At first Freya thought it had to be from someone outside the house, it was so shrill. Then she realized it came from one of her wards. The threat was so imminent that she sensed other angels changing course to get there as well, but Freya was the closest.

She didn't hesitate; moving back from the dining table, she opened out her wings.

The ward in danger was a man. He'd been at the wheel of his Citröen car for over six hours before he fell asleep. The regular motion of the wheels had lulled him, and he'd slumped forward, leaving his foot on the accelerator. By the time Freya arrived his car was heading towards the motorway's central reservation.

With the preternatural clarity of an angel, Freya was able to judge the exact way the car would react when it hit the concrete barrier. It would flip, perform a mid-air twist, and land on a vehicle on the other side of the road at an almost vertical angle.

I can do it, she thought. I can reach him in time, put myself between his car and the other vehicle, reduce the impact. Nobody has to die.

She was already in motion, seconds ahead of the disaster.

Then she remembered Hestron's words: her body was still part human. She was risking death.

What would any angel do?

She knew the answer.

She pictured her body being crunched between jagged sheets of exploding metal and glass.

Could you sacrifice your life? Mestraal's scornful remarks burst across her mind. *If you had to, could you do that?*

I *will* do it, she thought.

The car was veering crazily across the road now.

The man inside had woken but his reactions would not be quick enough to correct the car's trajectory.

Only Freya could manage it.

I will, she thought, cold fear ripping through her. I'll do it.

Her wings urged her toward the car, but she stayed above the road.

The man in the car threw the steering wheel forcefully left. The Citroen hit the central reservation at an oblique angle that sent it into a turn, travelling upward.

There was a Volkswagen 4-by-4 carrying a family of five on the other side of the concrete partition. It was travelling at fifty-eight miles per hour. Freya, terrifyingly, found that she could instantly calculate the impact speed of the two vehicles.

A man, a woman and three children were in the 4-by-4. They were wearing seat belts, but at this collision speed that wouldn't save them all. The man in the Citröen had seen the other vehicle now. He was desperately twisting the steering wheel, even though his car was airborne and he had no control over it.

The woman driving the Volkswagen saw a huge mass rising above her, and braked sharply. Freya heard guardian angels of the people in the car screaming in unison from different parts of the world. All of them were too distant to get there in time.

There was still time, however, for Freya to intervene – barely.

Her life or theirs.

I can't, she realized.

She was too afraid.

Perhaps they would survive anyway.

No, she knew. Not all would.

The wind whistled through Freya's perfect wings. They urged her on. Mestraal's challenge echoed hollowly through her bones.

Her feathers begged her to act, but she couldn't.

And then another angel arrived.

Male.

A slightly faded umbra of light.

Not quite so handsome as he had once been.

Hestron spread himself between the Citröen and the 4-by-4. His shining body interposed itself between the vehicles, and it was enough, just, to cushion the severity of the impact.

The Citröen hit the side of the 4-by-4, ripping off the Volkswagen's bumper. Two of the Volkswagen's rear windows imploded, showering the children with glass. The side-on collision smashed the front end of the Citröen entirely, crunching the left side-impact bars, but they held because Hestron had lessened the impact. The man in the Citröen felt the dashboard of the car enter his hip. A shard of plastic split off from the speaker-system to penetrate his thigh.

He lay there, gasping but alive.

For a few seconds there was the squeal of brakes and skidding tyres as other motorway drivers fought to avoid a collision and came to a stop. Then, after the momentary silence and shock that always follows a major road crash, people were jumping out of their cars and racing across to see what they could do for the injured.

Freya saw the mother who had been driving the 4-by-4 sitting upright in her seat, white-faced, panting with shock. The children in the back had suffered no serious damage. Her husband, having checked them, was trying to get his door open to reach the man in the Citröen, but others were already there, prizing him out of the car.

Unseen by any of them, an immaculate set of wings clung to the car door. For a moment the mother in the 4-by-4, perched high in her raised seat, turned towards the bright figure, sensing something.

Hestron was there: stuck between the vehicles, his body embedded in complex ways inside the metal.

Then he managed to slide to the ground, and lay still.

Another angel, which had been frantically trying to make it in time, raced to Hestron's side before Freya could reach him. A further angel glided past her shoulder.

Hestron did not seem to be moving. Then Freya saw a single feather, one of his outers, lower itself to caress his face.

Be alive, she thought.

The other two angels were spread across Hestron now, whispering urgently in high voices Freya could not understand. And then one of them shook his head, and Freya somehow knew what it meant. Even so, the two angels stayed there, bent across Hestron, holding his body together, trying to save him.

Further angels arrived. Freya was left outside their circle, unable to see Hestron. Finally, on a vast swoop of wings, Mestraal's ragged black body beat a path through them to Hestron's side. As the other angels parted for him, Freya felt an unfathomable shame. The last thing she wanted was for Mestraal to look at her. He didn't. Instead, he stayed by Hestron's side, directing increasingly urgent instructions at the other angels around him.

A shining hand reached feebly from deep under the car, touching Mestraal, making him stop. Freya heard a voice calling her name then, from somewhere inside that mess of feathers.

She didn't want to approach. She was too ashamed. But she did. She made herself.

Hestron was wounded beyond any hope of saving. Freya did not need angelic eyes to tell her that. His body was utterly smashed and twisted, his wings crushed, most of the feathers torn out. Only the left part of his face could still form any expression. One eye from that side swivelled, searching for her.

Freya stumbled forward, her wings dragging in disgrace behind her. The angels let her through. Looking at Hestron, Freya couldn't speak. The light from his halo was already fading.

'I am dying,' he said, from one side of his mouth only. 'Look upon me now.'

Freya felt her heart freeze.

There were people running in alarm all around the vehicles, unable to see any of this. Freya wanted them to leave. She suddenly couldn't stand all this activity bustling around him.

She knelt before Hestron.

'I did this,' she whispered.

'Listen to me,' Hestron said.

'Don't say it's not my fault.'

'Freya, I never expected you to give up your life.'

'No,' she murmured. 'You expected . . . something less of me, didn't you?'

Hestron's few remaining feathers that were not trapped between the vehicles reached for Freya. They stroked her face.

'I am dying in the service of a ward,' Hestron said, his voice rising a little with the effort it took to speak. 'I have saved a life, perhaps many. This is the death I wanted, and *there is still greatness in you.*' He gazed at her, all love. 'Forgive yourself this. And do not think you alone are blameworthy. I gave you a gift, but I had my own selfish intentions.'

'I can't believe you were selfish.'

'You are wrong. I have been, Freya . . .'

And then it happened quickly. The last of his light began to fade, and once more the angels drew close. Mestraal came closest of all, and words were spoken privately between them, and at some point during those words Hestron died.

His mind died first, followed by his body, and the last part of him to stop moving were the feathers. Like a slowly clenching wave they hardened from the base of the wing upward, a procession of light that finally dimmed somewhere near his throat. Two of the outers remained alive longer than the others. They swayed against Freya's face for as long as they could, holding her, knowing that was what Hestron would have wanted. Then they too stiffened and fell still.

Across the motorway there was silence. People stumbling about suddenly stopped, not knowing why. At the same time Freya heard distant sounds of fear, thousands of voices shouting – Hestron's wards throughout the world, sensing something precious was vanishing from their lives.

Freya looked down. There was no longer any light in Hestron's eyes. But they were twisted in her direction, as if at the end it was her his last thoughts had turned to.

Then there was a low murmur among the angels.

Freya tried to creep away, but a black wing held her. There was no anger in the look Mestraal gave her, only remorse and sadness. Freya expected hatred, even gloating. Hadn't she confirmed he was right all along about her? But Mestraal gathered her to him and said, 'No. Stay. I would not deny you this. Be with us.'

And the next moment, far from shunning Freya, the other

angels were suddenly surrounding her, all wings, all loving embraces and subtleness, all forgiveness, no malice, or bitter-ness, least of all from Mestraal, who stood higher than the rest, drawing them all together.

Freya saw the way the other angels looked up to him.

Her gaze was held by him as well. She wanted to look else-where, but could not.

Mestraal unfurled his wings. His vast dark light lit up the whole motorway. Cars and people were lost inside it, birds flew in confusion, breezes stilled. And although it was painful to be inside that dark light, there was beauty there as well, and Freya suddenly needed it, had to be closer to him and the pain of all that darkness. She found herself edging forward to do so, along with the other angels. Gazing at Mestraal, wanting to be closer still, Freya understood at last why Hestron had called him beloved.

The angels left the motorway. Carrying Freya and the dead body of his brother from the car, Mestraal flew into the sky. Hestron's long wings drooped slackly below his body, but four angels caught them and held them aloft. As Freya watched, his feath-ers reflected the sun's rays for a moment, blooming anew with life, as if Hestron was somehow waking, opening out his love to them again. But it was not so, and Mestraal, still carrying Freya, bore his brother up, beyond the motorway, beyond the city, beyond the clouds or the cares of all wards, to the vacuum of space. There he left Hestron, gently buoyed up by sunlight.

It was then that Freya heard a sound so beautiful she almost slipped from Mestraal's grasp. It was a multilayered choir-like chant. Freya had read about this sound before. It was reported occasionally in angelic texts, and was generally assumed to be the rapture of joyful singing. Freya now realized the truth – it was a song to mark the passing of an angel.

Other angels, too distant to make it to Hestron before he died, were now approaching at tremendous speed across the darkness of space to be with him. Mestraal greeted them all. They came, until eventually all the angels had come except those with wards too urgent to leave. They comforted each other, comforted Mestraal and also Freya. Not one of them cast an accusing glance at her. Not one stung her with a look of blame. Mestraal's dark wings enfolded her. As she gradually began to comprehend the magnitude of what had happened, the warmth of those wings, the lack of accusation in his gaze, only made it worse for Freya. But Mestraal understood her despair. He held her more tightly, as if he could sense her love for Hestron stirring madly, waiting to engulf her.

'We all loved him,' he whispered. 'Remote from flesh, sometimes it seemed as if Hestron could cradle the whole world in his wings, all giving, asking nothing of it in return. Weep with me.'

And Freya did.

27

Stephanie never saw Freya's note offering friendship.

Her mother kept it secret, fearing more contact would make her behave even more wildly than before. But it was a mistake. Stephanie couldn't bear not knowing what was happening to Freya. All she could think about was the dark angel, and what it might be doing.

Her parents kept her door locked most of the time, as before. That evening, in the hope that they would unlock it overnight and she could escape, Stephanie stopped ranting about dark angels. Over dinner she behaved herself. Her father spoke about troubles at the office, as if this was any other day, and she nodded dutifully. But she knew she wasn't fooling her mother, who reluctantly locked her inside her room again after they had eaten.

After that, Stephanie couldn't contain herself any longer and yelled to be let out. A little later, her mother came into her room and tried reasoning with her. Stephanie barely listened. She was more convinced than ever that evil forces of the dark angel were conspiring to prevent her assisting Freya.

That meant she had to see her, take any risk.

Her mother, seeing that desperate look in her eye, went

downstairs and re-opened Freya's note. After agonizing over the matter for a few seconds, she crossed out the final lines where Freya offered her friendship – she didn't want Stephanie associated with someone who could disturb her this much – then showed Stephanie the note.

Stephanie read it with a trembling hand.

Dear Mrs Rice,
I'm really sorry to have caused you and Stephanie so much anxiety about the dark angel. It wasn't what I thought.

Stephanie saw Freya's address.

Above that, there were some heavily crossed-out lines in a different pen.

'What did they say?' she demanded.

'Nothing,' her mother lied. 'They were like that when we received the note. Freya must have done it herself.'

Stephanie suspected her mother was lying, but couldn't think of a reason why she would do so. Unless the dark angel was scheming against her parents as well. Was that possible? The note didn't feel true. It said almost nothing, as if it was only intended to keep her away from Freya.

I don't believe it, Stephanie thought. Either Freya didn't write it, or she's being forced to hide the fact that she's in trouble.

She pretended to be relieved to get the news. Her mother sighed, the creases around her eyes relaxing a little.

'Will you be able to sleep now?' she asked.

Stephanie nodded, but kept her mother talking, knowing

she was concealing something from her. She had never known her mother do that before, and it frightened her.

I have to find Freya, she thought. To know she's all right. To hear it from her own lips.

Later, she heard her mother downstairs, engaged in urgent discussion with her father. Stephanie didn't wait this time to see what doors were left unlocked. There was no chance of sneaking out.

She needed to be bold.

It was a fifteen foot drop from her bedroom window to the garden. There was no trellis or ledge she could climb down, nothing to break her fall. Taking one long final look at the portrait of Nadiel on her wall, she threw her rucksack containing Freya's gift into the garden and eased her legs over the window ledge. Lowering herself down as far as she could with her arms, she dropped. She landed unevenly, more on her left leg than her right, spraining an ankle, but not badly enough to stop her leaving. She could still walk on it.

I'm meant to get there, she thought. Nadiel wants me to. I wouldn't have landed safely otherwise.

Her feet were bare. She wasn't wearing a coat, either; she'd been in such a hurry to get out that she hadn't thought to check how cold it was. She didn't care. Freya's house was a couple of miles away. Stephanie vaguely knew the address on the note. That was enough of a guide. She'd find her way there somehow, even in the dark.

Folding her bare arms against her chest, she quietly opened

the catch on the garden gate and began limping in that direction.

Despite Mestraal's words, Freya knew she was responsible for Hestron's death, and she couldn't bear it. She wanted to be back with the first of her wards again, when the world had seemed full of possibilities, not here in the deeps of space with Hestron's dead body mocking her.

In the end her shame overcame everything else and she glided like a wraith back down to earth to be alone.

Part of her wanted to die, because at least that would bring her closer to Hestron. And didn't she deserve to die? She suddenly hated herself, hated her gift. Mestraal was right; she didn't belong among angels. The part of her that was human desperately wanted just to be a girl again, tucked up in bed, not knowing anything about the places her wings could take her. But Freya also knew that she couldn't hide from her angelic side, not now. In her heart, she didn't want to either. She couldn't live any more without angels in her life. The idea of giving all that up to be just an ordinary girl again was unbearable.

Arriving outside the front door of her house she stood there, crying. Dad, back long ago, saw her through the window. He noticed she had no jacket on, and assumed she'd been wandering the streets for hours.

'Oh, Freya . . .' He guided her inside, and Freya managed a formless smile. It took all her energy just to do that.

She wanted to hug him, tell him everything, so thankful that he was back home again. But she couldn't talk. She couldn't even enjoy seeing him again. She didn't deserve that pleasure. She'd killed today. She'd murdered someone she loved. It's all right, Dad, she thought. There won't be any more angel visits. I won't be an angel any more. I won't be doing that. Just let me go upstairs.

'Freya . . .'

'Dad, please . . .' She was crying.

He hesitated, then let her go. Freya saw him wander shakily into the kitchen. Soon after, Luke caught her at the top of the stairs.

'What's wrong?' he asked.

Freya shook her head. 'I can't talk about it. Let me go.'

'Wait. Speak to Dad. He needs you to speak to him right now. It can't wait. I've persuaded him to let you know what's going on.'

'I can't now . . . I can't . . .'

She forced her way past Luke and lay on her bed in the darkness, staring rigidly up at the ceiling. She didn't want to do anything except cry. She wished she'd never seen Hestron's last look. She wished his feathers had never touched her. She knew that would haunt her forever.

About an hour later, Dad knocked softly on the door.

'Can I come in?' he asked.

'No. Could you leave me alone, please.'

He opened the door anyway, hovering half in and half out of the entrance.

'Dad, no, just go away!' she shouted. 'Please!'

His big frame waited there, silhouetted against the wall.

'You've been seeing angels again, haven't you?'

She glanced up, feebly trying to wave him away. 'How do you know it's angels?'

'There's just something about your face . . .' He stepped into the room. 'Something gorgeous happens to it whenever you think angels are near you. Don't you know that?'

Freya, deeply affected, but not able to talk, muttered something about being tired and –

'Don't lie to me,' he said. 'I can tell you're about to. Look, I think we have to ring the hospital again. I know you don't want to go back, but – ' He kept his voice calm. His face, however, was far from calm.

Freya tried to hide her head under a pillow.

Seeing that, he said, 'It's all right, we'll deal with it together. We've done it before. I'm here.'

'Dad, please. Leave me alone . . . I can't talk about this . . .'

He hesitated a moment, then retreated back to the doorway.

Freya dashed the tears out of her eyes. 'Wait,' she said. 'I know you've been over Janice's. Are you OK?'

He nearly said something, then nodded and smiled. 'I'm fine. Absolutely fine.'

Freya knew she should ask again, but she lacked the willpower to pursue it. Her dad left and she closed her eyes, furious with herself.

But somehow the conversation with Dad seemed perversely right as well. Not fit to be an angel. Not fit to be a daughter, either. Freya felt her mind imploding. She deserved more pain. She almost wanted more destruction. What was left for her to wreck?

She glanced down. Her wings were visible in the glow from the street light outside the house, and weren't they a darker shade? The edges were certainly darker. It made sense: wanting to be like Hestron, she was more like Mestraal.

Outside, she knew there were wards she should be responding to, but had ignored. She felt them calling to her like struggling birds, and remembered what Hestron had warned her about: that she would never be rid of their voices. She tried to shut her mind to them, failed. The thought of taking up her angelic duties again was intolerable.

Lying in bed, the quilt pulled over her head, Freya let the tears fall. Downstairs, she could vaguely hear Luke's and Dad's voices in the living room. Not listening, she tried to summon up a future she could live in. How about going all out to make closer, better friends? But that didn't even sound real. What insane kind of life would that be, when every second her wards would be calling frantically and her wings aching to be used?

There would also be more despair in the world, thanks to her. Hestron's wards were alone again. In time other angels would take on the additional burden of them, but that would only stretch the small number of angels even further. And what about friends, anyway? None of her friends at school were genuine. Amy, Gemma, Vicky – they were never true friends. Even Adam was just excited by a kiss after a chase. Only one person really wanted to be her friend: a mixed-up girl who'd never lived in the real world.

I can't help you, Stephanie, Freya thought. I'm dangerous to be near. Stay away. Don't get close.

Stephanie journeyed painfully on her sprained ankle across town. On the way she gained two excruciating cuts on her sole from a broken glass. Having nothing to stem the bleeding with, she limped on. Finally, after more than an hour of making mistakes and getting lost, she found Freya's house. For a while she simply stood there in the cold wind, checking and rechecking the number, hardly able to believe she'd made it.

'Nadiel! Nadiel!' she cried, giving thanks.

There were small pebbles along the garden's border. She picked one up, guessing which upstairs room might be Freya's. When she got no response from that, she tried the next.

Lying in the dark, Freya heard a skitter against her window pane.

She ignored it. Two more stones followed.

'Freya!' A frantic voice. 'It's me! Are you in?'

Freya prayed Stephanie would go away. She couldn't face her now. She couldn't face anybody.

'Hey!' Another stone clattered the glass. 'Please. It's cold. I haven't got any shoes on. I have important information for you about the dark angel!'

Freya parted the curtains and opened her window. She

couldn't believe the state Stephanie was in – half-dressed, her hair in disarray – but she couldn't let her in. She thought she might lose her mind if she talked to her now.

Stephanie's eyes, seeing Freya, glowed with happiness.

'I had to climb out of my bedroom window!' she said. 'I forgot my coat! Stupid of me . . .'. She gazed up keenly, shivering now that she'd stopped moving, the bottom of her T-shirt flapping in the wind. 'I went to school. I waited for you, you know. Why didn't you come? Was it the dark angel keeping you away from me?'

'I'm sick,' Freya said feebly. She couldn't see the smear Stephanie's bleeding foot left on the garden path.

'I know,' Stephanie called up. 'It must be the dark angel. Let me stay with you. I can help.'

'No.' Freya shook her head. 'I'm just ill, Stephanie. It's not the dark angel. I don't want to talk to you now. I can't. Really, I can't. Not now. I'm all right. Go home. Please, Stephanie!'

'I have something for you,' Stephanie whispered. 'Here.' She peeled the rucksack off her back and held out a little parcel wrapped in plain brown paper. 'I made it for you!'

'It's not the kind of angel you think it is,' Freya said, ignoring Stephanie's outstretched hand. 'Try to understand. I can't talk now.'

Stephanie blinked, about to throw the gift up. 'All right,' she said, staring at Freya. 'I'll shut up about the angel. Is that what you want me to do?' She crouched down, hunching her shoulders. 'It's cold, Freya. I'm cold . . . I'm . . .'

Freya wanted to comfort her, but not now. If she let her in, what would they do except talk about angels? She couldn't do that tonight. She'd go crazy if she did.

'Go home,' she implored her.

'Wait!' Stephanie yelled, as Freya started to close the window. 'I know . . . know you don't want to have anything to do with me socially.' She managed a smile. 'I just want you to listen a minute, that's all. At school I'll stay away from you. I promise. But it's really important you listen to me about the dark angel. It –'

'Stephanie, stop talking about angels! Leave me alone! Just go!'

A slack look of disbelief fell across Stephanie's face, but the smile was still hideously in place. She stumbled, fell onto the lawn, half-collapsing, but still holding out her little gift in the breeze.

'I don't want to lose you,' she burst out, favouring her right leg, so the injured foot had less pressure on it. 'What do you want me to do?' She put her gift on the grass so Freya could see it clearly. 'I'll be anything you want. I'll do anything. Just . . . please . . . just don't leave me out here.' She saw Freya standing at the window, weeping. 'Is it difficult for you to see me now? Is that the reason you're sending me away? What's wrong? I'll wait here if you like, until a better time. I can wait in the garden . . . until the morning . . . if you just give me something to wear. It's cold. Can you just do that?'

A huge part of Freya wanted to bring Stephanie in and comfort her, to warm her up, to be with her, but not tonight.

'Here!' she said, throwing down a coat and some socks. 'I

don't want you to freeze, but please Stephanie, I need you to go.'

But Stephanie didn't react as Freya expected. She didn't pick up the clothing. She just kept smiling and nodding, her head a little to one side. 'It's the dark angel,' she ventured weakly. 'He's making you say this.'

'No, it's not the dark angel! I'm all right! How many times do I have to tell you?' Freya screamed it out this time, her mind in torment. She had to get rid of Stephanie before she fell apart. What would make her leave?

'I know what I'm saying,' she called from the window. 'It's not the dark angel. It's *you*, Stephanie. Why don't you get it? How can you expect me to be your friend? You're too weird! Coming out here half-dressed! Talking angels all the time! Just stop!'

At those words, Stephanie looked as if she was about to be sick. For a moment she held a hand across her mouth, then a great cry broke from her throat and she clenched her teeth to hold it in. Somehow she gathered herself again.

'You . . . you come down to me,' she said, sagging on the lawn. 'I've got all the evidence here about the dark angel.' Her voice was barely a whisper now. 'It's in my head. It's . . . it's all here . . . in my head . . .' Stephanie tapped her skull repeatedly, as if that would make her meaning clear. 'In my bag, I've got evidence as well. No, I've left my bag at home. But it's OK, you don't believe in dark angels anyway. Forget that.' Stephanie giggled, a horrible, defeated sound. 'Come back home with me. Oh no, you don't want to do that.' She giggled again, slumping down on the freezing lawn.

'Freya?' It was Dad, entering the room. 'Who on earth are you talking to?'

She turned on him.

'Shut up!' she yelled, losing all control. 'Leave me alone, all of you! What do you want to hear, Dad? That I'm becoming obsessed with angels again? Of course I am! When will you understand that you can't do anything about it? You never could! Only I'm not even allowed to say that, am I? Because you're so ill, I can't even say that to you, can I?'

Dad stood rooted at the door, mouth wide.

Freya, her mind in a frenzy, turned back to the window. Stephanie now stood shivering, listening in.

'Look at you!' Freya wailed. 'Look at you! Standing outside in your bare feet, begging to be with me. Just go home, Stephanie! Go back to your crazy mum and dad!'

A strong pair of arms pulled her back inside her room.

'Freya, what the hell are you doing?' It wasn't Dad. He'd already left the room. It was Luke. 'What's going on?' he shouted at her. Glancing out of the window, he saw Stephanie fall over again. 'What's the girl's name?' he demanded. Freya made a noise in her throat. Once he had the name, Luke pushed the window wide, but Stephanie was already gone, jumping up with a strangled sob and running back the way she'd come. She held a hand across her face. Her feet slapped the pavement.

'Hey!' Luke called.

Stephanie didn't turn. She ran as fast as she could, still trailing spots of blood.

Luke closed the window and faced Freya.

'I can't believe you said that!' he thundered. 'I can't believe it!'

Freya made a strangled sound, her voice barely emerging. 'I'm . . .' The words she'd said to Stephanie reverberated in her mind. She suddenly felt so ashamed of them that she couldn't even look at Luke. 'I didn't mean it to come out like that with Stephanie. I'm –'

'Not what you said to her!' he bellowed. 'I mean Dad, you idiot!'

'I . . .' Freya wept, burying her face in a pillow. 'I didn't . . . He shouldn't have come in then. He –'

'You're pathetic,' Luke said, shaking his head. 'I'm ashamed of you. I never thought I'd say that, but I am. I'm ashamed of you.'

He strode out of her room, slamming the door.

Freya lay in the dark, a pillow over her head, so many feelings shooting through her that she thought her chest would explode.

'Self-pity now, is it?'

Mestraal. He stood over her bed, his body almost filling the room, his shadow obliterating all the light. 'Is this what you do best then, Freya Harrison? Break people's hearts? Is that the remarkable gift Hestron saw shining so brightly?'

'Go away!' Freya could barely speak.

'Don't want to be an angel any more? Well, you're not the only one who's given up on humanity. I hope you like the new darker shade of your wings. Better get used to them.'

Freya lifted the pillow and faced him.

'I hate you,' she said from the bottom of her soul.

Mestraal laughed. 'No, I don't think it's me you hate at all.' He flexed a wing, deliberately knocking the pillow away from Freya. 'Come on. Your wards are calling. Get up. Help them!'

'No!' Freya looked into his black eyes. She saw his abandoned wards there, including one he had withheld from her until now.

'See anyone you recognize?' Mestraal asked.

It was Stephanie, running across a rubbish-strewn car park on her way back home.

Mestraal sighed deeply, all energy and fight suddenly gone. His wings raked the floor, as if he could hardly be bothered to go on.

'Hestron risked everything to help you realize your extraordinary gift,' he said. 'He did it partly for you but also because, being Hestron, he never lost hope that he could somehow direct me back to my former path. He hoped that by showing me what a human could achieve he could guide me back to the light.'

'I tried,' she murmured.

'You *tried*?'

'I . . .' Freya winced, not wanting to hear anything else. 'Hestron said . . . I had greatness.'

Mestraal's feathers pointed stiffly at Freya. 'What greatness have you shown? Tonight did you show it?'

'With your wards, I tried . . .'

'When it was easy. When you were enjoying it. When it fulfilled your romantic vision of being an angel.'

'No,' Freya said weakly. 'Please stop, please . . .'

'You didn't. When Stephanie wanted the words to stop, you carried on.'

Freya buried her head in her hands. 'Please . . .'

'What about your father? You think he's bathing in the light you give out? You want to hear what he's saying right now?'

Mestraal asked it so quietly that Freya was afraid.

She shook her head.

'No? But he had to listen to *you*.'

'I love my dad. He knows I do. He knows!'

'Does he?'

Freya was transported unseen to the living room.

There she saw Luke sitting next to Dad on the sofa. Freya had never seen her dad look quite so vulnerable as he did now. In fact, she realized, she'd rarely seen him look vulnerable at all. He'd kept such things from her.

'Luke!' He was furious, unable to sit still. 'I asked you not to tell her! I wanted to do it at the right moment.'

'She had to know some time,' Luke snapped back, still angry with Freya.

'But not while she's going through all this!'

'When then?' Luke demanded. 'She's gone off the deep end again, hasn't she? She might be stuck there with her angels for ages. How long were you going to wait?' Luke hesitated, suddenly noticing how ill his dad looked.

'It's OK,' Dad said, reading Luke's concern. 'The latest tests indicate I'm going to last a while yet. I just wish I wasn't so damned tired, that's all. This illness has come at the worst possible time, with Freya the way she is.'

'You think she's noticed how bad you are?'

'That's not fair, Luke. You've no idea what courage it's taken her to get to this point. Most of the doctors didn't give her a hope. They thought she'd be institutionalized for ever. But she did it. On her own.'

'No. Not on her own.' Luke looked at him almost defiantly. 'You don't get it, do you? Don't you know what a great dad you are?'

Freya, watching, felt her heart snap.

But I love you, too, she thought. I love you as well. Didn't I tell you that?

Luke left the living room. Freya watched as he trudged upstairs. For a moment he paused on the landing, nearly knocked on her door. Then he changed his mind and went into his own room.

Freya avoided looking at Mestraal.

I haven't been there for Dad, she thought, her heart shriveling. Only Luke has. How many nights had Luke stayed downstairs with him recently while she was doing something else? She allowed Mestraal to guide her back to her own room. She opened the window and let the wind blow against her face. The same wind, she realized, was blowing Stephanie home. With her angelic eyes she could see Stephanie clearly now, still running.

Mestraal left.

Downstairs, Freya could hear her dad crying.

Stephanie stood outside her house, her foot still bleeding, not caring. She knocked at the door. Her mother answered, peeking suspiciously through the keyhole in her usual way. Stephanie smiled faintly at the look of disbelief she got.

'I'm back,' was all she said to her father's questions.

Her mother stayed with her for an hour or so, warming her up and disinfecting her foot wounds. As she washed her clothes, she tried gently questioning Stephanie about what had happened. 'Nothing', 'no', 'yes', was all Stephanie offered – monosyllabic answers that gave nothing away, meant nothing at all.

'Stephanie, talk to me,' her mother implored her at one point, trying to make sense of what she was saying.

'I'm weird,' Stephanie said, a small smile appearing on her face. 'Don't you know that?'

After her mother left her alone Stephanie tried to sleep, but Freya's rejection was an all-consuming wound. It wasn't possible for Stephanie to recover, not from those words. On the return home, she'd replayed them over and over. I can't be your friend. You're too weird. I know what I'm saying. It's you, Stephanie. You're too weird. I mean it. You're too weird. You're too weird.

Stephanie went through the motions of getting into her nightclothes. She cleaned her teeth and slid into bed. She didn't lie back, though, except when her mother came to check on her. Twice in the night she hurried to the bathroom to be sick, as quietly as she could. After the second time, she walked back into her bedroom and lit a pure white candle. White for absolute cleansing. It was always the first thing she did when she was desperate for Nadiel's help.

'I forgive you, Freya, for not being what I wanted you to be,' she said. 'I forgive you.' But even as she said the words, Stephanie knew she didn't mean them.

Too weird. You're too weird. It was true. It wasn't just Freya who'd said it. None of the other kids could stand her. Too weird. Looking hard at herself in the mirror, Stephanie jabbed a finger at her face in several places. You stupid girl, she thought. Freya's right to reject you. They all are. Odd little Stephanie, trying to be normal. You never will be.

Before she went to sleep, Stephanie took the portrait of Nadiel down off her wall and cut it with a knife.

Throughout the night Freya sensed her wards. She couldn't stop feeling them at the edge of her mind. They kept her awake, they would not stop. But she accepted that, because it was easier to think about them than to deal with her feelings about what she'd said to Dad and Stephanie. She had no idea how to correct so much, how to unsay things. Stephanie was out there somewhere, in the dark, and Freya knew she could have assumed her angelic aspect and sought her out, but she was too afraid of what she'd find.

The next morning Dad left for work early, making up for hours lost to hospital appointments. Freya heard him rise and go to the bathroom, but she was still too ashamed to face him. Instead, she hid in bed and got up at the same time as Luke, just wanting to see him, at least to have one thing normal.

Luke ignored her when she sat down at the kitchen table.

'I want to talk to you,' she said.

He didn't reply. Freya accepted that. But gradually she realized that something apart from his silence was making her feel uneasy. It was nothing she could name, nothing to do with last night. She looked up at Luke, watching him more closely.

'What are you doing today?'

'Nothing.' He shrugged her off.

'Just going to school?'

'Um.'

'What time will you be back?'

'Since when have you cared about that?' He still wouldn't look at her. But before he left to go to school, he handed her a package covered in brown paper. 'That girl last night left this for you. Well, it was on the lawn this morning anyway.'

Freya studied the package. The wrapping paper was still soaking wet after last night's showers, and the delicate yellow bow tying it had come partly undone.

Inside there was a string necklace with a pendant. Cut and fixed onto a thick cardboard backing was a picture of her, hand drawn with a heart in her chest. Inside the heart, in tiny, almost insignificant writing, Stephanie had put the symbol of her own sigil.

Luke watched Freya carry the necklace up to her room, then left for school. He had no idea what was going on between Freya and Stephanie, or the long-term effect Freya's words would have on Dad, but right now he had other matters on his mind.

As he walked down Cardigan Street and onto Devon Road, past the town hall building, he felt strangely alone. He couldn't put his finger on why, until he realized it was the absence of Sam. He'd grown so used to being with him that it felt odd walking to school without him.

At least one of us won't get hurt today, he thought.

His plan was to reach the area around Inkerman Street an hour early and find out what Tate had in mind. If the situation looked dangerous, he wouldn't go near the place. On the other hand, if he could find a way to get Tate alone he'd take it.

The day passed in a slow trudge of lessons. A couple of his friends noticed he looked unusually tense, and questioned him about it. Luke deflected their concerns. At half past three he headed off in the direction of home, then detoured in a long arc towards the town centre and Inkerman Street.

There was a block of flats with a good view over the intersection of roads in this part of town. The problem was getting buzzed through the security entrance. In the end he simply waited outside the flats for someone to leave the building, gave them a big smile as if he lived there and made his way inside.

He took the dingy steel lift to the seventh floor, sat on the balcony and waited for Tate to show himself.

The idea of making a bonfire of all her angel paraphernalia came to Stephanie just after midday. A great conflagration – real, earnest fire – seemed the appropriate way forward. Time to burn away all the vestiges of her old life.

It took her over an hour to gather everything together. She'd collected a lot over the past couple of years, stashing it in every corner and crack of her room. Most of her reference books were covered in protective plastic folders she'd made herself. The plastic would certainly burn well. She had no doubt about that.

Not bothering to change out of her nightgown, she brought the whole lot together and formed them into a nice tidy bonfire-sized heap in the middle of her bedroom floor. Around the edge of the pile she placed her shiny affirmation cards, all fifty-two of the wonders. Just in front of the affirmation cards she dumped some gaudy pictures of purple-clothed angels she'd found in a charity shop over a year ago. To those she added all the drawings she'd recently done herself of angels, angels in pencil, crayon, ink, whatever, mostly little line drawings of her and Nadiel together.

She discovered a bottle of lavender oil in one of her drawers. Sniffing it, she poured the contents randomly over the pile in the middle of the room, and for a while the air smelled achingly sweet. Pride of place on the heap she gave to her portrait of Nadiel. She'd already cut it up during the night, a kind of random hack. She couldn't decide the best way to mutilate it further. Searching around her room, she spotted a picture of Freya she'd drawn a few days ago, and put it next to Nadiel in the centre of the pile.

She had no real plans or thoughts about what would happen after she set light to everything. No doubt the lavender oil would burn quickly enough, and so would the paper and plastic. She didn't really care what happened after that. One thing she was sure about: Nadiel wouldn't intervene. If he'd been her guardian angel, he would never have allowed last night to take place. That meant one of two things. Either that Nadiel did not care what happened to her. Or – and this was most likely, after all – that guardian angels did not exist. Neither alternative was bearable to Stephanie, and the idea of the fire had come not long after.

I'll offer you one more chance to save me, she thought, giving Nadiel's portrait a tight smile.

Picking up his slashed picture, she found one part not so badly damaged. It was the area showing Nadiel's right hand, holding the dove. Stephanie gave it one last farewell kiss. Then she waited for her mother to leave the house to pick her father up from work before she sent the dove's wings up in smoke.

From his perch on the outer wall high up in the block of flats, Luke had a clear view over most of Inkerman Street. He felt tense but ready, and fairly safe; it was unlikely Tate would spot him up here. He didn't see the two people Tate had hidden east and south, behind him, but he got a perfect view of Tate himself and four other big kids loitering in nearby doorways. Tate's face looked a mess. Even from this distance, Luke could see the plaster across the bridge of his nose, and he took some pleasure in that.

He checked the time: four-thirty. Watching closely, he looked to see if any other boys from Tate's gang were hanging around. No one was visible, but he couldn't be sure they weren't there, either. If Tate had brought four extra kids, he might have others as well. Better to go home and wait for an easier opportunity to take Tate on one-on-one.

Comfortable with that decision, Luke waited to see what Tate would do once the deadline passed. No doubt if there were other kids involved they'd start turning up then as well. It would be useful to see who they were, in case he met them again.

Five o'clock went by. Five-past-five. Five-fifteen. The light grew dim as dusk set in. Tate stood next to the pet shop looking increasingly restless.

Then, on a skid of small heels, someone else appeared.

Sam Davenport was running down Inkerman Street.

*

Freya had been in the house all day, an increasingly uneasy feeling stirring her blood. At first she assumed it was just a general edginess caused by the state of her wards, and last night's awful treatment of Stephanie and Dad. But as the day lengthened she grew more perturbed.

Something else was wrong. Her angelic aspect sensed it, but her human side resisted whatever she was being warned about.

Then she felt a warm flush run right through her body.

Her senses tautened, suddenly becoming extraordinarily alert.

Even on a day with decent traffic conditions, Stephanie thought, it takes Mother a minimum of twenty minutes to pick Father up from work and bring him back home.

Plenty of time, then.

She felt curiously relaxed about what she was about to do. She didn't worry about getting hurt. It didn't seem to matter whether she did or not. It seemed far more important to burn things in the right order. That dove first, of course. It would never get out of dear old Nadiel's hand now.

She lit the first match and the dove burned with a wonderful speed, followed by Nadiel's smiling lips. Stephanie held his portrait for as long as she could, then dropped it when a rush of pain in her fingers left her breathless.

Nadiel's blazing face fell on top of one of her old diaries. The paper was old and dry and caught light at once.

Freya knew it was Stephanie. Her angelic instinct told her the second the fire was lit. Her feathers responded at once, offering Freya their strength, urging her skyward. Just see what's happening, they coaxed. That's all. Just see.

Freya cautiously launched herself. Within a few seconds of taking flight, she was over Stephanie's house, hearing the smoke detector blaring. From high above the roof she could feel the heat emanating from an upstairs room.

There were no other angels nearby. Freya was on her own.

The fire, she could tell, was already out of control. But Stephanie was alive; Freya sensed her heart beating at a tremendous speed, though for some reason she was making no effort to get away from the flames.

If I go in there I'll be burned, Freya realized.

She hesitated, forced herself towards the smoke, backed off again.

Then she became aware of another ward in danger at a different location. It was Luke – running from someone.

Freya couldn't be with them both. She had to choose.

Stephanie was in the greater danger, but if she chose Luke there appeared to be no danger to herself.

She chose Stephanie.

Luke couldn't believe what he was seeing – Sam pelting down Inkerman Street, closely followed by his mum, trying to catch him.

He's come to help me, he realized. To help me take Tate on.

'Sam!' he yelled.

Sam stopped, squinted up, not sure who was calling. Luke had to lean over the edge of the block of flats to make sure he saw him. At the same time that Sam spotted him, so did Tate.

'I'm OK!' Luke shouted. 'Get away! Go back with your mum! I'm OK!'

Sam stopped, shielded his eyes, looking for a way into the flats. That gave his mum a chance to catch up and take a firm grasp of his wrist. She led him – kicking and yelling – away.

Luke saw one of the lads with Tate laughing, but Tate

wasn't laughing. He motioned for the two closest boys to get moving, and they headed towards the flats. Tate flicked open his mobile phone. A moment later Luke's own mobile rang. He knew it was Tate, trying to occupy him, delay his leaving. Luke estimated he had about a minute at most to get out of the flats, or they'd have him trapped inside.

He ignored the ringing phone. He didn't take the lift – the wait was too risky. Instead he ran at full speed down the stairwell, thinking about emergency exits. There had to be another way out of this building apart from the main door. Reaching ground level, he saw a steel partition linked to a corridor and a rear entrance. There was a fire escape there. Luke slammed into it, bursting out of the building.

A narrow alley led away from the exit. It was empty. Luke had no clue where it led, but ran up it. The path took a winding route.

Then, behind him, he heard the scuff of shoes.

Tate had found the fire exit, and seen him. Two boys from his gang were just behind.

Luke raced ahead, searching for a road or path, anything that might take him away. If he could reach the busy town centre he could lose Tate or seek refuge inside a shop. But the narrow path just carried on, apparently leading nowhere.

Then he got a whiff of the river. He didn't want to go that way – not enough people – but he couldn't double back. He ran fast. What was it that Sam had told him the other day? That several pursuers always catch a single target given enough time, as they expend less nervous energy. Luke found himself thinking about that now.

At last – a road to the left. He veered down it, still running, until he reached the river bank. There wasn't much light left in the sky. If he could evade Tate for a little longer the gathering darkness would help. If they caught him after it was dark, things would go worse for him. A scattering of young kids were playing in a small dirty playground nearby. No help there. He ran on. Tate and the others were closing in. On Luke's right, the river flowed swift and dark.

Shrieks were coming now from Stephanie's room – terrifying, high-pitched wails. Neighbours, hearing them, raced out of the nearest houses, some calling for the ambulance service, others arguing about what to do. One man cut through the talk and threw himself at the front door, trying to break it down. The door held, even when a second man co-ordinated his effort with the first.

Freya dropped from the sky to the level of Stephanie's window. She raised a wing in front of her eyes, steeled herself for the impact and flew straight through it. The window frame was thicker than she expected and shattered the leading edge of her wing. Enduring the pain, she heaved herself inside. Her body, travelling so fast, sucked in a huge tide of air and glass with it, and for a moment the extra oxygen in the room fed the flames, obscuring Freya's vision of what was happening inside.

Then she saw an unconscious girl lying near the door. Stephanie had obviously tried at the last moment to get out, and been overcome with smoke. The hem of her nightgown was smouldering.

Freya lifted her up. She held her in her arms and prepared to fly the way she'd come in, but the heat was too great. A pillar of orange flame had sprung up around the curtains. Freya couldn't even see the window properly, there was so much fire. She staggered as a whoosh of hot air seared her eyes.

Dropping Stephanie, she fell to the floor. Her hands broke her fall, but one landed on a shard of glass from the broken portrait of Nadiel. As Freya clutched at something to steady herself, two of her fingers came into contact with the red-hot iron frame of Stephanie's bed. Screaming, she ripped the skin away. Then she bent down to pick Stephanie up again. 'Help me,' she begged, but there was no response. Shielding Stephanie's face, Freya dragged her to the bedroom doorway and down the staircase. She didn't know her wings were on fire until the feathers started to scream.

At the bottom of the staircase Freya needed to take a breath, but there was no air. She staggered to the front door. Through all the smoke she couldn't see the door handle, so she felt for where it must be, found it. The handle turned, but wouldn't open.

Freya couldn't hold her breath any longer. As soon as she drew in air, thick smoke entered her lungs. She fell down, coughing. Outside, the two men were still pounding into the wooden door, but it held. Freya nearly blacked out as she reached down again for Stephanie.

'Wings,' she murmured.

The wing that was not shattered took control. The individual feathers, mastering their fear, beat against the heavy, curling smoke and used the walls for leverage, pushing Freya back upstairs.

A solid wall of fire stood between Freya and the open window.

She shut her eyes and flew through it. As she passed beyond the window, flames flowed behind her, a trail of burning debris and dying feathers streaming over the garden.

She landed on the lawn and deposited Stephanie. The damp grass sizzled and cracked as her wings touched it. For a moment people thought they saw two girls: one unconscious, the other flaming beside her. Had the unconscious girl jumped from her window, shedding all this fire?

Freya used her hands to beat out the flames licking at the underside of her wings. There were excruciatingly painful burns across her legs and body. Her wings told her they could still make it safely into the air. They were lying, but she knew why.

Luke was dying.

Luke had nearly made his escape when it happened. He'd reached a broader stretch of the river, with a bridge that would take him straight into the middle of town. There was even an open grocery shop no more than thirty yards or so away. He could see the strip lights on, the unshaven owner – Luke was close enough to see his bristles – dipping grubby fingers into a crate of oranges.

What happened next seemed to take place in a kind of

slow-motion. Luke's right foot slipped on something, and his weight fell to that side. His body automatically reacted by throwing him to the left. For a couple of seconds he teetered on the edge, between safety and the river, and it could have gone either way, but he ended up falling into the water.

The river in this part of the town was shallow and Luke was a decent swimmer. If he'd landed directly in the water, even in the gathering dark he could easily have swum to the other bank and escaped before Tate and the others made it over the bridge. But instead of landing in the water the side of his head struck a supermarket trolley under the surface.

Luke felt the clunking impact on his temple.

For a moment he blacked out completely, mouth open wide. Then his body's survival mechanism kicked in, and the choking woke him. He turned in the water, disorientated, his vision blurry, unable to see anything. Thrashing his arms, he looked for the nearest bank, but the current carried him out towards the centre of the stream.

He was aware of Tate somewhere behind him, laughing. Blood poured down Luke's face and into his eyes and he felt sick. He passed out again for a few seconds, swallowing more water. His head felt wrong. He couldn't hold it up. The opposite bank was briefly within grasping distance, a ridiculously short arm-length, but he couldn't reach it.

Tate was still laughing, but one of the other boys realized what was happening.

'He's drowning.'

'Don't be stupid,' Tate replied. 'That water's only three feet deep.'

'He is,' the other boy said. 'Look at him.'

They all stared at Luke. To go from the pleasure of the chase to seeing him struggle disorientated them. They couldn't make the immediate switch to life-saving mode. Luke's face slid under the water.

The boys gazed at him, doing nothing.

Freya flew across town. Flying haphazardly, smashing into buildings, she fell from the sky, got up, rose again, and flew on, all the while battling the searing pains in her legs. There had to be a way to make it to Luke in time.

Only three undamaged feathers held the leading edge of her broken right wing in place. Those feathers urged her on, holding that immense weight. But long before she reached the river Freya knew she might not survive if she entered the water. Her lungs were appallingly damaged from the fire and smoke. Once her wings were drenched in water, she wasn't sure she would be able to lift them again.

Tate and the others on the bank saw – well, what did they see? An angel? If that's what it was, they would never have admitted it to each other. In any case, they were never quite sure when they recalled it afterwards. But something was near the river beside Luke, and it wasn't entirely human.

Freya swung over the river and crashed into the water. She stood there, barely able to keep herself upright in the fast-moving current. Fanning her wings for balance, she held Luke's head up.

Luke struggled feebly against her, thinking it was Tate. His efforts to fight her off were just enough to drain the last of Freya's strength. She managed to heave him up the opposite bank and out of the water, but couldn't drag herself out as well. It was her wings: saturated with water, they were pulling her down.

Freya lunged forward, trying to make the bank, but she couldn't, and then it was all she could do just to stop herself tipping backwards. Under the river her damaged feathers, realizing that they were responsible, beat wildly, but the water entered them, displacing the air. The wings became heavier and heavier until they were like metal sheets tying her to the river bed, and finally Freya toppled backwards, her straining head going under.

On the opposite bank, Tate and the others were mesmerized by the thrashing they saw. Was it some huge bird in there? Seeing that Luke was safe on the other bank, Tate urged the others after him, but the rest of the boys were in no mood for the fight any more. Anyway, they were too occupied by what was happening in the river.

'What is it?' one of them muttered.

'Dunno,' Tate said. 'Don't care. Let's stone it.'

He picked up a rock lying near the bank.

But while he drew his arm back, and raised it, he never brought it forward. Because something strong held him. Tate didn't know what it was, but for the rest of his life whenever he drew back his arm he felt frightened, and the next thing he saw made him cringe against the ground. It was a carpet of eyes moving toward the river. Tate put up his hands, screaming with fear, but whatever was there merely brushed past him. It entered the river with a speed that drenched the boys, and then the waters came up.

Tate stuffed his fist in his mouth as first the thrashing thing in the water and then, impossibly, Luke was lifted too, was lifted clean off the bank and away. Then something seething with energy and innumerable eyes stopped to stare at Tate and the other boys. It waited until they shook and cried like children. Then the shape moved purposefully up and into the air, still holding its burden.

The man in the grocer's looked up from his oranges. A sudden shadow had come over the bright fruit in front of him. He glanced out of the window and saw four boys shaking with fear. There was a shadow over them, a heavy light deeper than darkness. It extended upwards, a grey shimmer that splintered and spread like a cone of night for a moment across the whole town, then was gone.

Freya burned. River water dribbled from her soaking hair into the corners of her mouth, and she burned. Although she was no longer near the wet, slippery soil of the river bank she didn't know that yet, and with one hand she kept trying to drag herself further away from the water. Her other hand fumbled for Luke. Where was he?

Then she felt something enclose her. At first Freya wasn't even sure what it was. But as the wings gathered her in, taking all her pain into themselves, she stopped kicking and scrabbling. She fell still: a girl with a dark angel breathing life back into her.

Gradually the scalding subsided to a bearable level, and Freya pushed at Mestraal's wings to free herself.

She saw the change in him.

Mestraal gazed back but he didn't understand what he had done: not quite, not yet. And then he looked at himself, at the perfection of his wings.

Freya pulled him to her and kissed him.

Luke, from high above the river bank, felt disorientated. What was going on? 'Freya, is that you?' All he could see was a pool of light to which his own eyes had no admittance.

Coughing up water, he tried to see through the light to what was beyond it, unable to understand what he was seeing. Shading his eyes, he looked again. And this time he faintly detected two sweeping outlines attached to a pair of shoulders, bright things that couldn't possibly be there.

'He can see you,' Freya murmured to Mestraal.

'No,' Mestraal replied. 'I have no light to speak of yet. Don't you understand? It's *your light* he sees. How could he miss you?'

Stephanie lay for a long time in a hospital bed. While Freya's angelic body quickly recovered, new feathers replacing the damaged ones, it was weeks before Stephanie was strong enough to stagger unaided through the hospital corridors, and even then she had to borrow a frame and hobble to the bathroom just to get some privacy. The burn scars on her inner thighs tightened and made her wince every time she walked.

That pain, however, was nothing compared to the agony of her throat whenever her parents visited. The smoke inhalation injuries to her lungs meant it was misery to talk at all. But her mother blamed herself for what had happened, and during each visit sign language was never enough, and Stephanie ended up rasping apologies and reassurances, and for hours afterwards her throat felt as if it was still on fire.

The first day she could properly speak again a visitor came to the Burns Ward. The girl paused for a moment at the well-lit entrance, then walked tentatively down the corridor.

The ward receptionist smiled up at her.

Stephanie's groans of anger went unheard.

'Not you!' she croaked, as soon as Freya was within earshot. 'Anyone but you!' The sound that emerged strained her vocal cords, but she didn't care. 'Get out! Get out!'

'Stephanie, please . . . I'm so sorry . . .'

'No. Out! I never want to see you again.'

Unable to scream, Stephanie shook the bed. Her arms clattered and slapped against the various machines she was attached to. It was bad enough seeing Freya at all; worse that she had the gall to wear the sigil pendant she'd made for her. It hung casually around Freya's neck, like a direct insult.

'Come here,' Stephanie murmured more gently, inviting her closer. 'No, nearer, so I can say something in your ear.' When Freya was beside her, bending down, Stephanie followed the line of her neck, hooked the chain of the pendant around her own heavily-bandaged hand and tore it from Freya's throat.

Freya was appalled at her stupidity in displaying the sigil pendant on that first visit. She'd been wearing it all the time recently, while she waited for Stephanie's voice to recover. The wait had been hard, but it was only right that she waited: Stephanie deserved to have a voice with which to confront her. After the terrible things Freya had said that night in the garden, she wanted Stephanie to be able to say whatever she liked.

The following week she visited the Burns Ward twice more, trying to apologize, but each time Stephanie turned her head away. The third time the ward nurses had instructions to keep Freya out, and she returned home feeling desperate.

Luke was in when she got back. He looked well. Following

a brief convalescent stay in hospital, being monitored after the impact to his head, he was fully recovered. Freya even sensed a lightness to his step that had been missing lately. He had no memory of what he'd seen at the river, either. The blow to his head seemed to have made him forget or misremember those critical minutes, and Freya was grateful for that. She liked just being his kid sister. Being the butt of a few Lukey jokes didn't bother her. It was infinitely preferable to the way Dad was looking at her these days.

Because somehow Dad knew. She'd hidden her angelic identity from him as best she could, but she'd caught him studying her when he thought she wasn't looking. Once she even found him holding his breath. And another time, right in front of her, he became flustered, tongue-tied. It was the last thing Freya wanted. She was losing the normal relationship with Dad she craved. She couldn't allow that, not after everything that had happened. She had to do something about it. But what?

The next evening she waited until he was alone in his room, and knocked on his door. When Dad invited her in she sat on the corner of his bed, facing him. He moved towards the window. It was as if he wanted to get a look at her from another angle. Observing her for a moment, he smiled. Then he strode up and felt her shoulder blades.

'So where are they then?'

'What?'

'Are you still trying to convince me you're something else?'

Freya was about to try, but he stopped her.

'I can sense the difference, Freya. Even if I can't see the wings, I can tell you're not the same.'

The following Monday, Freya visited Stephanie again. As she'd done so many times already, she made her way down the now-familiar scuffed wooden corridor to the Burns Ward. This time she persuaded the ward nurse to let her go through.

Stephanie's voice had improved lately. She was able to shout.

'You talked to my parents!' she yelled, as soon as Freya was in range. 'You told them what you said to me in the garden! I can't believe you did that. And Mother *liked* you,' she added incredulously.

'Stephanie, those things I said –'

'Don't pretend you didn't mean them.'

Freya could have lifted her wings a fraction. In that moment, she could have done it easily, just enough to show Stephanie what she was. But she didn't. She wanted Stephanie to choose to be with her on her own terms, not impressed by some trick. She didn't want anyone gazing at her the way Dad was.

'Stephanie, please listen,' she said, before she could be stopped. 'I just want to say one thing. I know you came into school to see me about the dark angel. I never thanked you for that. Or for facing Amy the way you did.'

Stephanie stared at her fiercely. 'Compared to facing you that night, Amy was easy.'

Freya lowered her eyes. 'Can't find the words?' Stephanie

asked. 'Don't bother saying you'll make it up to me.'

'What I'm trying to say is . . .'

'Yes?'

Freya kept her eyes lowered. 'That . . . if you'll have me . . . I want to be your friend.'

'My friend?' There was disbelief in Stephanie's voice. 'I'm too weird, remember.'

'I'm weird, too.'

Freya smiled faintly, but Stephanie did not.

'I *believed* in you,' she murmured. 'You said you would help me.'

'I will.' Freya tentatively approached Stephanie. 'I've talked to the teachers at Ashcroft High. Mrs Baldwin wants you to come back.'

Stephanie shook her head. 'They'll never accept me.'

'They will. And if they don't, *I* will.'

For the first time Stephanie looked at her properly.

'You hurt me, Freya Harrison, don't you know that? You hurt me. *You really, really hurt me.*'

Freya reached out for one of Stephanie's bandaged hands. She held it, knowing that if she didn't persuade her today she would come again tomorrow, and the day after that if she had to, and the next. 'Please,' she said. 'Don't make me return to that school on my own, Stephanie. I don't want to go back there without you.'

Later that day, at the start of a misty, cloud-filled evening, Freya sat in her own room, perched on the edge of her bed, gazing from the window. Dad was tired again, and she was determined to talk to him about it. But first she listened closely, just to be sure.

Holding her head to one side, she tilted it one way, then another. Then she smiled. There had been no sound from her wards since the fire. She knew why; Mestraal was with them again. Their calls were being answered before she could even hear them.

But she missed their voices.

Tentatively her newly-grown outer feathers were whispering in her ears. It was an intimate conversation aimed at persuading her to use them. But the new feathers weren't sure of themselves yet. They were eager, greedy for the skies, but had never flown before; they were nervous. The older feathers that had survived the fire were more patient, awaiting Freya's own decision, but even they were restless. Sometimes, while she slept, they stirred secretly, stretching towards her open window.

Freya thought of Stephanie, and more than anything wanted to be with her.

'So you want to take on one of my wards?'

It was Mestraal, huge but no longer black. He stood by her window, and he looked like Hestron; the resemblance was clearer now. It almost made Freya cry to see it.

'You did this,' he murmured.

Freya shook her head, but he held it solemnly.

'We are equals now,' he said.

'No,' Freya answered. How could she be equal in power to Mestraal? That wasn't possible.

'You're wrong,' he whispered. 'There has been no one like you.'

'But Sandolphon . . . Metatron . . .'

'Not even them,' Mestraal assured her. 'I knew it when I saw what you did for Davina. No angel apart from me or Hestron had ever reached her so well, and that night you were only underway, only starting out.'

Freya and Mestraal's wings set the air moving in her bedroom, flow and counter flow, a wild breeze. From the heart of that turbulence one angel faced another. Across the world, Freya sensed all the other angels listening in on their conversation.

'I want to take on a ward,' she said.

'Your father?'

'Yes.'

'You cannot heal his physical condition,' Mestraal told her. 'Not even an angel can do so.'

'I realize that.'

'Do you know who his guardian was?'

Of course she did. She felt the influence of Hestron in everything he said and did.

As Mestraal smiled, Freya looked out into the dark night. 'I want more of Hestron's wards as well,' she said. 'I know I'm inexperienced, but I'd like to take on as many as I can. You choose how many. You decide who I can't cope with.'

'There is no one you cannot cope with,' Mestraal said. His wings held her in an embrace. 'You only thought there was.'

Mestraal departed, and Freya was alone in her room. But not alone. Not really. She would never be alone again. Her wards were everywhere around her, and whenever she journeyed in their minds there would always be an echo of Hestron.

She opened the window fully. One of her wings extended out to the street, as if testing the air. Dad was downstairs, resting. Freya wondered if she would ever tell him she had become his guardian. She doubted it, but perhaps, in time, there was one person her own age she would tell; it would be their shared secret.

To the south of her and to the east, and to the west and the north, her wards were waiting. Freya lifted a single elegant outer as an antennae to gauge their need, and at the same moment she felt the whole natural world extend in sympathy with her, winter trying to rush away.

Her wings suddenly curved upward, a slight rising tide of motion. Freya knew it was in response to another angel, gliding overhead. She smiled as her feathers asked if they could be alongside, sharing the same space. When she told them not yet, her outers, no longer willing to wait, burst from her back, urging the rest of the feathers to follow.

Freya wanted to fly, but first she had something else to do. She quieted her rebellious outers with a promise, and went downstairs.

Dad was in the kitchen, stirring some stew Freya had made earlier.

'Hey, I said I'd do that,' she chided him. She finished preparing the meal, laid out the plates and cutlery. Then she called

Luke out of his room and the three of them sat down at the table. They ate, chatting about nothing in particular.

Throughout the meal Dad kept glancing sidelong at Freya, then away again whenever she caught him doing it.

After dinner, Freya asked Luke if he would leave them alone together, and she sat down in the living room with Dad, bringing in some coffee and a slice of Madeira cake on a small tray.

'You're being very attentive tonight,' he said, laughing. 'Cake as well. What's all this in aid of? Are you after something?'

'Yes,' Freya said.

She sat next to Dad on the sofa, and handed him the coffee. Dad waited for her to tell him what she wanted, but Freya was just using that as an excuse to keep him with her and talk to her.

For the first time she properly asked him about his illness. He stalled her for a while, but she gently pressed him and kept on pressing until she knew he'd held nothing back.

As soon as her attention wasn't focused on him, he was anxious to return to her own welfare.

'So,' he said nervously, putting down his coffee, 'what am I supposed to call you now? What really are you now?'

'I'm just a daughter,' she replied. 'Just your little girl.'

'I'm sorry I haven't been there for you recently,' he said. 'I've been so . . .'

She put her fingers to his lips. 'You've always been there for me.'

He shrugged, those words strange coming from Freya. She knew he was embarrassed, but she didn't care. She slowly placed both her hands on his shoulders and made him look into her eyes.

'Dad,' she said, 'don't you know how much I love you?'

Also by Cliff McNish

Breathe: a Ghost Story

Jack is used to danger. His asthma has nearly killed him more than once. But his new home has a danger he's never known before – the spirits of the dead.

They can't breathe . . .

But in Jack's house they can . . .

> *CHASE*
>> *HIDE*
>>> *SCREAM*

Only Jack can see them. Only he can hear them. And only he can learn their secrets in time to save his mother – and himself . . .

'a true ghost story – the kind that lays its cold fingers on you, grips tight and doesn't let you go even when the last page has been turned . . . Wonderfully spine-chilling . . .' *The Bookseller*